PENGUIN BOOKS

THE BUILD-UP SEASON

Megan Jacobson grew up in Darwin and the far north coast of New South Wales, but now lives in Sydney, where she works in TV news production at the ABC. She has a degree in journalism and has worked as a question writer for TV game shows, and as an in-house script storyliner and script editor for several Australian television dramas. Her short stories have been published in the *Sydney Morning Herald*, aired on ABC radio, appeared in the UTS writers' anthology *I can see my house from here* and in the *Review of Australian Fiction*. Her first novel, *Yellow*, was shortlisted in the Older Readers category of the 2017 CBCA Book of the Year Awards.

THE
BUILD-UP
SEASON

MEGAN·JACOBSON

PENGUIN BOOKS

PENGUIN BOOKS

UK | USA | Canada | Ireland | Australia
India | New Zealand | South Africa | China

Penguin Books is part of the Penguin Random House group of companies
whose addresses can be found at global.penguinrandomhouse.com.

Penguin
Random House
Australia

First published by Penguin Random House Australia Pty Ltd, 2017.

1 3 5 7 9 10 8 6 4 2

Text copyright © Megan Jacobson 2017.

The moral right of the author has been asserted.

Design by Marina Messiha © Penguin Random House Australia Pty Ltd.
Cover photograph courtesy of Getty Images/Cryingjune and Marina Messiha.
Printed and bound in Australia by Griffin Press, an accredited ISO AS/NZS
14001 Environmental Management Systems printer.

National Library of Australia
Cataloguing-in-Publication data:

Jacobson, Megan, author.
The Build-up Season / Megan Jacobson

ISBN: 9780143573388 (paperback)
Young adult fiction.

penguin.com.au

MIX
Paper from
responsible sources
FSC® C009448

one

He's back.

The monster.

It's the middle of the night and I'm awake, because even though I'm seventeen I still haven't outgrown the childhood monster that haunts you in the dark. I haven't outgrown it, because when I was a child, the monster was real.

He was my father.

But the thing is, the monster was the person I was closest to in the whole world, closer than I've been to anyone since.

That will tell you everything you need to know about me.

And still, I wouldn't hesitate to kill the monster.

That will tell you even more about me.

I hear the footsteps creak along the polished wooden floorboards and my heart crashes inside my chest like a pair of sneakers in a dryer. He's meant to be in jail. Mum and

Nan went to the hearing, he got six years for breaking my mother's ribs. That was four years ago, but could he have been given parole already? Could he have found us? The darkness presses down onto my skin and I slide out of bed, all my nerve endings tight and twitching. The panic inside of me claws, and I search desperately for a weapon. The only thing I can find is the glass next to my bed. You can slit a throat with shattered glass.

Trembling, I pad down the hallway towards the living room, and I can hear the wind chime tinkling. It's so delicate, like the eerie soundtrack to a horror movie. Taking a deep breath, I grip the glass and have it poised to smash against the wall. I switch the light on.

To see my mother. She jumps.

'Iliad, my God you scared me. What are you doing still awake?'

The moon is bright outside and in the glow Mum's dragged a chair across the living room to fix the tangled threads of the wind chime that hangs next to the window. I almost can't breathe, the air feels as thick as the ground and I have to rest my right hand against my chest to know that my lungs are still working, and I hate being like this. Vulnerable. Like my armour has slipped and anyone can wound me. My left knuckles are white, still gripping the glass.

'I didn't turn any of the lights on because I didn't want to wake you,' Mum continues, deaf to the thundering of my heart. 'Are you still not sleeping? You're in year twelve now and you need rest to concentrate, darling. You barely passed your last science exam.'

She's trying to pry loose a knot and the wind chime is clanging now and it matches the ringing in my ears, from where the blood is pounding. I snap at her. I do that when I'm afraid. The fight response trumps flight response every time. 'Yes, well, according to my science teacher, energy doesn't come from crystals, Mum. Or reiki or chakras or whatever hocus-pocus crap you peddle. Apparently, physics is a *thing*!'

She stops concentrating on the wind chime now and looks down at me. She runs her fingers through her long dark hair, hair that I wish I hadn't inherited, wild curls to her waist, but I avoid her gaze and stomp over to the front door, making sure it's locked. It isn't. It swings open when I try the handle and so I slam it shut, bolting it this time.

'You left it unlocked!' I shout it, an accusation, and I run my own fingers through my hair, which I've kept long and curly on the left side and shorn on the lower half of the right, clipping the hair into a number two down to my neck. Mum gets down from the chair, so she's eye to eye with me. She goes to step forward, but stops. I don't move towards her. The ghost of my father is prowling that space between us, like it always has, snapping before we get too close.

Nan walks in, woken by the ruckus, her hair a white mess and her shrivelled sultana eyes blinking in the light. She moved in just before Dad went to jail, before they escaped from Queensland to live here, in Darwin, and just before they shipped me off to the first of the many boarding schools in Melbourne that I was expelled from. She bustles past us, breaking the tension. Nan and I have a begrudging respect for each other as formidable adversaries but that's as close to affection as we're ever going to get. She's tough as half-chewed gristly meat and she looks like it too.

'I guess we're all having a midnight tea party,' Nan says as she switches on the kettle.

'Darling, I just came back from a walk, I couldn't sleep. Please stop with the hostility.' That's my mother. The bells on her ankle bracelet chime as she nervously jiggles her legs. My heart hasn't stopped pounding.

'You named me Iliad after a book filled cover to cover with war, Mum! How can I be anything but hostile?'

The glass jumps from my hand without me realising. It flings itself onto the ground and shatters. Mum stiffens. I've scared her with my anger. I want to say sorry, but I never can. There's a memory that forces itself into my brain. My mother, after my dad has hit her. Because she didn't cook his food the way he likes it. Because she said something in the wrong tone of voice. Because I'd stupidly snuggled up to her, instead of him, on those rare occasions, and according to my father that meant she was attempting to use me to gang up against him. Because I was *his*. That led to the worst beatings. I learnt early to keep away from her.

After he'd hit her, he'd make her apologise.

'You made me do this,' he'd say to her, fist raised, face twisted so he looked more in pain than she did. 'You made me do this. *Apologise*, Eve.'

She'd say sorry. She always said sorry. And only then, after she'd apologised, did he slowly lower his fist. Like he was the victim.

I remember watching this, helpless, and I remember making a promise to myself. I would never be like her. I would never be a person who apologised.

Mum looks hard at me, then she turns to make her way to her bedroom, ignoring the tea steeping on the kitchen bench, her ankle bracelet jangling softer and softer until she's gone, and I slump down to rest on the oak coffee table. My heart starts to slow. Nan sits on the lounge and places the two teas down beside me, the mugs cutting circles into the old, unvarnished wood. I know Nan's added a dash of whisky to her own tea so I go to take a sip of it. She cuffs me on the back of my head and swipes it back.

'Keep out of it. That's my medicine. I've got a weak constitution.'

I roll my eyes. 'The only thing wrong with you is possible cirrhosis of the liver.'

'Bah!' she mutters, then she takes a swig and smacks her thin lips before pinioning me with her mean old eyes. 'We aren't the enemy, Iliad Piper. Be nice to your mother.' I don't know what to say to that so I stick out my tongue and she sticks her tongue out back and then I just watch as she heaves herself up to hobble to her own bedroom, her whisky-infused tea in hand.

I take the broom and pan and start to sweep up the broken glass shards from the floor. When I was little I used to think that all things had a sound trapped somewhere in them, like the noise was just waiting there, stuck inside atoms, and it was only when the thing was broken that the sound was given a chance to escape. I used to think that when my dad threw a plate, or when he punched a hole in the wall, the sound that I heard wasn't him. It wasn't his fist. I used to think that the shattering that rang in my ears was actually the plate or the wall finally being allowed to scream.

As I scrape the shards into the bin I wonder if that's why I'm always shouting. I wonder if it's because, long ago, something inside of me broke, and the crack from the breaking means that the sound inside of me can now escape. Sometimes it feels like it can't *not* escape.

I can't say sorry.

I can never say sorry.

But I climb the chair that Mum's left next to the windowpane. I reach and begin to untangle the threads of the wind chime. It's the only way I can apologise for being me.

two

'You keep your nose stuck up in the air like you do because you're sniffing for trouble, girly,' my nan always says to me. It's not untrue. I mean, in four years I've been expelled from five boarding schools. Now, Mum and Nan have run out of options and for year twelve they have to actually deal with having a teenager in the house.

It's funny, you skip school because you don't want to be there, and they think that expulsion's a punishment? For places that are all about 'educational excellence', those boarding schools really aren't that smart. On my first day of seniors college six months ago I saw Mia Tran sitting by herself at the back of the science lab, the tip of her tongue out in concentration, dismantling a Walkman from the 90s. I sat next to her and without looking up at me she pointed out the circuit boards, which she said looked like tiny houses, and the wires, which she said looked like their highways.

'It's like a little city,' she'd explained. 'It's like the people who live there are singing to us.'

She didn't flinch when I gave her a weird look, she just glanced up from her Walkman and met my stare like it had been the most normal thing in the world to say. I'd thought that lack of flinch meant something deliberately defiant about her, not that she was totally clueless. There's no school uniform at the public seniors college and Mia was wearing oversized 80s stonewash denim cut-off overalls with mismatched socks, jelly sandals and an ironic Britney singlet. It was only later that I realised none of this was ironic. She isn't a careful study of Björk. Mia just happens to dress like she was walking past an op shop as a cyclone whipped past and blew random clothes onto her. A black, asymmetrical pixie fringe frames her face, and her interest in uncool things doesn't come from a desire to be different.

She is different.

She is uncool.

She's an accidental hipster whose crooked fringe comes from her mother cutting her hair badly with sewing scissors, and the most rebellious thing she's ever done in her life is to score an A- once instead of an A+. She's unlike anyone I've ever known and I didn't want her as a friend.

I've never *done* friends.

But somehow here she is.

Mia's lying on the grass where we hang out before the first school bell. She's on her belly, knees bent, and she's kicking the sky with some seriously ugly orange Crocs. Her hair is pulled up into two little black buns on either side of her head so that they remind me of animal ears, and her fingers flutter expertly along the ground as she searches for four-leaf clovers. I'm listening to The Smiths on my phone and trying to avoid eye contact with the teacher who marches about on duty, pointing at rubbish that needs picking up, and then I see him. The dreamy guy. Mia looks over and clocks my expression, then sighs.

'You're still in love with the principal's son?'

I watch the boy slice his way through the schoolyard, all sharp bones and high cheekbones. With his James Dean quiff, black torn jeans and a crisp white t-shirt, he's seriously got a dishevelled old-school movie-star vibe going on. He graduated last year, but he goes to the nearby university and he sometimes shortcuts through the school grounds after sharing a ride with his mum, Principal Lovett.

Mia waves her hands in front of my eyes. They've unfocused themselves.

'No, I'm not in love. Lust. There's a very important difference. I don't believe in love.'

She scrunches her nose up at me.

'Love isn't the tooth fairy, Ily. I'm pretty certain it's of this world and not imaginary.'

I look down and notice a dying caterpillar near my foot. It's writhing and greedy ants are crawling all over it. Gross. I kick it away. 'In seventeen years I've never seen proof of either. Actually, the tooth fairy did leave behind money, so I take it back – the tooth fairy's existence is debatable.'

We sit there, me picking at the grass, Mia swinging her calves and looking intently at the clover patch.

'I still can't believe you're not dead, though – you did show your mum your last exam mark, right? The one you almost failed? I thought for sure you'd be dead today, and then you would have haunted your mother for killing you. I can see you as the poltergeist type. She'd have to get an exorcist.'

She plucks a clover and hands it over to me but I ignore

her and keep picking at the grass.

'An exorcist is for demon possession. She'd need a sage smudge-stick to get rid of ghosts. Apparently. And I'm alive. My mother's just happy that I turn up to class.'

'If I even got a B my mother would kill me. Actually, she'd lock me in the cupboard while she completed a first-aid course. Then she'd kill me just so she could resuscitate me and kill me again. And again. And again.'

'Lucky that's never going to happen. The B, I mean. And Mia, I'll tell you the secret of not getting into trouble. Just set low expectations of yourself.'

Mia rolls onto her side, cupping her cheek in her hand, and she scrunches her nose as though my life is a maths problem that she can't quite twist her brain around. Although Mia can figure out all things maths. She's dux of the year, every year. I roll my eyes and shove my earphones back in, pretending that she's not staring at me like a creeper now.

The first bell rings and we get up, brushing the grass from our knees and picking up our bags. Mine is slung sloppily over one shoulder while Mia's sits high in the middle of her back, her thumbs looped around the straps under her arms. She only lets go to pick at the hibiscus bushes that dot the schoolyard, flamboyant with colour. She hands one across to me but I flick it away.

'Mia. For the last time, I do not do flowers.'

She shrugs and picks it up, tucking it in the elastic band holding up one of her animal-ear buns.

'Honestly, Ily. Who hates flowers?'

Hamish McDiarmid lumbers past, from over near the janitor's shed where the footy heads sit. He's a rugby player and is therefore shaped like a big toe with a face drawn on it. He has a football crammed under his meaty arm and he's batting away a couple of dragonflies that thrum about whenever the dry season sets in. My eyes dart around to see where Max Selwyn is, because he and Hamish are a two-for-one deal, always punching each other on the shoulders and seeing who can out-insult the other. Six months in and I'm still not used to being at school with the male of the species. None of them are like the dreamy guy. I mean, over near the scribbly gum there are a couple of guys from the year below, faces covered in flesh-coloured Clearasil, and I can hear them having a competition to see who can burp the loudest. The sharp tang of unwashed undies wafts by as we pass them.

A whistle makes me look up into the branches of a nearby mango tree and damn it, there he is. Max. All gangly brown legs and defiant hair, and he's up in the tree for a reason.

The reason is me.

If I was a superhero then Max Selwyn would be cast as my obnoxious super-villain. It's not like it's my fault.

I mean, not really.

He was my second friend at this school, but only for a couple of hours.

I'd gotten lost on my way to last period. It was art, and everyone sits around these giant, rectangular tables instead of at individual desks. There were only two spaces left. One at the very back corner, and another right at the front. Obviously I plonked my bag down at the back corner and waited for the teacher to arrive. I wasn't the only late one. A few seconds later a girl sashayed in. She had over-plucked eyebrows and a ponytail so tight she was giving herself a facelift. I'd later find out her name is Jasmine, and it really doesn't suit her. If she had to be named after a plant I'd choose poison ivy. She looked unimpressed at the seat up-front, then scanned the room, saw me, and stomped

11

over to where I was graffitiing my notebook.

'That's where I'm sitting.' She'd said it like she actually expected me to give a damn.

I just rolled my eyes and stretched my arms out like I was pretending to yawn, and I settled myself into the seat.

'Weird. Because I'm the one sitting in it. You're standing. And by the way, those shoes that you're standing in are hideous.'

To her credit, she didn't scurry away. Instead she glared at me, tapping her ugly chunky wedges and arching those woefully diminished eyebrows.

'You better watch out, new girl, or people are going to think you're a bitch.'

I leant across the desk, giving her my most evil eye. 'No, you'd better watch out, or you'll find out just how much of a bitch I really am.'

She looked at me warily, not used to not being able to bully someone into submission.

'Rah!' I snarled at her, and she almost tripped backwards over her stupid wedges. When she begrudgingly sat down at the front I could hear her whispering loudly to the girl next to her.

'Like she can judge anyone's fashion. I mean, what's with her haircut? She looks like she got half her head stuck under a lawn mower.'

Ugh.

I returned to my graffiti. The guy next to me leaned across, a grin cracking open his face.

'You went to a lot of effort to stay sitting next to me, hey. I have that effect on women.'

I looked over to see who it was, and I rolled my eyes.

'Dork.'

12

But I was kind of glad he'd talked to me. I'd first noticed him in English, and I watched him muck around and laze across his seat and I thought he was the type of person I could maybe want to hang with. He has these swampy-coloured green eyes, the kind of swamp that you just know would have dangerous creatures lurking there below the surface. His collar-length, tangled dark hair is the sort that wouldn't ever let anyone tell it what to do, and he's Indigenous, so his skin is the kind of brown that catches and throws out the light. I was interested, but it's not like I'd let him know that.

'I'm Max,' he said. I ignored him. He swiped my notebook and read my name aloud from the front cover.

'Ily Piper. Heaps nice of you to introduce yourself.'

I snatched my book back.

'Why are you even talking to me?'

'Dunno. People who can match my eye-rolling ability intrigue me?'

Despite myself, a small smile escaped from my scowl and I went back to sketching in my notebook. I drew a creature with a gargoyle head wielding a sword, mid-swing, although its long claws would be enough to do damage on their own. It was covered in armadillo armour, with spikes shooting from its skin. Weapons were slung across its back, and its face was twisted angrily, hissing with a long, forked tongue that extended past the fangs. Max leant over me to look at it.

'That drawing's deadly.'

Deadly is a Darwin word. It basically means something's really great. Queensland has its own words as well – I used to say *togs* instead of *swimmers* until I got teased at boarding school for calling them that. I used to say *yeww* to show I

13

was excited by something until I was teased for that too. I'd gotten out of the habit of saying all the local slang when I was sent to Melbourne and the girls there looked at me like I was speaking some primitive foreign language whenever I spoke. When those girls rolled the Queensland words around in their mouths they acted as though they were tasting something rotten and foul. There are so many words I stopped using when I went away. I shouldn't have minded so much what those girls thought of me, those were girls who had cash registers for souls, but I did, back then, and by the time I'd stopped caring I had shaken so much of my home town from me that using my old mannerisms felt like I was trying to force on garments that didn't fit me anymore. I felt like nothing fit me anymore.

Darwin has its own language, I've discovered. As well as *deadly*, there's *budju*, which means a hot person, and *gammon*, which pretty much means something isn't true, or it's insincere or uncool. I knew what Max meant, but I shrugged and kept drawing.

'It's my Patronus.'

He blinked, then he laughed, running his fingers through that hair of his, which looked like it was allergic to brushes.

'Na, I don't buy it,' he'd replied when he'd stopped laughing. 'Pottermore lied to you. That looks way too friendly to be yours.'

For the rest of art we ignored the theory we were supposed to be listening to and rolled our eyes in unison. I hate theory, the way the experts tell you what an artwork is supposed to mean, because the way I see it, the whole point of art is in the way you react to it, how that reaction is all your own, and that's important, because sometimes there's not much else in the whole world you can lay claim to. I'll probably never own a Jackson Pollock painting, but I own the way his work makes me feel as though I'm looking at the way I'd paint myself if I'd never seen a mirror. The art theorists can't know that.

I learnt that Max hated most of the same things. I've always thought that shared disdain was the best way to bond with a person. He made me really warm to the mysterious Y chromosome.

The final bell rang and we were gathering our books.

'You're Eve Piper's daughter, aren't you?' he asked, but it wasn't really a question. 'I can tell by the hair.'

I sighed and shoved my pencil case in my bag and zipped it up.

'Unfortunately.'

His grin barged out of his face again.

'The girl next door, hey? We moved into the property next to yours last year. You weren't on the bus here so you drive, right? You can give me a lift home.'

I'd inherited my nan's old Toyota after her eyesight became too bad to drive and she accidentally ran off the road and decimated a termite mound. The bus to our place does take at least twice as long as driving, but I wasn't in the habit of doing people favours.

'Why would I do that?'

He just grinned wider.

'Because I reckon that underneath that mean look you're giving me, deep down you're the kind of girl who gives lifts to people in need.'

My scowl cracked again, just a little, and I sighed as he raised his eyebrows at me, hopefully.

'You're a terrible judge of character.'

He kept up that hopeful look.

'Okay. *Fine*.'

We drove out of the city limits towards home, to where the scrub straddles the highway, looking like it belongs to the dinosaur era, all turkey bush and spiky-leaved pandanus, with the occasional wallaby corpse, sad and flattened against the asphalt. Max kept trying to turn the radio onto the hip-hop station and I kept whacking him and returning it to Triple J. His skin felt nice on my skin.

'Do you always dress so colourfully?' he asked me, his hair tangling as the wind barrelled in through the open window. He was talking about my black nail polish, black jeans, black Cons and my black Velvet Underground t-shirt.

'I like this shade of black. I feel it really brings out the colour of my soul.'

He cocked his head to the side and shot me a crooked smile and I swear I could see the snout of a crocodile bob up from those swamp pools in his eyes.

'So, did a hairbrush or scissors do something to insult you once?' I asked, indicating to pass a campervan full of tourists. It was his turn to roll his eyes at me then.

'I like my hair to reflect my life.'

'What, don't tell me. *Wild*?'

I said wild sarcastically. Obviously. Max just shook his head and something soft swam across his face. Just for a second, and then it was gone.

'Na,' he said. 'Messy.'

He leant his head against the window frame and his hair rioted and we kept on driving, in silence for a bit.

'Hey, since you're the girl next door, you should swing

around mine this arvo,' he said, eventually. I raised my eyebrow. He went on. 'I'll show you my *python*.'

I gripped the steering wheel angrily, trying to compute what he was saying. His python?

Gross.

What a stupid nickname for his penis. He clocked my unimpressed face and just replied with a grin and tapped tunes onto his legs and kept on talking. 'It might freak you out though, it's huge.'

That was it.

His words scraped against my ears like matches against a matchbox and there was a spark and then a flame and then everything around me turned to fire. Max didn't notice he was sitting inside a fireball. He didn't notice that the world had turned red, that the plastic seats were melting and that the metal around us was turning to cinder. He didn't notice the flames clawing up and out the car window and setting the sky ablaze.

He didn't notice.

I skidded the car to a halt.

'Get out,' I hissed.

'What?' His stupid grin fell away and his eyebrows knitted together, confused.

'Get the hell out of my car.'

He stayed put, trying to figure out if I was playing some joke, waiting for the punchline that never came. The flames crackled. The sky burned. I reached over and unclicked his seatbelt and leant across to yank open his door.

'Get out.'

'Oi, settle down. We're in the middle of nowhere.'

'Not my problem,' I muttered, and then I shoved him.

He fell.

The earth caught him just fine.

I pressed the accelerator and watched him get smaller and smaller in the rear-view mirror. Slowly, the flames stopped licking at me. Slowly, the fire turned to embers, and by the time I reached home, the fire was out.

I felt scorched.

I felt spent.

And then, thankfully, after a while, I stopped feeling altogether, and it was only then that I could be calm.

So that was how Max became my nemesis.

That was the beginning of the prank war.

And now he's up in a tree, waiting for me, and I know that no good can come of this.

'Missing something?' Max calls down to me, and I can see him smirking through the mango tree leaves, waving a jumper of mine victoriously above his head. I recognise it as the one I'd worn when we went for an excursion to the art gallery the other day and they'd cranked up the air conditioner. Even though it's my regulation black, the jumper's hideous, all crocheted with loose, bell sleeves. Mum bought it for me when I was living down in Melbourne and it repulses me so much that I'd left it behind on the bus deliberately. I roll my eyes and watch Max as he straddles the bough and struggles to tie the sleeves around the branch above him. This is one of his more stupid prank attempts and retrieving the jumper doesn't interest me a bit.

What does interest me, however, is the way he's not aware that his head is getting closer and closer to a green-ant nest that's dangling just behind him. Despite their name, green ants aren't green, they're orange with green bums, and instead of living under the ground like most ants do, they live up in trees, and they weave leaves together with larval silk to make football-shaped hanging nests. The nests adorn the trees like giant Christmas baubles, except inside they're full of thousands of ants and larvae. The ants don't usually bite unless you're threatening their nest, then they swarm, and Max is just about to discover this.

Ha!

His head knocks back against the thing and I watch as they begin to crawl all through his messy hair. It takes him a little while to notice, but when he does, he really notices. His swearwords come tumbling down from the branches, along with my jumper, which I ignore, and he bats the nest away furiously after a bunch of ants have bitten him. After a vigorous thwack the nest falls down onto the ground with a light thud and splits open slightly, revealing the larvae and insects like it's some ant piñata. Max is too distracted by the bites and flicking the creatures from his skin to remember he's left his schoolbag on the ground. He doesn't notice me casually pick up his bag and unzip it. He doesn't notice as I kick the ant nest from where it'd fallen on the ground into his school bag, and then re-zip it.

Until he does.

Oh, he notices.

'No, you didn't just do that! Ily Piper, you are going *down*!' He's scrambling from the branches, thrashing at the ants. A smile plays on my lips as I turn my back to him and start walking to class. He swears some more and I reply by giving him the finger, and I sort of wish that it wasn't just my black, chipped nail polish facing him because the next minute I hear him fall the last metre to the ground. It's a satisfying kind of sound. Mia winces.

'Okay, so if your mother doesn't kill you, then I'm guessing Max will.'

I shrug.

'He started it.'

'You made him walk an hour home. Back when it was the wet season. Just before it stormed. Ily, I love you but that was kind of subpar behaviour.'

In the wet season the thunder shakes the whole horizon, and the rain's so heavy that each drop could take out a blowfly. Max was half-drowned by the time he'd reached home, apparently.

'Well, he shouldn't have invited me to check out his python.'

Mia cups her head into her hands dramatically.

'He owns a pet python – everyone knows that. It's called Fluffy and it lives in a fish tank next to his bed.'

I roll my eyes, unmoved.

'How was I supposed to know he was being literal?'

Mia releases her head and sighs, then picks some more flowers from a vine strangling the perimeter fence.

'All right, but maybe you should have just let him egg your car that first time and been done with it.'

'Mia, for someone who wins so many awards, you sound a lot like a defeatist.'

She peels back strands of crooked fringe that the morning sweat's already pasted onto her forehead.

'It's not a matter of defeat. It's an optimal strategy to learn what's statistically in your favour.'

I deadpan her. 'Speak English, not robot.'

'Pick your battles.'

I think of my name and how it suits me. How there's always a sort of fighting going on inside me, and how I sure

20

as hell won't put down my weapons for anyone, especially not to make peace with the likes of Max Selwyn.

'See these black clothes, Mia? It's because I'm secretly a ninja. Ninjas are made for battle. All I'm saying is that Max had better sleep with one eye open.'

three

Class is excruciating, like it always is. I keep doing this thing where my eyes randomly go out of focus, but I'm too lazy to focus them, so I just have a glazed sort of stare. Whenever I do it at home Mum thinks I'm meditating and she gets all excited about it. That's how most of my days pass at school. People wonder why I haven't quit school already, since I hate it so much. Part of it is because of art. I don't know if I'm stupid or not, but the thing is, it's hard to concentrate in school when you're only little and you don't know if your dad's going to be hurting your mum and you're not there to take his hand and calm him down. By the time we left him I was so far behind the rest of the class that it feels like I can never catch up.

Words and numbers tangle up inside of me and whenever I try to say them or write them they come out upside down, or arranged the wrong way, and they scrape inside my skull, stuck. When I make art, it's like I can scoop out what's inside my head and let it escape into the world. It's like a pressure valve being released. It transports me and it's always been the closest thing I have to running away without going anywhere. I want to study art at university, I could even cope with the theory if I got to create, and if that means putting up with maths and English and zoning out for six hours a day, so be it.

The second reason I haven't quit yet is probably the main reason. It's because everyone has always expected me to quit and to fail. I've found that there's only one emotion that's more powerful than hate, and no, it's not love.

It's spite.

I so badly want to finish year twelve to spite everyone who thinks I can't. That's pretty much everyone, if we're keeping score here. My mum doesn't think these are very good emotions to be compelled by and she tries to tell me that I should be motivated by love and forgiveness and all of that, but this is a woman who also believes in coffee enemas to ward off cancer. I'm not convinced that a person who advocates shoving coffee up your arse is somebody who you should be taking any sort of advice from.

Right now I'm in English and the clock that hangs beside the blackboard yawns at me as Mr Salmon tries to inspire us to love *Macbeth*. He uses the class as his own personal captive audience as he bungs on a bad Shakespearean accent, caresses his thick ginger beard and walks around the classroom like it's a stage made just for him. He wears his socks up to where his shorts reach his knees and he has a wardrobe full of whacky shirts. We all roll our eyes and stab the desks with our compasses. Mr Salmon's theatrical talents are really wasted on this school. At the moment he's quoting Lady Macbeth.

> *Come, you spirits*
> *That tend on mortal thoughts, unsex me here,*
> *And fill me from the crown to the toe top-full*
> *Of direst cruelty!*

Everybody cracks up when he says 'unsex'.

Morons.

'Enough, enough with your snickering, lift your minds up to loftier places. Let them soar. Max, what do you think Lady Macbeth is trying to tell us?'

Max looks up from blowing at the green ants crawling over his notebook. He slouches back in his chair and taps his teeth with the end of his chewed-up pen and tips his head upwards with all the confidence of the popular.

'That some girls are angry and insane? Isn't that right, Ily?'

He tears a green-ant–riddled page from the book in front of him and scrunches it into a ball, then throws it at my head. A terrible throw, surprising for a footballer. I think he was distracted by a biting ant. Mr Salmon picks it from the floor and pegs it back at Max, knocking him right between the eyes.

'You might find, young Maximus, that if several women aren't smitten by your charms, then perhaps they aren't insane and that indeed it's you that's the common denominator?'

The class cracks up again but Max just rolls his eyes and grins a lazy grin. I ignore everyone and pick at a piece of organic buckwheat porridge that must have fallen onto my jeans during breakfast. It peels off in chunks. I swear the only thing I miss about boarding school is eating meals filled with sugar and preservatives.

'Iliad, a retort from you?'

I slide my eyes across to grip Max's bog-coloured gaze with my own and try to stare him down.

'I think Lady Macbeth is saying that it sucks being a woman in a world run by idiot men and if she has to act like a mega bitch in order to deal with them, so be it.'

'An interesting feminist reading of the text, Iliad, but you do know that it's school policy to grant automatic after-hours detention for using that kind of language during class, yes?'

I'm about to protest, but Mr Salmon raises his hand like he doesn't want to hear it.

'Detention. And if you must swear in the future, you should take your cues from Shakespeare. They're much more eloquent – *thou clay-brained guts, thou knotty-pated fool, thou whoreson, obscene, grease tallow-catch*.'

I glare at Max, but he just smirks at me.

Jerk.

I'm stomping back to the car park after detention and the hallways echo with emptiness. I'm taking my year twelve major work from the art studio home and it's heavy under my arm. I'm making a sort of self-portrait for my major assessment, but instead of using paint I've been collecting all the war figurines I can find over the past six months. I've been riffling through Vinnies and rummaging through garage sales and stealing from doctors' waiting rooms in search of tin soldiers, G.I. Joes, those little green plastic army men and Lego people holding swords and guns. I've sorted them into colours and I've drawn a huge sketch outline of my head and shoulders onto a great big piece of wood veneer, filling it in with all the different figurines. It's something on a scale to rival the tales of Achilles, Paris and Hector from Homer's book *The Iliad*, which I'm named after. A war inside of me. I'm three quarters done and I wish I could show it to my English teacher to prove to him that I do actually know what a metaphor is, even if I can never put it down into pretty-sounding sentences.

And I almost drop the whole thing when I hear a violent crash nearby.

Dad.

My heart does the automatic *kerthump, kerthump, kerthump*.

Everything tightens under the grip of my nerves.

My eyes dart to see where the noise is coming from.

And it's okay.

It's okay.

I try to tell my panicked body that everything's okay.

There's a bunch of crates stacked near the big rubbish skips that sit next to the car park, and dreamy guy, other-wise known as the principal's son, is kicking at the pile of crates, lifting them above his head, and crashing them down below. They're plastic so they just bounce, indestructible. He looks hurt and angry and raw, like all that is inside of him has crawled out to sit there on top of his skin for anyone to see. It startles me.

So I stand there, frozen, my art piece under my arm, until a crate comes flying and rests at my feet and he sees me, standing there like a creeper. He jumps, surprised, and I know he's about to start on me, because that's what peo-ple do when they feel vulnerable. I know. Fighting against

26

someone else is easier than letting the humiliation slay you. We both stand there, ready to snarl.

When the principal walks out. Her eyes sweep the carnage before her.

'Is this how you react to our discussion, Jared? How mature.'

So his name is Jared. I tuck that piece of information away in my pocket.

Whatever realness that had been sitting on his skin has been sucked back deep inside of him, and the mask he wears now is hard and impenetrable.

It's not the lust I feel towards him that makes me do what I do next, even though the boy has cheekbones that you could cut your fingertips on, willingly, and lashes that loop thickly around his storm-grey eyes. It's the something real I saw in him that compels me to act. It's the things I saw when he thought no one was looking.

I step forward.

'It was me.'

They both just stare at me now.

I speak louder. Chin up. Daring anyone to contradict me.

'I was the one who threw the crates.'

I can tell Mrs Lovett doesn't believe me, but she can hardly punish her son when someone else is owning up. And she can hardly punish me for something she knows I didn't do. She taps her feet.

'All right, Iliad Piper. Please pick up the crates and stack them neatly like they were. Jared, we'll discuss this further in the car.'

'No!' His voice is low and determined. 'I'll make my own way home.'

She taps her feet again.

'Oh, you will? You'll catch three buses? Don't be ridiculous.'

I speak up.

'I told him that I'd give him a lift.'

Jared looks curiously at me, but nods at his mother.

'Yep. I'm going with her.'

She sighs and then rummages through her handbag for keys as she turns to clip-clop over to her car.

'Fine, Iliad,' she says over her shoulder. 'You had after-school detention yet again today, didn't you? For a girl who's only quite new at this school, you've really tried your best to put yourself on my radar.'

four

Jared's glaring out the window and I try to focus on the road and not the fact the boy I've been lusting after these last few months is sitting less than a metre away from me.

'Which way's your house?' I ask, and he just keeps looking out the window at the flat, suburban streets and the palms that dot the lawns.

'I don't want to go home yet. Drive me into town?'

Okay. So dreamy guy's not really a talker. I indicate to switch lanes and we're silent except for the indie song playing on Triple J, and I'm nervous. I wish I was someone who got smiley when they were nervous, but when I pull my lips away from my teeth I just look like a growling dog, not a friendly person. My words come out like barks and snarls, and people move away from me. It's strange, how my personality veers so wildly between crippling anxiety and not giving a damn about anything at all, and both these personalities are so jumbled inside of me that I'm not sure which of the two is the real me. Jared finally breaks the silence.

'So your name's really Iliad? Like, the books by Homer, *The Iliad* and *The Odyssey*?'

I've heard this question a thousand times and I roll my eyes.

'Yeah, but everyone calls me Ily. And it's not like I had any say in what I was called. I was named after my father.'

He turns to me, one brow raised incredulously.

'Your dad's named Iliad?'

I keep my eyes on the road and my voice neutral.

'No, his name's Troy. They thought they were having a boy, so I was nothing but Troy Junior until I was born missing that all-important Y chromosome. My mum came up with my name. So, like, Ilium is another name for the ancient Greek city of Troy, and Iliad, like the book, means "in relation to Troy". So I'm unfortunately forever defined by my father.'

He rests his head back on the window frame, staring out at the shifting landscape.

'Everyone's always unfortunately defined by their parents, whether we're named after them or not.'

A metal song starts playing and Jared fiddles with the radio knobs to change stations, then he turns to look over to where my artwork rests on the flattened back seats. He whistles through his teeth, impressed.

'Did you make that?'

I nod and keep my gaze forward.

'It's not finished yet. It's my art major work.'

I'm almost at the mall in town, where I was planning to drop him off, but Jared's still looking back at the piece.

30

'Don't stop here. I've got a better idea,' he tells me. 'Keep going out to East Point.'

I pull over when we get to East Point. It's a reserve not far from the city centre, a vast strip of public parkland set against the ocean. There's nobody around except for a man in the distance in a reflector vest who's riding a mower across the yellowed, dry-season grass. The buzz from the distant mower sort of sounds like the insects that are droning all around us. We get out and Jared's already making his way towards the beach. He jumps down from the embankment. I follow him and sit at the edge while he's kicking at the pebbly sand. I watch as the sun dazzles over the bright blue water and bounces over the ripples of the flat Arafura Sea. The horizon's so vast you can almost imagine you can see Indonesia, if you squint.

'What are you doing?' I ask as he crouches and digs his hands down so that the sand swallows them up. After a bit, he stands back up and opens his palm flat towards me. I slide off the embankment and step forward to see what he's got. It's a rusted old bullet shell.

'There're heaps of these around if you look for them. Down the other end of the reserve are a bunch of old army bunkers from World War Two from when the Japanese invaded. They bombed the place as well. The far north is the only part of Australia that's been attacked by foreign forces, well, since white people arrived anyway, but most people don't know about any of it, not southerners. All around here is riddled with World War Two bullet cartridges.' He tries to look nonchalant, like he doesn't really care, and he shrugs. 'Thought the bullets would look cool. If you wanted to use

31

them, you know, for your major work.'

It's perfect. I take the bullet casing from him and his touch zings through me. I don't know how to react to that, so I just snatch my hand back and I know my face is probably looking pinched and mean so I concentrate hard on kicking through the sand as he joins me in the search for more bullets. We've found six shells before we're done. The heat's pressing down on us here with no shelter to stifle the sun that's all puffed and smug and smearing everything in a glaze of sweat. I'm glad when Jared finally suggests we drive into town to get drinks.

We grab a couple of iced coffees from the shop and we're walking along the footpath when I see Mum's car. The street she's parked it on has parking meters, and I watch a parking inspector coming closer and closer. I can see his eyes light up when he spots it. What is it with parking inspectors getting so much glee out of inflicting misery? Before he has time to cross the street I dig into my pocket to slide a couple of coins into a nearby meter and then I stomp over and shove the ticket under her windscreen wipers. She'd forgotten to get one, of course, and I curse her under my breath, the way she gets so caught up in whatever hue her aura is at any given moment that she forgets to notice actual things like buying parking tickets. I raise my middle finger at the inspector as we walk off.

Jerk.

And then, of course, Mum appears. She's coming out of the nearby wholefood grocery and deli, distracted by her organic quinoa or goji berries or whatever disgustingly wholesome food she insists on inflicting upon me.

Shit.

I grab Jared's arm and race down an alleyway so she doesn't see me.

'What was that all about?' Jared asks when we've turned the corner and I've got my back rested against the wall, catching my breath.

'It's my mum. That was her car.'

He gives me a funny look.

'So you saved her from a fine. Why the hell are you hiding from her?'

I stub my toe into the concrete and try to put it into words.

'Do you know how you can always be trying to protect someone, and still sort of hate them at the same time? Like, you're so angry at them that you don't want to let them know that you care?'

He shrugs like he has no idea what I'm talking about, and I dig my fingernails into the brick wall behind me and wish I hadn't said anything. It's none of his business. We stand there in silence for a bit, but he's looking at me like he's trying to figure me out.

'You're not like everyone else, are you?' he asks, finally.

I scowl and step out from the alleyway onto the back street so I can loop around to my car and avoid Mum.

'Who says I want to be like everyone else?'

Jared keeps in step as I stomp along the footpath and he's looking at me curiously now, and when he draws his mouth into an amused half-smile I notice a dimple nuzzle its way into his cheek.

'Hey,' he says, as he grabs my arm to stop me.

'Who says I meant it like a bad thing?'

The way he says it is like we're in a secret club, like we

33

don't *want* to belong with the others. I just stare at him. The space between us feels like it's buzzing, and I have to take a long swig of iced coffee to keep my emotions in check. He keeps going.

'You know, I never said thank you. For what you did for me, with the crates and stuff.'

I screw my nose up, embarrassed.

'Don't worry about it. So what did the crates do, earlier today, to deserve your wrath?'

He looks up at the sky. It's streaked with sunset pinks and oranges now it's getting late.

'The crates were innocent. They're collateral damage. It's just. My parents. They think I'm still a kid and I just want to be my own person and make my own choices. I'm eighteen for Christ's sake. I want to be allowed to be an adult.'

I get it. I so badly want to shake my childhood off me and step away from it like it's an ugly, shoddy garment that I can leave behind on the floor and become someone else. Anyone else. I want to tell my childhood self to scram. I don't know if it's true or just a myth, but I heard once that each cell in your body only has a seven-year lifespan, so that even if you remember something from when you were little, in actual fact not even a single atom of who you are now was there, experiencing it. Not a single cell. I can't wait for seven years from now. I can't wait until not a single atom of the child-hood Ily exists anymore.

'Is that what the conversation with your mum was about this afternoon?' I ask him.

His face darkens and he nods.

'I told her I want to quit my accounting degree and move to Sydney next year to concentrate on acting. It's the only thing that I really want. They're so focused on me being like them, me having a stable career, but screw that. I would give up stability, I'd give up anything and anyone, if I could make it as an actor.'

I don't know what to say to that. My mum would support any career I chose. I don't know if she even cares. The sky keeps softening and mosquitoes descend, like they do every evening. We're silent, except for the sound we make when we slap at them. We can see Venus, the first star to wriggle through the sunset, though it's really a planet not a star. Jared reaches his hand up towards it, and he's got his forefinger and thumb poised, like he could pluck it right out of the sky.

'That's gonna be me one day. A star. People think it's arrogant to say it out loud – that, like, the chances of it happening are so low, but even if it's point zero zero zero one per cent or something, the chances of it coming true are still higher than if I didn't try at all, 'cos then it'd be zero, and I know it's stupid, but an old lady who reads tarot cards at the markets told me I'd be famous once, when I was a little kid. I've never forgotten it.'

'You are made out of star stuff, you know,' I tell him, after a long stretched-out moment. 'A science teacher told me this once. Hear me out. So almost every atom in everyone's bodies comes from stars that once exploded. Like, everything we're made of, oxygen and nitrogen and iron and carbon, all the building blocks, they were made in the belly of a star and those bits of us that came from the stars were once upon a time up in the sky there, shining like the rest of them. Isn't that cool?'

His smile is tight, but it still makes his dimples wink at me. I wish again I could be a girl who smiled back, one who laughed easily and who could flirt, but I'm not. He shakes his head like he doesn't agree.

'I don't want to be made of the same stuff as everyone else, Ily. You're not made of it either. I saw your art. You wouldn't be happy being ordinary.'

I roll my eyes, embarrassed again. He's half right. Happy isn't an adjective that could ever be used to describe me. I'm picking at my jeans when he reaches across and grabs my hand. I look up at him and I notice the dip at the centre of his perfect lips, and the way the quiff of his hair is being mussed about by the breeze.

'God, you're striking,' he tells me, and it's so unexpected that I want to scowl or roll my eyes but it feels like his intense gaze has hooked onto my soul and is reeling all of me out through my pupils. I don't do compliments, but it's not like he called me pretty, or beautiful, or any of those words that I know are just lies that guys use on girls when they want an easy hook-up. Guys use 'beautiful' like the word is a cheat code in a video game, one where they throw random adjectives at any girl-shaped thing in the hope that the right combination will result in getting laid. I might not be the cleverest girl, but I'm not stupid enough to fall for beautiful. *Striking* though. I could be that. I roll the word around my brain and try it on. Striking. The school counsellors called my behaviour *striking out* and I've never heard the word used as a positive thing before.

And then he leans down and kisses me.

Me.

Iliad Piper.

I'm being kissed by the dreamy guy.

I can taste the hint of iced coffee and it makes me buzz. The feel of his lips and the way his hand is brushing the curve of my waist makes me suddenly understand how softness can be beautiful. All my brittleness begins to melt under his touch, his fingers skimming under the hem of my shirt. I feel my armour slipping from where I always wear it, invisible there against my skin. The kiss lasts an eternity, but then an eternity is over, and it's strange how something can seem to last forever and still not be nearly long enough. He pulls away and I don't want him to, but I open my eyes and realise that he's only stopped because he's smiling, his head still dipped towards mine, and I can't quite believe that I'm able to coax out those dimples. Before I can say anything he leans in again, and his mouth silences me again. Me. The girl who's always shouting. But in this moment, all I want to be is quiet. Until right now, I never realised just how good quiet could be. The whole world goes silent except for my heart, which has never been so loud.

He puts his number in my phone and once I've dropped him off back at his place and I'm driving home, I think, *shit*.

When we left my dad, when I was first sent away to boarding school, I remember beginning to erect that wall I've got around my heart. Building it higher and higher, adding spikes and razor wire. Before I was sent away I had loved Mum, even if I was never allowed to show it. I'd loved the place in Queensland and the ferns there and the feeling of having a home, no matter how dysfunctional it might have been. And Dad too, I'd loved Dad fiercely, even in the times I was frightened of him, because I'd thought he was my best friend and children are stupidly generous with their hearts before they learn to be more careful about it.

At seventeen, though, I'd stopped loving things, because I learnt that every time you love something you give a little piece of your heart away. I learnt this lesson the hard way when everything I'd ever known and loved was taken away from me when I was sent to Melbourne and my heart felt shredded to pieces. After that, I was astonished by how I'd once just handed out love so recklessly. I'd stood in the dorm of that first boarding school and dropped my bags and looked around the cold, stark room and my fingers had flown to that place on my neck where you can feel your pulse. I had to stand like that for a while, feeling it thumping, just to convince myself I even had any heart left.

I'd stopped believing in love anymore.

I tell myself this, as I drive along the highway.

I don't believe in love.

But my heart is betraying me, the way I feel it skip a beat every time I think about this afternoon with Jared.

five

It's the weekend and I'm woken up by Mum blaring some CD with the sound of whale calls through the house. I groan and press the pillow against my ears, but then I remember yesterday, with the dreamy guy. I roll over to grab my phone from the bedside table and I scroll through the contacts to make sure it wasn't just some impossibly good dream. Nope. There's his name. A huge grin barges onto my face and I pull the sheet over my head and I kick my feet against the mattress because it's possible I've felt this happy before, at least once in my seventeen years, but if I have, I can't remember it, and the whale calls don't even annoy me anymore. I pad through the hallways and the nails poking out through the exposed timber floorboards keep nipping at my bare feet. Nana is making a ruckus with the pots and pans as she attempts to make us omelettes.

'Not those bloody damned whales again,' she says to

herself as I duck past her and turn the kettle on. She raises her voice. 'Eve, you don't even know what those whales are harping on about. They could be saying all sorts of uncouth things in that funny whale language for all you know.'

'Yeah,' I call out, 'or worse, they could be insulting Deepak Chopra.'

Mum enters from the next room, all Indian saffron scarves with her feet bound in rough-hewn leather sandals and her toenails painted lavender. She's carrying a feather duster and she bops me on the head with it as she steals the mug of green tea I've got steeping on the bench. I roll my eyes at her but I'm too happy to be really annoyed so I just switch the kettle back on.

'Blasphemy, Iliad,' says Mum. Deepak Chopra is like her god. When she speaks to her clients she sounds like one of those random Deepak Chopra quote generators you can find on the internet. She speaks in a jumble of random profound-sounding words which make little to no sense when you really think about them. My personal favourite is 'Your heart requires unbridled possibilities for quantum bliss'. Mum wasn't impressed when I sent her the quote generator link with the message – *Mum, is this you trapped in the computer??*

The kettle starts screeching and I make another cup of tea for myself.

'You're right,' I tell Mum. 'The whales wouldn't *dare* question Deepak. Whales really aren't smart enough to question *Deepak*, their brains being fish brains after all, so I can understand why you like them.'

Mum sighs her trademark sigh at me and runs her fingers through her long curly hair. 'Whales are mammals, Iliad, not fish.'

Nan lays out three plates and starts to serve up the omelettes. Mum purses her lips when she sees them.

'Mother, you know that I'm a vegan. How many times
have I asked you to use your own cookware if you're going
to insist on serving up animal products? Dead animals have
an energy, you know, and the energy of death seeps into the
metal and tampers with the vibration of the vegetables when
I go to cook them.'

When she says this, Mum pats herself down absentmindedly, her long hand tapping against her bones as though she's
feeling to make sure she's still there. I didn't inherit much
from my father. Looking at my mother is like looking at a
flesh mirror, except I'm the distorted reflection. It'd be a real
mirror if you cut me back to the bones, slicing away the small
pockets of fat from my hips and my cheeks and the slight
roundness from my belly. Surviving on nothing but air,
kombucha tea and kale is *so* not worth it though, and I take
the omelette from Nan and sit down at the kitchen table.

'The eggs are unfertilised, you ninny. There are no *death
vibrations*.' That's Nan. She doesn't truck with nonsense.

I pipe up with my mouth full. 'Mmmm, unfertilised
chicken period.'

Mum ignores Nan and shoots me an unimpressed look
as she adjusts the chunky crystal necklace that drapes against
her clavicles.

'Must you torment me, Iliad?' She sits down with us, her
plate empty. 'I'm having a Group Intensive over this next
couple of days. If you want petrol money this week you'll
help me this morning making the bungalows ready for
visitors.'

Mum is a self-styled spiritual therapist and since moving up to Darwin she's been supporting us by taking money

from the bored comfortable. I mean, on some of her meditation retreats people pay her loads of money to literally sit around and do nothing. I have to hand it to her, she's got a good racket going on, and the worst thing is, she actually believes she's doing good and helping people. On her website she doesn't use her real name, in case Dad googles her when he's let out. She calls herself 'Mystic Everbright – Crystal Healer, Reiki Practitioner, Homeopathic Pharmacist, Vibrations Diviner, Aura Cleanser and Spiritual Psychotherapist'.

Dad never let Mum work, and even though I'd never tell her, I secretly respect the fact she went back to study when I was away at boarding school, even if it was some online course about the magic crystals and chakras that have always fascinated her. I don't believe in it, but she does, and given that she charges higher rates than qualified and regulated psychologists and psychiatrists with actual medical degrees and peer-reviewed studies I'll grudgingly admit that there's a fortune to be made from woo peddling.

'I can't help you clean the bungalows. Soz. I have to work on my year-twelve art project. It's due soon,' I tell Mum between mouthfuls while I shovel the last of the egg into my mouth and slurp down the green tea. I say it in a *sorry not sorry* kind of way.

'Girly, for once in your life can you make your mother glad she endured a forty-hour labour?' barks Nan.

I glare at her. She's still eating and her cutlery is making these annoying, tinny scrapes as she cuts and scoops up her egg. I roll my eyes.

'That's really insulting,' I tell her.

'Your attitude is insulting,' she slings back at me. It's funny how quickly happiness can drain from you. I seem to have the kind of skin that can hold in all the bad stuff while the good stuff just leaks out of my pores so quickly.

'I'm here because Mum's got no other options, but why are you here?' I yell at her. 'Just go to a nursing home or something!'

She keeps chewing loudly and staring me down with her mean old eyes.

'Iliad, keep your voice down please.' That's Mum. She's nibbling at her nails and taking Nan's side, as usual. 'My mother paid for this roof over your head and she's a great help to me, and I'd appreciate it if you were too. Unless you decide to start taking the bus into school I know you'll need petrol money. So please, help with the bungalows.'

She has me there. I do need money. I get up and slam my dishes into the sink, not hard enough for them to break, but hard enough for them to clatter.

'What good has the roof of this house done me when you never wanted me living under it anyway?'

Mum looks hurt, and I wish I could take the padlock from my tongue and let a *sorry* escape, but I don't have the key. The *sorry* stays inside me.

'All right. You work on your art, I'll do it myself.'

Then she reaches out to touch me, but I flinch, unconsciously.

'I love you, daughter.'

I bite my lip, and I wish I could hug her, or say it back. Instead, I just nod, and walk outside.

I used to think my dad didn't mind that I was born a girl instead of Troy Junior. I used to think we were conspirators. When I was small he'd pick me up and place me on the Hills Hoist, up there with the drying knickers and his King Gee shorts and Mum's peasant skirts flapping in the wind, and he'd spin it around so that the world became dizzy and fun. He'd smell of beer on those occasions, but I didn't know that then. I just thought he smelt of fun dad. When Mum would come looking for me, he'd throw me over his shoulders and tell me, 'Let's hide from Mummy,' and we'd crouch down in a cluster of ferns, watching her worry. If she'd spot us we'd run. Laughter trailed behind me like blown bubbles in the breeze as I ran from her. It was our game.

'Tell Mummy she's a bitch,' Dad would say to me at other times. I knew it was a bad word, and I'd stop sucking my ice block to look up at him, unsure. If I hesitated, his face would cloud and turn a purple shade like a summer storm. 'Did you hear me, girl?' I knew better than to not hear him. I knew the backside of his hand. Not nearly as badly as Mum, because he loved me best, because I was part him, but I knew what slaps felt like. I'd pad over to where Mum was.

'You're a bitch.'

Dad would roar with laughter and tickle me so much that melted red Zooper Dooper would spill all over the tiles, and I'd laugh, because you can't not laugh when you're being tickled, but I didn't want to laugh. The bad words never seemed funny to me. Mum's face when I'd say those words to her never seemed funny to me.

I used to think Dad and I were conspirators, but we weren't. I used to think we were allies, but we weren't. I wasn't his ally against Mum. I know this now.

I was his weapon.

I know that mothers have to love their daughters, but you can hate and love someone at the same time. It's how I feel about my mum, and my nan, that hate mixed with love.

I wonder if the way I acted when I was little made Mum hate me. Am I a living reminder of my dad? I'm thinking these things as I run through the property, my feet pounding as harshly as my heart, and the canopy becomes a thick green mess against the sky. I wonder if that's why she sent me away.

six

We live on a property outside the city's edges. Nan sold her old place in Wollongong when she moved in with us, and with the proceeds of the sale she and Mum bought this place. Mum's an only child, like me, and Granddad died when I was just a baby, so there was nothing keeping Nan there and I guess there must have been a lot of cash left over because boarding school isn't cheap. The property is serene. I mean, it was a lot more serene when it didn't have a teenager in the house, but here I am. I discovered that up until a few years ago there wasn't even a legal speed limit around here, that's how untamed it is. You could have driven down the red dirt street at two hundred kilometres an hour and no policeman would have even batted an eyelid. Pretty soon after they moved in, when Mum really started getting gung-ho about her whole spiritualism thing, she ordered in a dozen bamboo and teak bungalows from Bali and dotted them around the property for people to stay in during her Group Intensive retreats.

The bungalows are nothing but fancy outdoor bedrooms really, and when Mum puts on these retreats we're all forced to share the bathroom in the main house with a hodgepodge of middle-aged people bedecked in too many bracelets. I'm guessing their flowing beaded kaftans are supposed to show that they're the sort of people who believe in loftier things than what this material world has to offer, but the designer price tags on those kaftans kind of contradicts that story. They all smell like they've been infused with patchouli, although I know that they do bathe. I know this because every time they're here they use up most of our tank water.

I can't say sorry with words, but I can do it with actions. While Mum's busy clearing the breakfast dishes I sneak into the linen cupboard and take the fresh sheets to help her with the bungalows.

'Stupid hippies,' I mutter to myself as I sweep the red dust from the bamboo floors and stomp at the geckos and skinks to scram.

'More money than sense,' I hiss as I bat at the cobwebs that tangle in the uppermost corners, and I squish the daddy-long-legs with the bristles of the broom.

'Kumbaya, my Lord' is a really dumb song, I think to myself as I wrangle the mattresses and pull new fitted sheets over the corner edges. Then I get the tune stuck in my head and it wriggles about in my ear, even though my mother doesn't actually sing that song. I walk the long way back to the main house, through a clearing in the brush. I'm giving all the ferns along the way a good thrashing when I hear a loud, rapid fire *ki-ki-ki-ki* alarm call and I know I'm about to get attacked by a plover.

For Christ's sake.

Plovers are native birds and it's their nesting season around about now. While I admire their maternal instincts I'm not going to kill their stupid babies and I don't know why this bird has to be taking its overprotective parenting beliefs out on my head. It swoops, filling the air with its high-pitched shrieks, and strikes at my scalp with its feet and then hovers and circles, diving down again to have a go at my neck with its spurred wing. I lash out and it soars back up to where I can't reach, circling, watching me with its evil yellow face before plummeting down once more like a crazed kamikaze pilot. I run towards the scrub with my head ducked low and my arms up protectively around my ears, the undergrowth grabbing at my sneakers and the thorns hooking at my jeans.

Finally I've run far enough to prove I'm not a threat anymore, but the bird still holds its ground and stands in the clearing, eyeing me off, daring me to take a step forward, all grey and white with a mask of yellow, like it's playing the part of some superhero vigilante, protecting the clearing from the likes of me.

'Smell my breath, little plover. Yeah, I ate eggs for breakfast. How do you like that? Huh? Better not piss me off or your babies might become tomorrow's omelette.'

The bird calls my bluff and takes a few angry steps towards me, tooting like a brass instrument, and with a jump I quickly take a few stumbles back and almost trip over a small palm.

'All right, all right. You win this one. Jerk.' The bird looks defiant. I'm about to circle around the perimeter to make my way back home when a flash of movement catches my eye and I see my nan through the fronds. She's sitting on an old, rusted upturned wheelbarrow and sucking heartily on a cigarette. I sneak up on her and she jumps when I yell, 'Boo!'

I hold out my hand for a cigarette. 'Give me one or I'll tell.'

'Christ, Iliad, you almost gave me a heart attack.'

'Hmmm. *Almost*. Worse luck.'

I stick my hand out again and she shows me her empty packet.

'Last one. Somebody stole my spare pack.' She says this accusingly and with her eyebrows raised, making yet another wrinkle in that face of hers, which is already as rippled as the muddy old dam when I hurl handfuls of rocks into it. The accusation is valid. I swiped the packet a week ago when I'd thought I'd seen my father in the mall and I was on the brink of a panic attack. I lost sight of the man in the crowd and it took everything I had to remind myself that he was safe behind bars, far away. It's not the smoke that calms me, I don't think, it's the long, steady inhalations I take as the carcinogens enter my bloodstream. I could probably go to one of Mum's mindful breathing classes but I'd rather risk cancer than admit to needing her help. I shrug and take the lit cigarette from her fingers as she's ashing it and I sit down next to her as I take a drag.

'I bet it was one of the hippies who did it.'

She doesn't believe that for a second and she watches me intently as I blow smoke from my nostrils. Like a dragon. *Roar.*

'You really need to stop being so attracted to things that bring you no good, you silly girl.'

'Oh don't worry, I'm not attracted to you. It's the cigarette that brought me over.'

'Bah!' she scoffs and she spits near our feet.

'So when are you going to catch cancer and die already? You've been smoking these for what? Fifty years now? Sixty?'

She swipes the cigarette back off me and it's almost a stub. The end glows furiously as she sucks the last remnants of tobacco.

'Don't tell Eve you caught me smoking. She's got enough to worry about with you as it is.'

I watch as she tosses the butt onto the ground and buries it into the dirt with the toe of her little leather lace-up shoe, then she kicks some leaf litter over the evidence for good measure. She reminds me of some old burrowing marsupial.

'If I didn't exist then my mother would find a million other things to worry about. It's her nature to worry. She chose to marry my dad, didn't she? I'm doing her a favour, really. Giving her something to focus on.'

Nan cuffs me on the back of my head and I rub where she smacked me, even though it didn't hurt. Without speaking we get up from the wheelbarrow and we start to pick our way back through the scrub.

'Come help me light the incense in the bungalows for when the visitors arrive. It'll cover our cigarette smell,' Nan says as she offers me a handful of joss sticks and a lighter.

'Good try. I've already helped out enough today. Suck it.' I stick my tongue out at her and I skip towards the dam.

I kick off my Cons and peel off my jeans and t-shirt, hanging them off the sinewy branches of the nearby rosewood. In just my sports bra and Bonds cottontails I dive in. The water swallows me up and I open my eyes in the murky depths and I watch as my hair fans about towards the surface, it's like strands of brown sea grass coiling all around me. I've always wished I could hold my breath forever, I've always liked it better under the water than out there in the real world, but right now I think of dreamy guy Jared, and I push off from the clay bottom, and the air tastes sweet when I gasp it in.

When I was little I used to believe in magic. Sometimes, when I'd hear my dad yelling at my mum, I would run down the stairs of the old Queenslander I grew up in, and I'd find a place in the garden where I was hidden and small, where the fronds made a nest around me and I could pretend that the world was green and lush and Iliad-sized, and I was a giant in this little world of grasshoppers and ants and fuzzy-backed caterpillars. I used to believe in magic words. I used to think that maybe, just maybe, if I said the right incantation, if I put the right syllables together in the right order, then I could cast a spell that'd stop the fighting. *Abracadabra* didn't work, obviously, and neither did *Presto*, or *Shazam*, so I'd try other ones. More secret ones.

'Zeebleoffirous!'

Nope.

'Stomprabbitshoopshoop!'

Nope.

I must have said tens of thousands of different sounds strung together over the years.

'Beeblebopzigglezaggle!'

Nope.

But there are no magic words, I discovered. Yelling 'Snorkwaffles!' at my father never saved my mother from a body full of bruises. You can work on your third eye all you want, but biology is a thing, and there are no corneas or irises or optic nerve centres in the middle of your forehead. There just aren't. Sometimes you just have to open the two eyes that you've already got and you have to use them to stare the real world in the face. Mum's chanting didn't make a jot of difference. It was my nan who did it. My nan who doesn't truck with nonsense. She drove Mum to the hospital and then down to the police station and made her file charges against my father, and it was only then that Mum finally left him, after all those years. I remember the day that Nan stormed into our house, a suitcase in tow, all toughness and gristle with her mean eyes that meant business. Or maybe, just maybe, my magic words had worked? Maybe it was some variation of 'Mushydooda!' that caused Nan to appear at our front door?

Christ.

If that's true, then it really is a prime example of the old saying *be careful what you wish for*. I'd hated being taken away from my dad, and it makes me ashamed to admit it, but I didn't want to leave, I just wanted him to stop getting angry. He wasn't always bad and after a fight he'd act so nice. He'd bring my mum flowers and his pockets would be full of sweets for me. I missed him when we left because I didn't know my mother. Not really. She was a shell back then, a husk of herself, and her eyes, it was if they had been taken out and put back in the wrong way around so that they gazed inwards rather than out at us like they should have been.

'He didn't just batter her body, he battered her spirit worse. But don't worry, girly, she'll get better,' my nan told me as she changed Mum's dressing at the noisy emergency shelter and I watched as she bound my mother, the cotton swallowing Mum's chest around and around and around, and it felt like my own chest was being wrapped up, too. I felt the tightness of it so much I couldn't breathe, and even though I was thirteen and too old for toys, I wanted my stuffed toy cat that I used to believe could protect me. I needed something from home in that cold, crowded place.

'Mr Whiskers. I forgot him. We have to go back.' I panicked.

Nan just kept bandaging my mother. 'We can't, Iliad.'

'I wasn't talking to you!' I'd snapped at her, and I crouched down by Mum.

'Mum, we *have* to go get him.'

But Mum couldn't really see me, she was too trapped inside herself. It felt like my own ribs were broken then, because they weren't a cage anymore. The hinges to my ribcage were open and it felt like they'd let the world in, and the world is a big and heavy thing when it's sharing space with your heart, and I reacted the only way I'd been taught to react.

'I want to be back with my dad! You're a bitch!' I spoke my father's words as the tears spilled from me. 'You're a stupid bitch! A worthless stupid bitch!' I felt the strings of my thirteen years with Dad pulling at me like I was his marionette. Then I slapped her. I'm so ashamed, but I slapped her. The force of it never jolted my mother's eyes back the right way around like I wanted it to, but it did get the attention of Nan.

'Stop this!' she'd barked, taking my wrist in her claws. Her beady eyes were fierce as she properly stared at me, my tears streaming, my chest heaving with panic. I look like my mother, but that day, with my behaviour, I know that she was only seeing my father in me.

'You need some stability, just until we've sorted things out,' Nan had told me, as she packed my things for the first boarding school.

My mum just sat there, with her vacant eyes and her bandaged chest.

She let me go.

She let Nan send me away instead of being a mother, for once.

And even when she got better and they moved somewhere far away and safe, and they found a proper home to live in, she never once asked to have me back.

I haven't thought about magic words in years, but I do today, when I think about Jared. After my skin has wrinkled from the dam I stomp back through the property until I find a space underneath a turkey bush, where the long grass grows higher than my head when I'm sitting down. Surrounded by grass, the world seems as small as the space that I'm sitting in, and above me the spiky pink turkey-bush blossoms tumble in the breeze. I can hear a lyrebird somewhere in the distance, and the woop-woop sounds of native pigeons, but that's it. That's all there is. I open my mouth and feel my breath hot on my lips as I try out the sounds.

'Krackenbracken!'

'Shongshing!'

'Elvishnelvish!'

I'm wishing that yesterday wasn't a fluke. As I try a hundred different words, I'm wishing with every syllable that someone like dreamy guy Jared could actually really like someone like me.

seven

My feet are stained a rust colour from the dirt as I march towards home. I haven't bothered to dress and I have my t-shirt tied like a turban around my head and my jeans tossed over my shoulder. My sneakers are tied together and I'm swinging them around like nunchaku as I walk, whipping the nearby branches with them and startling the birds. It's still the dry season so there aren't any clouds and the sky is so blue it looks chlorinated. If I could whistle I would whistle right now, but unfortunately when I pucker my lips together no sound comes out. Never has, no matter how many times I've practised in secret, making a stupid duck-face and blowing until I felt dizzy. Let's chalk it up as another thing I have no aptitude or talent for.

I must have misjudged the time because Mum's students have arrived. A dozen people are gathered around our patio, all with faces turned expectantly towards her.

Normally I wouldn't mind so much. This is a group of people who are extremely likely to embrace nudity, so being in my underwear would actually make me overdressed. It's not uncommon to find Mum's clients skinny-dipping in the dam, sunning their droopy breasts, burning their bald pates and displaying their floppy penises in that special gross and unselfconscious way of theirs. Mum says I should see their bodies as beautiful and not be brainwashed by the advertising industry's unrealistic body-shape ideals, but I'm not judging them. I mean, it's not like I'm going to be recruited as a Victoria's Secret Angel anytime soon. I just don't want the sight of fifty-year-old genitals burned into my retinas. Is that too much to ask? Needless to say, I avoid the dam whenever they're around. But it's not the hippies who bother me as I walk towards the group of them in my bra and undies. It's Max Selwyn, who's lurking around the outside of the cluster.

If he has taken the prank war into my home space then he is in for another world of retribution.

I am going to break his face.

'And this is my daughter, Iliad,' introduces Mum as I'm standing there, dripping and dirt encrusted, wearing a t-shirt for a turban and not much else. My mum says this proudly. She knows I helped with the bungalows, I'm forgiven, and I look at this moment like just the sort of child a hippie would want to lay claim to.

That is to say, I look weird.

Max smirks and I quickly yank the shirt from my head to pull it over me. Thankfully it's oversized.

'Peace out,' I mutter to the group, waving a two-fingered peace sign around and then excusing myself. I scoot into my bedroom and lean against the mahogany door, holding my head in my hands. I wonder if it's scientifically possible to die of shame.

It's only the rumbling of my stomach that forces me to venture out of my room again. Dressed, this time. Our house is large and wooden and stands on little stilts, creating a gap underneath just large enough for the chickens to scratch around in, the bones of the building creaking arthritically with the wind. My mother has a penchant for 70s paintings, old copper vases, Balinese carvings and ancient coins that clink about in mosaic bowls. I'm probably the youngest thing inside these walls. Bougainvillea vines strangle the outer beams and palm fronds scratch at the corrugated iron roof, and circling the whole thing is an expanse of wooden decking, and the decking is strewn with hammocks and heavy wooden furniture, wind chimes and tea lights and burning mosquito coils.

Right now, the clients are sitting in a circle, their eyes closed and heads bowed. They look so peaceful. Their upturned eye creases remind me of how a child might draw a smile with a pencil. Everyone's perched on throw cushions and alpaca rugs, and incense smoke curls hazily around them. In the middle of the circle is Mum's shrine, or if we're going to get technical about it, a pyramid of semi-precious crystals. At the centrepiece of this crystal pyramid is Mum's pride and joy: a giant amethyst that sits purple and sparkling inside of a large scooped-out rock. It's like a fairy's grotto and when I was little I thought that's exactly what it was. Little kids believe a lot of nonsense.

Most of us, however, grow out of it.

I notice as I pick my way around the group that Max isn't

sitting in the meditation circle. And neither is Mum.

Curious.

I walk through to the kitchen and I've just finished spreading manuka honey onto a slice of spelt sourdough when I glance up to the far kitchen window and I see them. They're standing on the decking. Mum is unbending, all straight backed and jutting bones. She's facing away from me and the ridges of her spine look like a skinny strip of corrugated iron underneath her taut skin. Max is leaning against the supporting beam and he's trying to make a case to her about something. He's waving his arms about, trying to convince her.

If this is prank based, then I have to hand it to him, he's really going to a lot of trouble.

Mum brings her hands to her hips, the way she does when she's not going to budge, and then Max's head flops down, as though his eyes have suddenly become really heavy. I suck the honey from my thumb and leave the knife perched on top of the jar as I pad closer to the window, my back scraping against the wall, out of view. Holding the sandwich in my teeth I creak the glass slats open so I can hear what they're saying.

'I'm sorry, Max, but I don't know how I can make this any clearer. If you don't have the funds then you simply can't participate.'

I stop, mid chew. Max Selwyn needs his aura cleansed? Ha!

He tries to bargain with her.

'I live next door, so it's not like I'd be taking up a bungalow. And I'll pay you back in instalments. I can do odd jobs around the property. Like, gardening, and helping with the fencing.'

My mother is curt.

'My daughter is quite capable of doing those things, thank you.'

Max's shoulders are slumped. He's searching my mother's face, his eyes darting, but her face can be icy sometimes.

She sighs her trademark sigh.

'Look now, let's be reasonable, it wouldn't be fair to the other clients. Each of them has invested a significant amount of money for this intimate workshop and I can't just divert energy from them to include another person. I appreciate your interest, Max. I really do. But perhaps you can come along to one of my more modestly priced seminars in the town hall later on in the year?'

Max shakes his mop of black curls, frustrated, then he straightens up and juts out his chin. He looks venomous.

'You reckon you're this deadly woman who's all about healing people and good karma. You reckon you're all about focusing on the inside, but I look around here, and what do I see? A bunch of bored, middle-class old whitefellas. That's what I see. You reckon you're all about doing good in this world but you'll only do good if they're paying you. That's not real goodness. It isn't, hey. You're *gammon*. If karma does exist then I hope it bites you on the bum, you old bitch!'

My sandwich is halfway to my mouth but I'm too shocked to take another bite and the piece that I'm swallowing right now turns to dough in my throat. It gets wedged and I choke on a cough and bang my chest to dislodge it. Max hears. His eyes flicker towards the window and his gaze touches mine.

Damn it.

If I'd thought he'd glared at me before, it's nothing like how he's glaring at me now. That look he gives me. If there really were dangerous creatures lurking underneath his swamp-green eyes then right now, at this moment, a water snake would surely have jumped out from them and it would have dug its fangs into my face. That is the kind of look he's giving me. I scowl back at him but even my best scowl is cheerful compared to Max. He swings around and he leaps down off the decking without bothering to use the stairs. I watch as he stalks his way towards the front gate, lashing out at the ferns, kicking at the rocks. Mum stands there for a bit, the wind mussing up her curls, then she smooths herself down and tugs at her necklace. After a few deep breaths she turns to walk back inside. I sprint, sliding along the floor-boards, toppling over a pot plant. I make it to my bedroom without having to run into her.

My art major work stays unfinished, flat on my floor. I can't concentrate on it. I'm lying on my bed throwing the beads from an old broken necklace at a gecko which is scaling the far wall and making *chk chk* sounds. I don't even come close to hitting it. I've never been good at hand–eye coordination.

Tick, something else to add to the list of things I'm not good at.

I keep thinking about the look Max gave me. It felt personal. He looked vulnerable. He looked like he'd opened his chest up the way that Clark Kent opens his suit to reveal the superman costume underneath, except instead of a superman costume, there was Max's heart. Fist-sized and bleeding. I wonder why he cared so much. I wonder why he thought my mother could help him. Chanting is happening outside in the living room and the voices seep through the crack under my bedroom door. I think about what Max said.

The clients are all retired business people or the wives of bankers; they're white and old and middle class. It's as though when Max looked at my mother and said those things, he was wearing my own eyes in his head as he was seeing her. I could almost feel him blinking.

I've said the same sort of words to her before. It was a couple of years ago and I was preparing to return to boarding school. Mum had given me two hundred dollars and we were going shopping for things that I'd need. New shoes and art supplies, mainly. I was chewing gum and dragging my feet and we'd stopped at the weekend markets. The air was stewing with the smells of laksa and satay chicken skewers, and buskers were juggling diabolos and tossing them at the sky, and stall owners were calling out at me to admire their painted glass or their homemade hacky sacks. Mia would have been there too, helping her mum at their noodle stall like she does most weekends, but I didn't know her then. She would have been just a stranger selling us lunch. Mum was distracted by a stall hawking glass-bead necklaces and when she was picking at the beads I'd wandered off from her, snaking through the crowd, until I saw an old Indigenous man sitting cross-legged against a wall. He was playing a didgeridoo and I sat next to him, feeling the guttural sounds of the instrument wash over me.

'Hey sista girl,' he'd said to me, when he'd stopped playing for a little bit to catch his breath. The occasional passers-by had thrown coins into either one of the two upturned hats he had placed by his feet but most people were ignoring him. I'd squished my gum into a dent in the brick wall and ripped open a packet of salty plums. My fingers were stained orange from eating them and when the man stopped playing I handed the packet over to him without saying a word.

He took one and we sat there licking the saltiness from the dried, preserved fruit and watching the forest of legs march back and forth. I pointed over towards the two battered old baseball caps he had put in front of him for collecting coins.

'What's with the two hats?'

'Just keepin' up with inflation, ay.' That made me laugh.

He told me he was from a community in the desert and he'd travelled for days to come to the big smoke for a cousin's funeral. Hotels were too expensive so he was sleeping with some of his mob in the long grass out of town. Then he told me that I had hair like his daughter and it didn't feel strange when he reached out to touch it. I hadn't shaved any of my head then, and it hung in dark curls down to my waist. He took out a battered old photo of her from his wallet and the way he looked down at the picture of his daughter . . .

That *love*.

It just made my heart heavy. Not heavy like I was carrying too much inside of my chest, it was strangely the opposite. I felt like my heart was hollow, filled with nothing but emptiness and air, but emptiness can weigh so much sometimes. It's strange how much it can weigh. I looked over at this man who was busking for a bus fare to return to his daughter and then my mum elbowed her way through the crowd and I looked up at this woman who was driving herself batty with preparations to send me away.

'Here you go,' I told him as I slipped my two hundred dollars into his old, rough hand. His smile was as big as the world.

'Bless you, cudgerie.'

I squeezed his hand and he squeezed mine back and then I unfolded myself from the ground to join my mother.

I had decided on a pair of black Nikes in the shoe store

when Mum realised I didn't have any money to pay for them. I could see the cords in her neck tense when I explained that I'd given the money away.

'It wasn't your money to give, Iliad.'

'Yes, it was. You're always saying I should pay it forward, and he needed to go home to his daughter. Plus, he was sleeping in the long grass and I get to sleep in a bed.'

'We pay taxes for homeless shelters. For goodness sake, Iliad.' Then she turned to the shoe salesman. 'I'm sorry, we're not taking these.' She dragged me out of the store by the elbow and she was pinching at my arm and we had to go to Kmart instead.

'I don't know why you're punishing me!' I yelled as she picked out some ugly, cheap, generic shoes with pink edging. *Pink*, for Christ's sake. 'You're always harping on about doing good for the universe. I did good, Mum! I'm racking up karma points! Why are you punishing me?'

'Karma points won't pay the bills,' she'd snapped back. And it crushed me. She had no money for a homeless man, but she had plenty of money to send me away. I let her buy the pink shoes, but I tossed them into the dam when we got home. I filled them with stones and it was satisfying to watch the shoes sink, and I didn't care when the PE teacher at the new school yelled at me for my inappropriate footwear. All my caring had packed its bags and left me behind without even leaving a note. I stopped believing in karma that day, too, because no good came to me from that donation. I didn't win the lotto. I didn't suddenly become popular. I wasn't allowed to leave boarding school and live back at home.

The man's smile, though, that was payment enough.

I remembered his smile as I was being yelled at and it was enough, because he wanted to be with his daughter, and is there anything sadder than a parent who doesn't want to be with their daughter?

eight

The cane toad temporarily stops me from obsessing about dreamy guy. It's been two days since we looked for bullet shells on the beach and he promised he'd message me once he knew when he'd be free to catch up. I've been trying to work on my art piece, but I've been distracted, checking my phone every few minutes to see if he's sent me a text yet. Nothing. So I'm checking my phone for the millionth time when I scream because a cane toad's crawled into the living room and I almost step on it as I'm heading to the kitchen for a glass of water. Gross. The ugly thing just stares back at me and I wonder what to do with it. They're an introduced pest that's wreaking havoc on the native wildlife and Nan always picks them up with a plastic bag and puts them in the freezer to kill them, but I can't bring myself to add this one to the growing number of corpses taking up space next to the frozen peas. It's not this toad's fault he was born in a place where he doesn't belong and isn't wanted. Instead, I grab the broom and begin to sweep him out the front door.

'Don't look so hard done by,' I tell him as he gets pushed around by the bristles. 'I'm doing you a favour, stupid thing.'

So I'm there, talking to a toad, when my phone starts buzzing in my pocket. I take it out and see Jared's name on the screen.

A grin makes its way onto my face. Maybe magic words do work, after all.

'Hello?' I answer, and I sweep the toad so hard he tumbles clumsily off the patio.

'Hey, Ily, how are you going?'

I grip the broom handle tightly to keep my emotions in check and I try to play it cool.

'Yeah, good. Hey, you do realise that our generation don't do phone calls. We text.' I say it as nonchalantly as I can, then I stick my tongue out at the toad, which is sprawled on the ground below looking dazed. I can almost hear the smile in Jared's voice when he replies.

'Yeah, apparently, but who says I want to be like everyone else?'

My smile keeps itself latched onto my face.

'Who says I meant it like a bad thing?'

We have our first in-joke!

'Ha, exactly. So,' he goes on, 'I was just thinking of how impressed you were with the way I completely massacred those crates and I thought I'd give you the opportunity to see how I deal with medieval royalty. The local theatre company's doing a production of the Scottish play next week and I'm playing the lead role if you wanna come along? Spoiler alert. I get kind of stabby.'

'*Macbeth*?'

He makes a tortured kind of sound.

'Don't say it out loud before the performance! Actors are a superstitious breed, you know. Our profession is precarious. We need to hang onto all the luck we've got.'

I laugh.

'I'm studying it in English, and yeah, for a guy who's only met me once, you've really got me pegged. I do prefer plays where nearly everyone gets murdered. I'll be there.'

'Cool,' he tells me.

'Cool.'

I hang up and bury my head in my hands like I can't believe what's just happened, and I call down at the toad making its way to the safety of a fern.

'You should go find someone to kiss you, little toad. You might not turn into a prince but it's still excellent!'

Mia's come with me to watch the play because, as she explained, 'We'll get to hang out together outside school for the first time, so that's socialising, but it's also curriculum-related, so it's like an optimisation of my time.'

I don't understand Mia, but I'm glad to have her with me as people throng about outside the theatre, waiting to be let in. I've found that you never feel quite so alone as you do in a crowd of happy people.

The local theatre is a beautiful old sandstone building, one of the very few structures in town that wasn't built after the 70s. Nearly every other building in town was blown away by Cyclone Tracy in 1974, so if you just judge a place by its architecture, Darwin looks like a city where the past doesn't really exist. I remember walking around the Cyclone Museum with Mum once, and the guide was showing us all the old photographs of the landscape just after it was flattened.

'Can you imagine?' He paused. 'Can you imagine having everything you'd ever known obliterated overnight?'

I stared at a giant black-and-white photo of mangled corrugated iron, torn palm fronds and timber strewn everywhere, but the thing I properly noticed was a child's teddy bear, half buried in the chaos. I didn't stop staring at it as the guide told us about how the city was rebuilt so much stronger, how they got all these scientists involved and introduced regulations so the new buildings we see now are able to withstand even the worst cyclones so what happened with Tracy will never happen again. As he spoke, I just wondered what had happened to the child who owned the teddy bear.

The bell rings and people start filing their way inside the theatre. I look around for Mia and see her crouching down to pick at a weed that's growing through the crack in the concrete. She places it in the elastic that holds up her ponytail and scurries over to me before I hand my ticket to the person at the door.

'You do know that's a weed, Mia?'

She looks at me seriously.

'A weed is still a flower, Ily, it's just one that nobody's bothered to appreciate before, so I'm going to,' and I watch the weed bob up and down as Mia skips inside to find our seats.

The theatre is small and the stage is stark, and the play's colour scheme is white and grey and red. The actors are decked in Shakespearean costumes and Jared wears tights well. Too well. I can't stop staring at them and it makes me feel like a creeper. Other than focusing on his tights, though, I can't stop my eyes from glazing over. I don't really understand the language, despite Mr Salmon trying to explain it in class. From what I can gather about the story, these witches tell this dude he's going to be king, and his wife *really* runs with the idea, so they go about murdering everyone until they're king and queen, but then they feel guilty because of all the killing, as you do, and then it turns out the witches weren't quite telling the truth when they made Macbeth think he was invincible, so then he and his wife get stabbed as well. The end. I think the moral of the story is that you shouldn't go around trusting witches? I mean, it's a valid point. The guy playing Macduff forgets his lines a couple of times, and you can hear Banquo whisper the prompts across at him. Jared says all the lines correctly, I think, and his cheekbones look glorious under the overhead lights. He's got real talent. I always used to think acting was like pretending, but it's not, I realise, as I watch him become Macbeth. To act well is like lying well – sometimes the measure of something isn't in the way it shows itself, but in the way it can carefully hide itself so you don't know they're doing it.

> *I have no spur*
> *To prick the sides of my intent, but only*
> *Vaulting ambition, which o'erleaps itself,*
> *And falls on th'other.*

As Jared proclaims these lines dramatically he struts about the stage. He wears his skin so comfortably up there, almost as well as his tights. Nobody could fault his passion. It radiates.

Afterwards I'm waiting outside with Mia for her parents to pick her up when I feel a pair of male hands grab me from behind, covering my face. A scream punches its way out of my lungs, and I suddenly feel like I'm small again, afraid that the monster has finally decided to come for me next.

'Scared you!' Jared grins and I can see his dimples.

My throat's too tied up in knots to talk and I just concentrate on breathing, but thankfully Mia babbles on for me in words I don't understand.

'Such a brave adaptation . . . about destruction wrought when ambition goes unchecked by moral constraints . . . so evocative and atmospheric . . . The witches' cauldron represented . . .'

Jared nods along, pleased, and when she's finally stopped talking my heart has returned to normal speed. He turns to me.

'I've got to go chat with people, but wanna grab a bite to eat after?'

I nod, and he plants a kiss on my lips and disappears into the crowd. Mia squeals and hugs me, and I have to pull her off.

'For the last time, Mia, I don't do hugs.'

She's bouncing from foot to foot, her ponytail swinging.

'Not only do you get to swap mouth fluids with dreamy guy, but he invites you to the theatre and dinner? I'm so so so so so happy for you!'

The grin she's wearing is so wide it doesn't even waver a little bit. Even after her dad comes to pick her up, she keeps her nose pressed to the car window, waving at me. I wonder what the world looks like to someone as pure as Mia. It makes me think of art, the way that two people can look at the one painting and even though the paint and brushstrokes and all the surface things are exactly the same, somewhere after the picture hits your cornea it transforms and becomes mixed up with all that is you so nobody else in the world can see the same picture you can see. Sometimes I wish I could pluck out Mia's eyes and wear them instead of my own so I could see the world like she does. I bet it'd be beautiful.

Jared and I go to have dinner at the nearby chicken take-away, and every time we reach for the tomato sauce bottle or the salt at the same time his touch zings through me. He tells me all about his family. His dad owns one of the mechanic shops in town, and his big brother, Toby, has done a business degree and is going to take over the garage one day, which is lucky because it lets Jared off the hook. I'm wondering why his family weren't there at the theatre when the front bell sings and Jared's face turns white. Two men walk in. The younger one beelines straight for Jared and calls out in a booming voice, 'G'day, little bro!' He's all brawn and stubbies with grease under his fingernails. You can see the resemblance except he's got a blunt, hulking handsomeness whereas Jared is more fine and chiselled. Jared glowers.

'Aren't you supposed to be out concussing yourself somewhere?'

Toby laughs heartily and dives in to give Jared a head-lock and a noogie, mussing up his little brother's carefully styled hair.

'Footy game's over. The Swampdogs didn't know what hit 'em.' Then he looks over at me and his smile is good-natured, his eyes crinkling at the sides even though he'd only be in his mid twenties. 'G'day, I'm Toby. Jared's punching above his weight, I see.'

He's such a liar, but he says it like he wants to put me at ease, so I take his hand when he offers it and it envelops mine.

'Ily.'

'Great to meet you, Ily! This is our dad, Wayne.'

The older man comes over now, having placed his order at the counter. He's a large man like Toby, and something about his presence makes him seem even larger still. He nods at me and steals a chip from Jared's plate.

'You missed a good game, son. You shoulda seen your brother. There he was, legs up, up the middle, and I was shouting "go you good thing" and that big Islander bloke from the Swampdogs almost had him but he made a dummy pass and then there he was, my boy, thundering over the tryline right between the goal posts.'

Wayne's face is ruddy with pride. Toby grins over at his dad while Jared sits watching them, his knuckles whitening as he grips the tabletop.

'I was performing my play, remember? I was the lead.'

'He was really good,' I say, daring his father to contradict me, but Wayne turns back to Jared.

'You still mucking around with that nonsense? You need to focus on your degree, son, or come help us out in the garage, make yourself useful.'

'I sincerely apologise for making you think I'm useless.' Jared's voice is sharp with the unsorriness of his words. The lady at the counter reads out a number and Wayne just leans a meaty arm to thump his eldest between the shoulderblades and walks away to pick up their order, leaving Toby.

'So little bro, we're heading home to watch the Wallabies play South Africa. You could come watch it with us. Build up those testosterone levels of yours. Ily, you're welcome too.'

Jared just says coldly, 'Sounds scintillating, but we're hanging out here for a bit.'

Toby shrugs like he expected that answer, then he digs into his bag and takes out a couple of cans of soft drinks.

'Fair enough. Hey, I forgot, these were left in the

clubhouse after a barbecue. Take 'em if you guys are thirsty.'

My mouth is so dry after all the chips I'm grateful, and I say, 'Yeah, thanks', just as Jared spits, 'No.'

I look sideways at him. What?

'Ily doesn't want to. *Do you, Ily?*' Jared says it like it's a warning, not a question, and it unsettles me. Toby doesn't put the cans back in the backpack, he holds them in the air and he waves them so they dance.

'Mate, you should get your hearing checked 'cause it sounded to me like she just said that she did. Grab one, Ily, if you like.'

I stare defiantly at Jared.

'Actually, I . . .'

'Ily, shut up!'

Underneath the table Jared grabs my wrist and it hurts. I'm so shocked I don't know how to react and I just sit there, blinking, wondering what the hell just happened to the guy I was crushing on so hard only a few minutes ago, and when I finally speak it's like the words aren't mine, they're someone else's, except they're crawling out of my own mouth.

'No, I don't actually want one. Thanks anyway, Toby.'

Jared releases me, and Toby's suddenly serious, like he's staring really hard at us. A tendril has escaped from the grip of Jared's hair gel and he flicks it from his eyes so that he can properly glare back at his big brother. I look about the room, at the pictures of cartoon chickens painted on the walls, at the salt and pepper shakers, at the woman dinging the bell at the counter. Anywhere but Toby's gaze.

'All right,' says Toby, after a long, stretched-out moment as he shoves the cans back in his bag. 'I'm putting them away because you just said you didn't want one, Ily. And I'll respect that. But little bro, if you speak to a woman in that tone again, you'll be making friends with the backside of my hand, you got it?'

After Toby leaves, I don't say anything to Jared. I don't need to. I just storm out the door and I feel my wrist smarting. This isn't how I wanted the date to go. The more I think about it, the angrier I get. I can feel the clash of swords inside me. Jared chases after me and I make up magic words under my breath, silent ones. Ones that'll rewind time because I so badly want it to be five minutes ago, before the dreamy guy became someone who I don't think I like.

'*Razzlecantankeramo.*'

'*Damslamkablam.*'

Jared keeps following. I walk faster.

Finally Jared catches up, and when he grabs my shoulder I shake him off angrily. Tears prickle at my lids but I blink them away. I will not let them fall. The streetlight's pouring its beams down onto Jared and he's got worried ripples in his forehead but I just keep my gaze latched onto the space where my car is, about ten metres away, and I know my face looks pinched and mean but I don't care. I can feel Jared trying to fix things. He takes a while before he speaks.

'I'm sorry about before, the way I spoke. It had nothing to do with you. It's Toby. I hate how he made me feel small in front of you.'

I run my fingers through my hair and take a breath to steady myself.

'That's an excuse, but it doesn't excuse you. You were angry at someone else but you directed it at me because it made you feel better, even though you knew it'd make me feel worse. What the *hell* is wrong with you?'

He kicks at the ground and I can see all the hurt from

way down deep starting to seep out of his pores.

'People aren't perfect, okay? You're not like everyone else, and that's a good thing, but I'm not like everyone else either. Yeah, I lose my temper, but you knew that, so you can't hold it against me now.'

Then he digs into his pocket and takes out an old bullet shell. It's still sandy when he places it into my hand. 'I went back looking for more of these because I've never met a girl like you before and I can't stop thinking about you, and yeah, we've only known each other a week, but I'm not imagining this connection between us and I'm pretty certain you can feel it too.'

I feel myself softening with each word he says, and my armour starts slipping. He reaches out to touch my shoulders and I can feel the electricity jolt from his fingertips into my veins and buzz around.

'I really like you, Ily, and I know that when you really like someone, you've got to accept all of them, not just the good parts. I wanna be with you. Do you feel the same?'

He's looking at me, pleading, and I can still feel his touch sending sparks all through my body. I hesitate a bit before I nod.

'Yeah.' I curl my fingers around the bullet shell and concentrate on the weight of it. 'But if you try to tell me what to do again, I'll break you.'

I can see the relief wash over Jared's face and he smiles so that his dimples wink at me, then he runs his hand through the shaved part of my hair, tipping my head up to face him.

'Hey girlfriend,' he whispers to me.

Despite myself, a smile creeps out from my scowl.

'Hey boyfriend.'

Then he leans down to kiss me and with it, he does that

thing, the way he makes my heart lurch so hard it loses balance, and then that feeling of vertigo, and then falling. I only know that I'm still upright because I'm aware of his arms around me, holding me steady, and I concentrate on the feel of lips against lips to remind myself that I'm still standing.

When he takes my hand as we walk back to my car I try to forget the way my wrist hurts. I think of how I can't blame Jared for the way that he acted, not really. It wasn't him speaking, it came from a kind of blackness that I can see sometimes swimming inside of him, and I can't blame him for that, you know?

I mean, he's obviously lived under Toby's shadow his whole life.

I just repeat the words over and over again in my head. My boyfriend. My first *boyfriend*. The dreamy guy's my actual boyfriend.

nine

'Talented little grommets, aren't you both? I swear, dudes, that's the only reasons I've put up with you two rolling your eyes and carrying on in class like you do.'

Our art teacher Mr Boaden is referring to the major works that Max and I have handed in. They've been placed next to each other, propped against the classroom wall, ready to be packed up and sent away to be assessed. It's only the end of August, but the art major works are due now, even though the exams aren't until October.

Mr Boaden uses words like *grommets* and *stoked* and *dude*. Even though he's old, like forty or something, he still wears Volcom or Mambo t-shirts and it's not uncommon to find him shredding down at the skate park. He's got this long black hair that hangs halfway down his back in a low ponytail and once when Max asked him why he didn't get a goatee, Mr Boaden replied without missing a beat, 'Because

I don't have a big enough yard-y.' He's that kind of teacher.

Max's work is brilliant, not that I'd ever tell him. It's a painting of a river, but it's way more than just a landscape. The brushstrokes are full of looseness and light and it's got something of a Van Gogh quality to it, the way the water and the sky swirl so the painting comes to life and almost dances off the canvas. The strokes become more and more separated and defined until the swirls start to look like the famous bush medicine leaf paintings by Gloria Petyarre – an Indigenous artist from the Utopia region of the Northern Territory that Mr Boaden has told us about. It's like the whole landscape is being tossed about before our eyes, and it reminds me of the way the knock-'em-down winds shake the leaves free from the trees every April to paint pictures in the sky. In the middle of the thrashing river is a crocodile, painted in an X-ray style, with an intricate series of lines to depict the creature's internal organs. Max says his work is inspired by his Bininj and Anmatyerre heritages.

'I reckon that both of you have a high chance of having your pieces selected for the Northern Territory showcase. Give us a high five, yeah?'

Max and I roll our eyes at his raised hand.

'I don't do high fives,' I tell him, deadpan. Mr Boaden shrugs like he was expecting that response, then he removes his hand from where it's hanging lonely in the air. He takes his wayfarers that are dangling from the front of his t-shirt and slips them on just as the bell rings. He turns to leave, his ponytail a straggly black line against his spine, but he calls back over his shoulder before he reaches the doorway.

'You know, you've really captured your personality with that self-portrait, Iliad.'

He meant it as an insulting kind of joke, but the art piece

does feel like me. The bullets were the perfect final touch. I used them to make a heart shape in the middle of my chest. The war in the book that I'm named after, *The Iliad*, all started because Helen fell in love with the wrong person. That was what started all the violence. Love. The shells are the perfect centrepiece for the little fighting figurines surrounding it, arranged on the canvas so they look like an outline of my face and shoulders, if you step back.

I'm surprised to see Max looking hard at my portrait, like he's lost in it. He's standing there, staring, then he catches me watching him, and it jolts him back from wherever he was. He scowls at me and I scowl back, meaner. Mean enough to make him shift his gaze, tossing hair from his face and picking up the old, graffitied bag at his feet.

'Mr Boaden was wrong, hey. It's nothing like your personality. It looks way too friendly to be yours.'

'It's to celebrate you handing in your major work,' Jared tells me when I meet up with him after school and he hands me a huge slice of chocolate-chip cheesecake from the patisserie in town. I take the paper bag from him and peer in.

'Seriously, you promise there's no secret vegetables mixed in here, or like, they haven't substituted sugar for dates or something disgusting like that?'

I know that Mum's baked me a cake as well, for when I get home, but it'll be vegan and gluten-free and any cake that can be classified as a health food forfeits any right to pass as a dessert.

'Nope, it's full of all the bad stuff.'

I scoop a spoonful of cake into my mouth and I close my eyes, relishing it. I'm not sure what feels better – the sugar rush, or the sense of having created something I'm proud of, and having it out there in the world.

We drive to the Nightcliff foreshore and Jared walks over to the cliff edge and stands there for a minute, the wind making little grabs at his shirt and flirting with his hair. I stay back, sitting on the park bench, watching him warily. I hate heights. After hurling a few stones into the blue he and I wander down towards the jetty. There's no real thought about where we're going, there never is. In the six weeks we've been dating, just being next to each other is enough, and anywhere that's away from our complicated families is enough. We share headphones as we walk, one in each ear, taking turns to choose the song, but it's more than just discovering the music of Sufjan Stevens or The Zombies or Loon Lake. We're secretly telling each other the truths of our souls with each tune.

Jared's been good since the night of the theatre.

So good.

So, so good.

Things I've discovered about having a boyfriend:

It's being pushed down the street in a trolley stolen from the shopping centre car park, feeling the air tangling its fingers in my hair, spreading my arms out wide so I could almost believe, when I shut my eyes, that I'm flying.

It's the way the nook of his neck is the perfect height for my head to meld into.

It's my scowl being nudged from its usual place on my face by chocolate-chip cheesecake, and knowing the smile I wear is the one he gave me.

When he's good, he's so, so good.

We're sitting on the jetty edge, kicking our feet and wearing the day like it fits us. Jared reaches over to his satchel and takes out a stack of paper.

'What's that?'

He holds the papers tight so that the wind doesn't snatch them away, skimming his thumb down the edge of the stack.

'It's a script. Silas Matthews, the director guy who always wins the Darwin short film festival, he's gonna be entering Shortfest this year and I've got an audition for the lead. Shortfest is, like, the biggest and best short film festival in the country. If I get the role, it could be my break, you know?'

We watch a fish puncture the surface, then disappear, leaving nothing but ripples. Jared turns to me, really seriously. 'If Silas's film makes the finals, it'll put me on the radar of all the best acting agents in Sydney, and it'll prove to my parents that I can really make it as an actor.'

He looks so intense. I nod. I get it. I want to move to Sydney next year too, to go to the College of Fine Arts. My marks for theory might not be good enough, but Mr Boaden thinks my portfolio might get me over the line. It's only been six weeks, but I can't stop thinking about Jared and me being together next year. I imagine the two of us living in Sydney, him an actor, me an art student, drinking cheap wine in the small bars of Surry Hills, exploring the alleyways of Newtown, and kissing up against the graffitied walls. Sometimes I fall so in love with how I imagine the future could be that I'm almost afraid of it happening, because when something's close up you can see the flaws. I don't want to know what the flaws might be. I don't want to be disappointed by reality. I listen as Jared talks about next year, when his life will really begin, and I hope with all my being that my life will begin then, too.

The build-up season's starting to kick in. That's what they call those disgustingly few months before the wet season rains properly begin, then it's all afternoon squalls and cyclone warnings.

I wake up extra early to the smell of fire. The first time this happened I panicked and thought my dad had broken out of prison and set the place ablaze to punish us for leaving him, and I sprinted out of my room to find the extinguisher. I know better now. I stand on the decking, blinking at the sunrise, perched on one foot with the other resting on my knee, eating my bowl of porridge.

I watch Mum's group as they're gathered around a smoky campfire. The flames skip about and throw funny shadows on people's faces. My mum has this healing ceremony that she does. One by one all the people in the group take turns around the circle. They talk about their addictions or their destructive habits, or they just generally talk about really sad stuff, then they pretend to scrunch those negative things up into imaginary balls and lob them into the fire. Some people are sobbing, their tears doing little dives off their chins and splattering the thirsty dirt. A man has his head in a woman's lap and she's petting his hair like he's a small child. There's something like jealousy that grips my heart when I watch it. I was never allowed to be held like that.

Mum catches me standing there and she clears her throat in a 'please leave now' kind of way. Another one of her clients, a regular called Bob, beams at me and invites me to join in. He's here pretty often, not only for these group things but he pays for one-on-one sessions every now and then. He's tall with kind eyes the colour of milky tea, and his laughter bubbles up from him so easily that I wonder why he needs to come to these things at all. Mum widens her eyes in a way that means 'don't even think about it' but I ignore her and I take a few steps forward so I'm at the edge of the decking, still chewing slowly. The group is looking up at me with eager, welcoming eyes. I clear my throat.

'I was addicted to the hokey-pokey, but I really turned myself around,' I say into my hands, then scrunch it up and pretend to fling it into the flames. Mum's face tells me to scram and I do. Bob just laughs.

'She's filled with spirit, that lass.'

'Hmmm. That's one way to put it,' Mum replies dryly.

It's biology and Mia doesn't realise that it's not a wise idea to enthusiastically answer every question the teacher asks when you're dressed the way she's dressed. It's like a blaring neon sign begging people to pick on her. I worry about her, despite myself. Innocence is an endangered species in the age of the internet. Today she's wearing what looks like 80s MC Hammer pants with an old man's vest, and crowning her hair is a daisy chain she made sitting on the oval before school started. It's been raining spitballs on her head all day and it pains me how it doesn't seem to bother her. I just want her to fight and to rage, not to dust the spitballs out of her hair as casually as if they were fallen leaves. The teacher, Mrs Patel, is discussing aquatic ecosystems when Jasmine, the queen of spitballs, pipes up from the back.

'Like, Mia, I know you're digging this because Asians love seaweed, you know, because of sushi and all that, but seriously, miss, can we stop talking about sea vegetation and get onto dolphins or something? Like, please?'

Jasmine thinks she's cool because she's got a fake ID and she used it to get an ugly tattoo of a dolphin jumping over her ankle. I snap from my usual zoned-out status and glare across at her.

'Wow, let's talk about stereotypes. You do know that dolphins are vicious and nasty, right? So, yeah, I think that ugly one on your ankle suits you fabulously.'

Jasmine's pissed off, but she's a bit scared of me so she's not as awful as she'd be if it were Mia saying it.

'Ooh, so the angry girl can speak? Yeah, I can see why you'd have a grudge against happy, peace-loving animals.'

Mum had really gotten into dolphins for a while there and I'd spent a day on Google researching them to better insult her with facts when she insisted on sending me to boarding school number three, even though I desperately didn't want to be sent away again. I can be productive when I want to.

'Actually, dolphins are known for isolating the females and gang raping them for days. They're also known for killing babies – porpoise babies and shark babies and even dolphin babies when they want to rape the mother. And, yeah, they have a reputation for just generally being arseholes. So I can see why you feel a connection to them.'

Jasmine looks at the teacher for backup but Mrs Patel just shrugs.

'All valid facts. Nice to see you taking an interest in marine biology, Iliad.'

It's only a matter of time before Jasmine and her group spread a rumour that I'm obsessed with dolphin rape.

So that's a great start to the day.

Then it's recess.

I have puddles of flowers surrounding me by the time I'm finished eating my sandwich. I have to tell Mia for the millionth time that I'm really not big on flowers.

Then Max happens.

I'm guessing the prank war is still on because a water balloon explodes on my head.

Max Selwyn is a jerk.

He's ducking behind a tree, lobbing balloon after balloon at me, laughing like it is the funniest thing in the world. I regret having felt sorry for him that time he'd come around to see my mum. I wish I could rewind the clock and spend all those minutes working on my art piece, or studying, or even watching cat videos on YouTube . . . anything other than feeling sorry for this waste of a human who's catapulting water bombs in my direction. The thing is, though, Max hasn't considered the fact that I'm standing next to the sprinkler tap. As I duck to avoid another direct hit I run to the tap and twist it to full. He's pelted by a half-dozen sprinklers scatter-gunning water in every direction.

We both arrive in art class equally drenched.

'I know that climate change is a thing, but a downpour this early in the season?' asks Mr Boaden, as we're standing there wringing the water from our clothes.

'It's his fault,' I say just as Max shouts, 'It's her fault!'

Mr Boaden sits on his desk and swings his legs back and forth, assessing us. He knows about the prank war. Max left an open tube of acrylic paint on my chair once and I had to walk around with a yellow bum for the rest of the day. Another time, I'd emptied a whole tube of superglue into Max's hat, and it's only due to the fact Mr Boaden caught me in the act that Max has any hair left on his head.

'Oh don't worry, I didn't presume for a second that either of you little grommets were innocent.'

It's double period so I'm assuming we're going to be

doing our theory questions because now that our major works have been handed in our trial exams are looming.

Mr Boaden stops us before we all settle down in our seats.

'So dudes, we're gonna take a break from our regularly scheduled programming for today. The trial exams are only a bit more than a month away, and I could go over the different movements again, from Surrealists to the Dadaists and the Abstract Expressionists . . .'

We all groan. *Theory.*

Mr Boaden raises his hands for us to settle down.

'Chill, guys. Take a chill pill. I'm not gonna do that, so you can all stop freaking out. I want to help you guys to realise that all art has a social, cultural and historical context to it. Just as each artist we're studying has been influenced by their own unique cultural and historical frameworks, so you guys are shaped by yours. So for today I've checked out a bunch of video cameras from the media room and you're all going to pair up and shoot a five-minute video on what the school environment looks like to you. I want you to discover what your individual perspectives are. No editing. You frame up each shot before you press record and you come back with five minutes of vision and five minutes only. You got it?'

I look around the room. Max and Hamish will pair up, and so will Jasmine and Shari. I'll probably be stuck with the guy who smells like cheese.

Super.

The class has started buddying up when Mr Boaden pierces the room with a two-fingered whistle. It's so high-pitched the sound of it scrapes down my spine. It gets everyone's attention and I'm a bit jealous of his whistling ability.

'Max, step away from Hamish. You and Ily are going

to be partners for today.'

Max's mouth swings open. 'Sir, are you high?'

'Don't perpetuate skater-slash-artist stereotypes, Max. No, I'm not high, and if you want to pass this class then you and Iliad are going to get along, if only for the next ninety minutes.'

Max shakes his feral black hair, then pretends to cough weakly.

'Actually, sir, I think I'm coming down with something. I think the wet clothes are making me catch a cold. I'm gonna have to go to the sick bay.'

Mr Boaden just taps his fingers on the desk. *Rat a tat tat.*

'Don't be such a douche, Max, or I'll give you something to be sick about. Iliad, don't just stand there, make your way over to Max. Now.'

Neither of us budge. Mr Boaden bites his tongue and moves across to the box filled with camera equipment and he begins distributing its contents among the class. When he goes to hand a camera to me I stand there with my arms hanging at my sides and I glare at Mr Boaden. My eyes aren't just shooting daggers, they're assault rifles. Mr Boaden jabs at my shoulder with the camera case.

'Look at those eyes of yours, Iliad Piper. Don't look so stoked, will you?'

I narrow my lids at him even more. 'I can't see my own eyes, sir. Duh.'

Max and I are trudging along the school grounds. I'm carrying the portable Canon camera and Max is lugging the tripod. It's hot and I'm ducking from shadow to shadow while Max glares straight ahead and powers through the heat in a dogged steady line. Finally I slice at the silence between us.

'Seriously, scram. Go to the sick bay. I'll do a better job on my own anyway.'

He stands there, shouldering both the tripod and the sun's glare on his lean shoulders. His brow is dripping.

'You'll do a better job than me? Ha. For someone who thinks she's so deadly and knows everything you don't know anything.'

He's wrong about me.

I don't think that I know everything, I *know* that I know nothing at all. I can barely even pass a test.

I don't tell Max this, obviously. Instead, I just roll my eyes and the crooked overhead branches shadow my face while Max sweats. We stare each other down.

'Ooh, what? You're going to film an AFL ball like the footy head you are? Pfft.'

Max stares at me, then turns to keep walking. He has the tripod so I have to chase after him. He hears me following him.

'Seriously Ily, stop being a know-it-all.'

'I can't help it. I do know it all. Don't hate me for my superior knowledge,' I lie.

Finally, he stops and turns. 'You don't know *me*.'

I've caught up to him. We're all the way over at the back oval and the sun is scratching at me now that there's nothing around for coverage. I scramble for something to say back to him.

'I know that your name suits you. You're a Max pain in the arse. You're Max annoying.'

Max rolls his eyes.

'Did you just do a dad joke? You did. *You just made a dad joke*.'

Oh my God, I did. How embarrassing. I pretend to ignore him.

'Seriously, just hand me the tripod so we can get this over and done with,' I snap, holding out my arms. He passes it across. 'Why are we even all the way out at the back oval here?'

Max looks at me like I'm an idiot.

'To shoot a wide establishing shot of the school. We set the scene and then we can do close-ups of the specifics.'

I have no idea how he knows all this but I'm not going to give him the satisfaction of asking. Instead, I just set up the tripod and I'm about to hit record on a wide shot of our school buildings when Max interrupts.

'Jesus. You haven't even done a white balance.'

I scowl over at him to hide my confusion. He explains.

'So before you start shooting you've gotta adjust the colour balance so the lighting isn't too blue or too yellow. Don't roll your eyes, I'm hating this as much as you. Just hold a piece of paper or something white in front of the camera so I can fix it, will ya?'

I roll my eyes anyway but I take out my notebook and stand in front of the camera and Max begins playing with the camera setting.

'Done,' says Max when he's satisfied. 'Now shoot the stupid wide shot.'

I press record and film a few seconds of the school from a distance. It does look better now the colour's corrected. Not that I'd ever tell him that, although I can't keep a lid on my curiosity anymore.

'How do you even know this crap?' I blurt when I press stop. He's smooth and easy with dismantling the tripod. He's done this before.

'Because not all of us are content to just sit around at the back of the class with their *gammon* weird haircuts and their snarky comments. I wanna make documentaries, I've got a camera and everything. AFTRS, the Australian Film, Television and Radio School, they do these Indigenous short courses and I went to one when they came up to Darwin last year and I'm applying to study directing there full-time next year. But, yeah, don't look so shocked, hey. Settle down, I probably won't get in.'

I just stare at him as he stalks his way back towards the buildings. I don't like it when people climb out of the boxes I've put them in. I'd never in a million years have imagined that Max dreamt of anything bigger than winning at footy on the weekend or passing a maths exam. Or suckering me in the face with a water bomb. The fact that Max has dreams bigger than what he is right now unnerves me. I can see all that wanting and hoping spill out of him, I can see it puddling on the ground, squelching underneath his toes, and I just want to scoop it up again and make him tuck it back into his pockets. I want him back in his box. It's easier to hate him that way.

We reach a cluster of trees closer to the buildings and Max has put the equipment down and he's looking around really intently. He gestures at me to be quiet. Obviously, that makes me want to be loud.

'What are we looking for?'

'Christ. Keep your voice down. Frill-necked lizards. You can find them around here sometimes.'

I bunch my hair up off my neck and then I notice that Max is standing directly underneath a green-ant nest. Slowly, quietly, I bend to pick up a rock from where it sits near my shoes. It's the size of my palm and heavy. I roll the weight of it around in my hand. Perfect. While Max is crouched down, peering into the undergrowth, I swing around and I lob the rock as hard as I can at the nest.

It's a terrible throw.

It misses by a mile, but Max looks at me confused, then looks up at the ant nest and scowls. I shrug.

'You can't blame a girl for trying. Anyway, why are we filming lizards? This assignment is supposed to reflect how we feel about school, right? Why the hell are you trying to make it an animal documentary? Seriously?'

Max keeps looking up at the ant nest and I can tell he's had it up to here with me.

'Says the girl who didn't even know what an establishing shot or a white balance was. Fine, snark at everything. You got a better suggestion? Hey?'

I don't actually have any suggestions but I don't want him to win. I scan my brain for a reply.

'Okay, so when I'm at school I'm not thinking of frill-necked lizards or the basketball court or anything that everyone else is probably going to make a montage of. All I'm doing is staring at the clock and my eyes are going in and out of focus because I'm so bored. Can we shoot that? Like, five minutes of a fuzzy clock and then this stupid assignment will be done within five minutes and we'll have an hour left to spare and I won't have to spend it watching you roll your eyes. Sound good?'

Max is ready to dismiss me, but then I can see the idea of it sort of swim about in his irises.

'That's kinda how I see school, too.'

'Great. Let's get this over and done with, yeah?' and I stomp towards the classrooms.

We find an empty unlocked room and Max makes me do another establishing shot. This time it's me sitting at a desk, shot from behind, so that you can see me looking at the clock above the blackboard for a couple of seconds. Then we set up the tripod and record a close-up of the clock ticking. Max plays with the focus so it blurs then sharpens then blurs again. I keep time. When the five minutes are up we rewind the footage and watch it back. It's actually interesting. It's actually good. It looks like something from a French art-house movie. Max presses stop on the playback monitor and I notice that we're sitting next to each other, leaning in like a pair of old bookends, our clothes still damp and clinging to us even this late after recess and I suddenly feel awkward. So we're sitting here, leaning into each other in this awkward but safe sort of silence when my phone beeps.

It's Jared.

It's a selfie of him bored in one of his lectures, his chin sort of dipped so he's making ripples in his forehead.

Damn he looks lovely.

I've had my phone confiscated too many times to count for texting him back under my desk during class. We spend every afternoon together and most weekends, and I sometimes feel sorry for everyone else in the whole world, the way they don't know how pointless their lives are because they're not being kissed by Jared Lovett.

Max's gaze slides across to my phone. I'm grinning and dippy, and before I have a chance to stop him he swipes the phone from my hands and jumps from the desk.

'Bwahhhahahahahahaha,' hoots Max as he looks at the selfie. He's half delirious with laughter. I keep grabbing for my phone but Max is ducking and weaving between the desks and making obstacles of the chairs and he bats me away like I'm a moth.

'Why is he making that face? Does he have something in his eyes?'

'Christ, he doesn't have anything in his eyes, okay?'

Finally I'm able to yank it back, but only because Max is now sprawled out on one of the desks, his legs dangling and his arms askew. He's panting and feeble from laughing so hard.

'Blue steel and a half, hey. That bloke thinks he's such a *budju*. Hahaha.'

'Yeah, keep on laughing. How's that tall poppy syndrome working out for you?'

Max rolls his head over to look at me.

'Me, jealous of Jared Loves Himself? Bwahahahaha.'

This sets him off again. The thorns of anger are beginning to prickle inside of me.

'Jared *Lovett*,' I spit. 'Just because he's going to be a famous actor . . .'

Max doesn't let me finish.

'Jared Loves Himself is never gonna be anything because most of the time he acts like a complete dickhead, and even then, he's just playing himself!'

Max is hurling laughter up at the ceiling. I grab the tripod and start dismantling it in angry, jagged jolts. Max can't stop himself. His laughter follows me as I stomp down the hallway, my middle finger raised back at him.

Max Selwyn is a jerk.

ten

I help Mum clean up after her most recent retreat, so I don't get to catch up with Jared until the evening, and when I see him he's jeopardising his perfect bone structure with attempted suicide. It's what he tells me dramatically, sort of tongue in cheek, but sort of not, after I've parked on his parents' street and walked over to meet him where he's lying sprawled out on the road, waiting for a passing truck. It's late but it's still fiercely hot. It's always hot. The default settings in this town are hot, bloody hot and Dante's inferno. I can practically see the asphalt panting. I sweep my eyes up and down the street and see the logistical flaws in his suicide plan. The first and foremost being a distinct lack of traffic. Jared's parents live on the quietest cul-de-sac on earth. A dozen mosquitoes hover around us as I scuff my shoes and stick my tongue out at him. He smiles back wryly.

'So, whatever problem you have, I'm guessing it's

temporary, right? And this solution you've come up with, it's kind of . . . *permanent*. Don't you think?'

'Don't feed the attention monster!' comes a call from under the hood of the car propped up on cinder blocks on his parents' lawn. Toby.

'Aren't all the Neanderthals supposed to have died out by now?' Jared calls back.

Toby just laughs good-naturedly and waves to me.

'Hey Ily.'

'Hey Tobes.'

Jared continues with his problematic suicide plan. I drop down to lie beside him and my hair fans out messily around me as I lay there, holding his hand. I roll my head towards his and drink in his profile like it's a cool glass of water. The sharp peaks and hollows of his cheeks. The faint purple smudges that are always just under his eyes like he's been up all night thinking of deep and important things.

'So, suicide. We'll take our cues from Romeo and Juliet, shall we?' I tell him. He squeezes my hand.

'We're so romantic.'

Toby emerges now from under the hood. The evening light's softening into darkness and moths are zigzagging around the streetlights that have just powered on. Toby scratches his back with the wrench and spits onto the ground. He grins paternally at his younger brother.

'It's getting late and I'm parched. Do you want me to bring you out a long glass of harden-the-hell up, little bro?'

Jared swears at him under his breath while the front door of the family home eats Toby up with a slam of the flyscreen.

'So what's up? I'll get it,' I say to Jared, drawing little circles around his palms.

'I didn't get cast in Silas's Shortfest film,' he admits.

Instead of the film being his break, Jared has to pretend he's not broken.

'Silas is clearly an idiot,' I tell him.

'Clearly. I'm gonna succeed with or without him, and screw him if he can't see talent. I'll just write my own script and it'll be so good that heaps of directors will be knocking on my door to film it and I'll enter the competition myself. Screw him.'

'Screw him,' I agree.

We're distracted from insulting Silas by the sound of tyres crunching on gravel and the bass of a subwoofer thumping the air around us. It's Jared's neighbour, the one who proudly sponges down his puke-green Subaru WRX on his front driveway every Sunday afternoon. He stops about a metre from our feet and the driver's side window whirrs down so that his terrible techno music has a chance to properly insult our ears.

'Oi, what do youse two think this is? A bed or something? Get off the road, ya muppets!'

Jared and I don't move. The neighbour beeps. My right hand is entwined with Jared's but I raise my left arm and stick my finger up at him in response. He beeps again. Long and whiny. *Beeeeeeeeeeeep.* I keep my middle finger raised. Toby's wandered back outside to see what the commotion is all about. He's topless now, with his greasy shirt swung over his shoulder and he's holding a surprisingly delicate cup of tea that he sips from as he watches us, amused.

'You need to back up and readjust, Andreas, to make sure the wheels properly go over his head when you accelerate,' Toby calls over to the Subaru guy. He says this while closing one eye and reaching out with the cup of tea as if to calculate the angle needed for maximum damage to Jared's skull.

'Youse are cracked, ay,' mutters Andreas as he winds the window up and begins reversing his car. Toby shrugs and sips at his tea before turning on his heels and disappearing back inside the house. Andreas steers around where we're sprawled, then he gets out of his car to face us.

'Lying on the street like that is not only dumb, it's a crime or something, ya couple of idiots. Next time I'll call the police.'

'Your taste in music is a crime!' I yell back.

Andreas pulls at his hair and is about to say something to me but then he thinks better of it because he just swears to himself and stomps up his driveway and slams his front door shut.

'You risked your life for me,' Jared tells me, very seriously, then he nuzzles his face into my neck so I laugh. I know all the blackness has lifted from him because he laughs too, and then he leans in and his lips silence us. When he finally moves away I look over at him. The stars have begun to turn on one by one, so the sky is powdered with them, and it hits me.

I'm in love with him.

I'm in love with Jared Lovett.

I roll the word around in my mouth.

Love.

It feels so much more potent than any combination of magic words I've ever spoken as a child. I realise that the razor-wire gates I've got guarding my heart have opened to let him in, and I can feel him there, with every thump. I don't know if he feels the same way, but I realise that it doesn't even matter if he doesn't, because that love that I feel, it's all my own. I hug it to my chest. I own it in the way I own a Jackson Pollock painting when I look at a picture of one in class and it makes me feel like it's just mine and I'm alone with it. Nobody can take that love I feel right now away from me, not even Jared himself. But still, I watch him as he lies on the street, staring at the stars and holding my hand, and I hope that he sees something in me to love back.

eleven

I know I should be concentrating on school more and taking it seriously, given that after class I'm mostly spending every spare minute with Jared instead of studying. And I really know I shouldn't have minded so much when Max hid a green tree frog in my lunch box last week, even if it did jump right onto my face when I lifted the lid. Jerk. I'm thinking this as I'm staring at the open fridge for long enough that Nan would give me a cuff on the back of the head if she was around to see it, and then I swipe the half carton of organic free-range eggs from the top shelf and put it in my bag.

Nothing changes the fact that the prank war is still oh so on.

Mia startles me as I'm waiting with my back against the brick wall of the janitor's shed, egg carton in hand, peeking around the corner to the place where the footy kids congregate before the first bell. I almost drop the carton when she taps me on the shoulder and my heart goes *kerthump* like it always does when I'm frightened.

'Jesus. Personal space, Mia!' I snap when I turn and see her body only a couple of centimetres from mine.

She doesn't move away. Today, she's bringing weird clothes to a whole new level. She's wearing an oversized hypercolour t-shirt from the 80s, a garish mash of yellow and pink. It's a man's shirt and on this bonsai-sized human it reaches almost to her knees. The neck of it swoops so low it drapes over her left shoulder and she's wearing a pink singlet underneath. To keep with the 80s theme she's wearing stonewash denim jeans that probably once belonged to a child and they're riddled with holes. Not designer holes. The denim literally is threadbare after decades of wear. Her mother has hacked at her fringe again and today it's particularly haphazard. She's pulled the rest of her hair up into those two shiny black buns that sit high like animal ears on either side of her head, and then to top it off there's a giant hibiscus flower tucked into the elastic of one of the buns. The best way to describe Mia, I think, is a kaleidoscope in human form.

Mia never looks ruffled when I snap at her and right now she doesn't flinch, she just cocks her head to the side and points at the egg carton.

'You're continuing with the projectiles, Ily? Do you honestly think this is the optimal strategy for revenge?'

I can see why Mia wants to study robotics at a Mechatronic Engineering course at university next year. She already speaks like a robot. I roll my eyes at her.

'No, it's not the optimal strategy. It'd be *optimal* if the eggs were rotten.'

I take a step backwards so that Mia's a normal person's distance away from me and I have breathing space, and then I turn to peer around the corner again, continuing to keep watch for Max. I feel a tap on my shoulder again but I ignore it. She doesn't let me ignore her.

'In my opinion you'd get much better marks if you gave all this war stuff up and spent your time a bit more constructively.'

I snap without looking at her.

'I never asked you for your opinion, Mia, nobody ever does, so I'm not sure why you have to always keep offering it!'

Mia doesn't say anything back for a long while and Mia's never quiet. I turn around and she's standing a few centimetres away again, her face upturned and as open as a sunflower. I've hurt her. She takes the hibiscus from her hair and she looks down as she begins to twirl it, watching it spin around and around.

'I know it's not me you're angry with, I'm just the person who happens to be standing here at the moment,' she says finally, not meeting my eye, 'so I'm going to pretend you didn't say that.'

I look at Mia properly. For someone with such questionable social skills it surprises me how perceptive she can be sometimes.

'Hey . . .' I want to say sorry but I can't coax it out. Mia looks up at me and I force a small smile. 'You're right,' I tell her. 'You're always right. That's why you're dux of the year every year, huh?'

She smiles back and forgives me. I worry about her sometimes, how she doesn't mind being trampled on. She just springs right back up again from where she's been crushed underfoot, and she never even thinks about maybe growing thorns this time. She's about to say something when I hear it.

Max's loud, obnoxious laugh.

This is it!

I forget about Mia and I snatch an egg from the carton and I jump out from behind the wall and I peg it at him, then I grab another and I hurl that one at him too.

Both terrible throws.

I've never been good at hand—eye coordination.

Unfortunately Max stays egg-free. Hamish, however, is standing next to him, and I've clocked him two good ones, one right in the middle of his chest and the other on his forehead. Two proper bullseyes. He's dripping with yolk.

Damn it.

Hamish looks confused as he wipes his forehead and stares down at his eggy fingers, but Max meets my gaze.

Shit.

I drop the carton and turn to make a sprint for it, but Max is a footy player and he's used to running. Within a few strides he's caught up to me and he yanks me back by the elbow and frogmarches me to Hamish.

'Get your hands off me. This is assault, you know!' I hiss as I struggle to break free from his grip. He just rolls his eyes.

'Uh-huh. Like I'm the violent one in this situation. Apologise,' Max orders, yanking at my elbow.

I glare at Max, then turn to Hamish.

'I'm sorry that you had to be collateral damage, Hamish. I'm really sorry that it wasn't Max's annoying face I smashed with an egg. Truly.'

But Hamish doesn't notice me. Mia's taken off her oversized hypercolour t-shirt so she's just standing there in the pink singlet and torn jeans and she hands the shirt to Hamish.

'Here you go, it's clean, and it'll fit you,' she offers.

He looks down at her and smiles. Then he whips off his eggy shirt and uses it to wipe off his forehead and he pulls on the ugly yellow and pink one. He doesn't even seem embarrassed. He and Mia turn to face us. They both look ridiculous in a matching kind of way.

'Mate, this prank war, it's spilled over into civilian life and I'm not too happy about it,' he says to Max.

I've got out of this scot-free.

Ha!

Mia looks stern as well. She has her tiny fists on her tiny hips.

'Agreed. You guys have been like the Arab–Israeli crisis all year. Somebody needs to step in and be the UN.'

'It's her fault,' mutters Max just as I'm saying, 'It's his fault!'

Mia and Hamish look at each other, then before we know it Mia's opened the door nearby and Hamish shoves us both inside the janitor's shed. Two giant shoves. They slam the door after us and Hamish is leaning against it and he's built like a human version of a brick shed so there's no way we're getting that door back open. Max and I shoulder-barge it anyway.

Nope.

Nothing but shoulder bruises.

'Mates don't lock mates in sheds with crazy girls!' Max yells out through the crack.

I'm offended.

'Crazy? *Pffft*. Hating on you is all the proof anyone needs to show that I'm totally sane.'

He rolls his eyes at me and looks unimpressed. We bang at the door but it's no good.

'This is an intervention!' calls out Mia and I immediately regret having just felt sorry for her. No wonder she doesn't have any other friends.

'You guys have until first period to sort it out,' yells Hamish.

I check my watch and that's another fifteen minutes. Great.

My eyes have adjusted to the dark and I pace the dusty space, kicking at ladders and lawnmowers. Max has slid down so he's sitting with his back against the door, his gangly legs all askew.

'You started it,' I tell him after I've finished pacing and have sat down on the ride-on mower, feet up against the dashboard.

'If I knew you were gonna react so unreasonably about reptiles I wouldn't have offered for you to come around. Believe me, hey.'

We glare at each other. The seconds tick by angrily. Ten more minutes to wait. Max is tapping some tune on his legs and it's really annoying. I'm stuck in this space with him and it's as good a time as any to ask him about the fight he had with my mum.

'So why did you come around to my mum's retreat that time, anyway?' I ask him, after we've both tried to out-glare the other in the squinty darkness for a ridiculous amount of time. 'If that was prank-war based, eggs are gonna be the least of your worries. I will break you.'

Max runs his fingers through his messy long hair.

'Not everything is about you, Ily. I know that's really hard for you to comprehend, hey, but bear with me. I . . . I just wanted to learn about her healing stuff. Livers, mostly.'

I laugh.

'Ha! You and Hamish go to that many parties and drink so much that you need my mum to cleanse your liver for you?'

The laughs are shaking me, I'm doubled over and stomping my feet into the dashboard. This is gold. Max stands up and throws a pair of gardening gloves at the wall.

'Shut up!'

'Max the party animal!'

'Shut up, Ily. How do you know? You never go out anyway.'

I shake the curls from my eyes.

'That's because I don't need to go out. I have Jared.'

Max bangs the door again. It's no good. Our prison wardens are sadistic. We really should reassess our choices in best friends. He slides back down to the ground, then he sighs.

'Jared's a dickhead, Ily. Jesus. I'm helping out with filming Silas's Shortfest film and Jared had such an attitude when he auditioned that nobody in their right mind would want to work with him, and then he kept calling and texting about it even after Silas said no. It's like, seriously, dude, stop trying to control everyone, you can't just hassle people when you don't get what you want.'

Max goes back to tapping that annoying tune on his legs and I'm flicking the levers on the ride-on mower and then it hits me.

I could learn to film.

I could film the Shortfest script Jared's writing, and he could star in it, and we could maybe even win, then his parents would have to be supportive.

I turn back to Max.

'You have a camera and you know how to shoot, right?' I ask him. He raises his eyebrows.

'Yeah...'

I pick at my nails and kick at the dashboard again, trying to find the right words.

'So,' I begin, focusing on my nails, 'you were over at my house and you want your liver cured, or your aura cleaned, or whatever, yeah? Well I was raised on that crap. You know I could teach you all about it? I've been hearing it all my life.'

Max stops tapping at his legs and he's looking at me like he doesn't know where I'm going.

'What's the catch?'

I flick my torn pinkie nail onto the ground and meet his eyes.

'You teach me how to shoot the Shortfest film Jared's writing and lend me your equipment and I promise I'll teach you all the hocus-pocus crap you want to know. You will have the most sparkly aura ever. Ha!'

Max stands up and starts to pace the room.

'You'll teach me everything?' he asks me.

'Everything.' We meet each other's gaze.

'You know that even if I say yes, this doesn't mean that the prank war's over,' he warns me.

I roll my eyes. 'Oh, don't worry. I never said it was.'

He's silent for a bit and he narrows his eyes at me, trying to work me out, and the swamps of them seem even murkier in this light, but then he nods. It's so slight, you would hardly notice it, but it's a nod. And that's it. There's no hand shaking or any of that. I just nod back, ever so slightly. And that's how we make our pact.

Then the school bell rings and we race to the door and slam it open. I don't pay any attention to Mia as she runs after me.

Mia is a jerk.

twelve

I'm starving when I get home. For the millionth time I miss the food from my boarding schools, even if I miss nothing else about those places. What I would give for sugar and preservatives. I grab an apple and practically inhale it while leaning against the fridge, enjoying the cool against my back, and I check Facebook on my phone. Mum's Mystic Ever-bright Spiritual Healing page comes up in my newsfeed and somebody called Warrior X has posted on her wall. He hasn't uploaded a profile picture.

Bitch. You owe me. I never forget. You can't take what's mine and get away with it.
Whore.

I drop my apple and watch it roll along the floorboards. Another one.

Mum's received comments like this from made-up accounts for years. She usually deletes them as soon as she's seen them, but I thought they'd stopped ages ago.

'Is Dad out of jail?' My hands are shaking as I walk out to the back decking and hold out my phone for Mum to see the post.

Mum's doing her sun salutes and she stiffens mid *chaturanga dandasana*.

'Is he?!' I yell.

She folds herself down into a cross-legged position, forgetting all about her yoga practice now. She stares up at me and shakes her head.

'No, darling. How many times do I have to tell you? We're safe. We're always safe now.'

I try to convince my thumping heart that it was only a disgruntled customer who wrote those things. I guess hippies, like dolphins, aren't as peace-loving as everyone makes them out to be. I plonk myself down on the hammock and swing back and forth, ignoring my stupid heart, ignoring my stupid nerves. Mum's gaze is sympathetic, like I'm a victim, and I'm not. I refuse to ever be a victim. I refuse to be like she was. Whenever I'm scared or upset I fight and right now I can feel the swords sharpening inside of me, gouging my veins, freeing the blood so it floods and turns everything red, and I blame her. I blame her for making me into a person who reacts so irrationally to internet trolls. I blame her for raising me in a violent environment and then not being there for me when we could maybe discover each other in a space of peace. Mostly, though, I blame her because my dad isn't here to blame.

'Seriously, you should offer refunds or something,' I snap. I hold out my phone again for her once my hands have stopped shaking. 'Exhibit A, yet another unhappy customer. People seem to really hate it when you fail to realign their chakra or whatever. It's almost as if . . . as if . . . you're charging them ridiculous amounts of money for hocus-pocus cures that you couldn't possibly hope to deliver on.'

Mum's brows knit, but then she smooths her face into a fake serene mask, so you can't see what's really underneath.

'You should be studying and not spending so much time on the internet, Iliad. You're hardly ever home as it is and your exams are coming up.'

'Yeah, my internet usage is the first thing I'd worry about if I saw this sort of comment.'

She cricks her neck and then deflects the subject. 'Mother couldn't make breakfast this morning because somebody had taken all the eggs.'

It's an accusation. I kick my feet against the ground so I swing higher in the hammock and I meet her questioning gaze head on.

'I was hungry. I'm a growing young woman, you know.'

Mum doesn't believe me.

'Uh-huh. You're telling me you ate the whole half carton of eggs by yourself in one morning?'

'Yep. Are you shaming me for my appetite? That attitude is how girls develop eating disorders – you know that, don't you?'

Mum sighs her trademark sigh and then unfolds her long spindly limbs to return to her downward dog.

'I am not shaming you. If you tell me you ate all the eggs, then I'll accept that.'

Mum's cleansed her crystal collection in a tub of salt water after a group therapy session and now she's re-energising them in the sunlight. They glint next to her in the September afternoon glare.

'I ate the eggs,' I lie, then I hop out of the hammock to squat down and run my fingers through her crystals. I think of what to say next.

'So . . .' I begin. 'My friend has been drinking a lot and he wants his liver cleansed. What should I tell him to do?' I ask without looking up at her, feeling the coolness of the crystals slip against my fingers. They clink and tinkle. Mum stays put in her downward dog.

'Stop mocking me, Iliad.'

I place the crystals back into the pile.

'I'm not mocking you. I'm trying to connect here. Will you let me?'

Mum stretches out her neck so I can see the cords in her throat, then she rolls over onto her back and looks over at me.

'You really want to know?'

'Yes, I asked you, didn't I?'

She stares at me for a good long moment, then scooches over to where I'm sitting at the crystal pile. With her long hands she sweeps through the clinking crystals to pick out a green aventurine and a purple-blue lolite.

'These two are particularly healing for the liver,' she tells me. 'For regeneration and detoxing.'

'Aventurine and lolite,' I say. She's shocked that I know their names and she looks over at me with such enthusiasm that I almost recoil from her gaze. It doesn't dazzle, it burns.

'So you do listen to me, daughter?'

'I don't listen, but I can't help hearing sometimes.'

She sighs.

'All right, Iliad. Well, I guess I'll take what I can get from you.'

She picks around the pile until she finds an emerald-green shard and she holds it up into the light.

'This one, too,' she tells me. 'Dioptase is especially beneficial for the liver.'

I take that one from her. I think she's done, but then she rummages through the pile until she finds another one. A tigereye. It's all different sorts of brown and not nearly as pretty as the others.

'This one's for you,' she tells me as she presses it into my palm. 'It always reminds me of you.'

'Because it's ugly?'

Mum sighs again, unimpressed by me.

'Don't be ridiculous, you're anything but ugly. Tigereye represents strength and courage, practicality and groundedness. It'll bring you protection. Please keep it with you, Iliad, as a favour to me.'

I roll my eyes and think of how panicked my heart was only moments ago.

'Yeah, I'm the ridiculous one here. Next time I'm being chased by an axe murderer or getting attacked by a crocodile I'll just whip out my magic crystal and it'll protect me, will it?'

I shove it into my pocket anyway. Mum stretches her legs out and wiggles her lilac-painted toes.

'Also, tell your friend to take milk thistle for detox, chicory root for its cleansing abilities, dandelion root to stimulate bile flow and organic turmeric for regeneration of the liver.' This last part is muffled by her hair, because by now she's completely folded, her cheek resting against her knees. I will never, ever be that bendy. Ever. 'Reiki will also help,' she goes on, 'and Iliad, the liver is the seat of anger and primitive emotions. Tell him to fix that root cause. It'll help.'

I nod. Mum unfolds herself and looks hard at me, then before I can react she reaches her arm forward and runs her fingers through the shaved part of my head. I recoil from her touch. I can't help it, it's an automatic reaction whenever she gets too near. My father taught me to be by his side, not hers.

'Don't pet me, I'm not a dog.'

She snatches her hand back as though I've bitten her. I don't know what to say and she doesn't know what to say and thankfully that bitey silence is interrupted by a car crunching up the driveway. It's Bob, her client with the kind, milky-tea eyes.

'Hello lassie!' he calls out to me.

'Christ. I'm *not* a dog,' I mutter again, then I stand up too quickly and hit my head on a wind chime. It jangles. Mum pulls at her necklace and flashes a smile at Bob as she gets up off the ground with all the languid grace of a tigress.

'Please run along, Iliad. I'm doing a cleansing ceremony. I need space and silence to pluck the toxins from an aura.'

I slide my gaze between the two of them.

'Really? Another session?' I ask, then I rest my head against the support beam and watch Bob climb the stairs. 'Seriously, what are you even doing to get such a filthy aura, Bob? I bet you kill puppies in your spare time for fun, don't you?'

Mum isn't impressed. 'Scram!' she tells me, and she whacks me on the bum for good measure. I stick my tongue out at her and she widens her eyes in a warning but before she has time to say anything else I turn and skip inside. The crystals clink in my pocket and they feel like a passport to somewhere better. Somewhere that involves Jared and me living in Sydney next year, him as an actor, me an artist. And kissing. Lots of kissing.

thirteen

'You had a fight with your mum again?' Jared asks when he comes to meet me and he's watching as I stick yet another one of Mum's Mystic Everbright flyers onto a cafe corkboard – there's only a handful of them left after I've spent half the morning trudging around all the cafes in town handing them out. We exit the cafe, away from the air-conditioning, and the humidity grips us with its clammy hand.

'It's easier to just say sorry, you know,' he tells me. I shrug and keep \alking along the footpath and our thongs slap our feet in a steady rhythm. I'm about to enter the next cafe but Jared stops me to lean down for a kiss, then when I'm distracted he swipes the flyers from my hand.

'Hey!' I go to shoot him a dirty look but he just flashes those dimples and pulls me close enough to drape his arm around my neck.

'I don't like it when you spend your Saturday doing this.

I missed you. You should be with me.'

I let him direct me away from the shops and across the street to a park, and we sit down on the bench under a banyan tree, a tall, gnarled old thing strewn with vines that sway like streamers above our heads whenever the wind weaves through them. It feels cosy, sitting side by side with Jared. I notice again how my head fits in the nook of his neck like we're puzzle pieces.

'The S word isn't in my vocabulary,' I remind him. I feel bad about yelling at my mum yesterday, and distributing her flyers was the only way I could think of to make up for it. I take back one from where Jared's placed them on the bench and use it to fan myself, handing another over to him to do the same. Instead, he starts to read it.

'Your mum can read tarot and auras and stuff? That's so cool.'

I roll my eyes. 'You mispronounced bullshit.'

Suddenly Jared whacks the hand I'm using to fan myself and the flyer hurtles from me and onto the ground. I'm shocked and confused and I'm about to protest, but I see how angry Jared looks and it silences me.

'It's not fucking bullshit,' he explains, slowly and clearly like he's talking to someone irrational. 'I mean, have you ever considered that maybe you're just too narrow-minded to believe?'

'Why do you care? You hit me!' My hands are shaking.

'Stop overreacting, I hardly touched you. And just to let you know, the tarot lady I went to when I was little, the one who told me I was gonna be a famous actor, like, she knew so much other stuff about my family and everything. So stop making this all about you, okay? You can be really offensive sometimes.'

I get why the tarot means so much to him. His family don't believe in his dreams, so he's got to cling on to whatever he can to believe in them himself. I feel guilty, but it's all clogged up with surprise and hurt. My emotions are clotting inside me so my throat feels lumpy, but maybe he's right? Maybe I am being irrationally upset at him? It's hard to say. I used to trust my emotions, but right now I can't trust they're telling the truth. Jared says that they're wrong and it's a strange thing, not being able to believe the thumping of your own chest.

The storm clouds have lifted from his eyes and he's looking gently at me now. I'm silent, rubbing my hand where he whacked me. Not hard, but that's not the point. Jared puts his arm around me, like he cares.

'So what did you do to your mum that you feel like you have to spend your Saturday handing out flyers?'

I might not be able to trust the beating of my heart, but I do trust how nothing feels as good as when he's got his arms around me. That's the stupid thing about being in love with someone, I've discovered. You want to yell and push them away when they hurt you, but then you realise that having them away from you would hurt so much more than anything else, and that desperate fear of not having them anymore padlocks your tongue and glues you to the spot. I look up at him and I don't know much, but I know that his face feels like home and everywhere else feels like I'm lost.

'I yelled at her yesterday. Again,' I admit. 'I just got so scared my dad was going to come back and get her that I lashed out.'

He knows about my dad, and he hugs me tighter.

'Didn't you say he's got another two years of jail to go? And he doesn't know where you guys are?'

I watch a black cockatoo land on one of the branches above us and it looks like some punk prince when it fans its crest. I try to find the words to explain how I feel.

'The thing is, though, fear doesn't respond to logic. It's like my rational brain and my nerves speak completely different languages.'

Jared jumps off the bench so the flyers scatter to lie discarded among the leaf litter and he reaches out his hand to me.

'C'mon, I've got an idea.'

We've pulled up at East Point, further back from where the beach and bullet shells are, and in the distance you can see the old army bunkers. This spot is cut with sandstone cliffs, not high ones, but high enough to do damage if you fell at low tide onto the rocks below. Today it's high tide and the blue water is so bright it dazzles with gold where the sun skips across it. Jared walks over to the cliff side and he picks up a rock from his foot and hurtles it into the void. I stay back and sit at the perimeter fence, in the spot where the wood bends a little like the crook of an elbow.

'What are you doing?' I call over to him. 'Get away from the edge, you're making me nervous.'

He just grins back at me.

'Psychology, Ily. So you're scared your dad's gonna come back, even though it doesn't make sense. The only way to counteract an irrational fear is to replace it with a rational one. You're scared of heights, so come stand here.'

Vertigo and I aren't on good terms, so I stay where I am. Jared stomps the ground with his foot.

'It's solid!' he promises.

'I don't trust that it'll stay solid! That's the trick with being okay with heights. You need to trust.'

Jared walks over to me and grabs my hand, and drags me unwillingly to the edge. I curl my toes and try to focus on Jared's face, the dip at the centre of his lip, the hint of a dimple that's just begging for you to coax it out, and I feel our fingers laced together.

'You're wrong,' he tells me. 'The trick with being okay with heights isn't about trusting if the ground'll stay solid. The trick is – you just have to not care if you fall. Are you scared about your dad anymore?'

I just want to get away from the edge. I shake my head. No. Jared holds my hand tighter.

I concentrate on his fingers around mine and my heart's panicked bleats begin to quiet.

And then he jumps.

The water comes crashing towards me and I scream until the blue swallows me up and then it's silent as I sink, a gash of white bubbles marking my descent. I've lost my thongs I realise as I kick, and then I'm at the surface, gasping and stunned. Jared's already treading water and laughing and he shakes his head so droplets go flying.

'See, Ily,' he tells me as he swims a lazy freestyle over to me and wraps me in his arms. He whispers into my ear. 'There was nothing to be scared of.' His lips taste of salt as he kisses me and I don't know if my chest is pounding from the fear or from the way he always makes my heart go wild whenever our mouths touch.

We make our way back to shore. It's not quite box jellyfish season yet, but you can't be too careful – they're so poisonous they can stop your heart if you're unlucky, and if you survive they say the pain's so bad you would hardly call it luck. There're crocodiles too, not many, not often, but one is all it takes.

'People jump from there all the time,' he tells me as I flounder about in the water as fast as I can in my jeans and sodden t-shirt that bubbles up around me so I look like a jellyfish myself.

'People are crazy!' I call back, and he laughs, and I can't help it, a small smile cracks my scowl. I splash water at him and he whale spits a mouthful back, and the stillness of the day settles down on us as we paddle back.

When we get back to the car, all barefoot and sopping, Jared takes my phone from where I'd left it in the glovebox.

'We need to take a selfie to commemorate this conquering of fears.'

He stands so the cliff edge is behind and he pulls me into him and starts snapping, slightly adjusting his chin every shot.

'You really know your angles,' I laugh at him, and he grins, then kisses me.

'Just practising for my professional headshots next year, when we move to Sydney.'

I'm sitting on the bonnet wringing the water out of my hair and Jared's looking through the photos to pick the best shot and send it to himself.

'The highest privacy settings if you're going to put it on Facebook. And don't use my real name,' I remind him. Mum and I use pseudonyms on social media. She's strict about that, if nothing else, so Dad can never find us.

'I know. For the millionth time, I know,' he tells me. I rest my chin on his shoulder to look at the images, my hand around his waist, and I can feel his stomach muscles through his wet shirt. The hardness of it reminds me of the ridges that form on the red dirt roads around my house, the ones that make the car bump enough to set your teeth on edge. There're a couple of good photos that he zooms in on, but then he keeps swiping past the ones we've taken.

'Stop, that's private!'

I'm pretty certain there are some embarrassing selfies I've taken, and I try to grab the phone back off him, but he grabs my wrist so I can't reach it.

'Don't you trust me?'

'Of course I do.'

'So let me look.'

I'm still struggling against his grip when suddenly he lets me go, and even though the sun burns angrily above us it feels like the temperature's dropped when I clock Jared's face.

'Who's this?' he demands as he holds out my phone, so close to my nose that I have to jump from the bonnet and step back to see what it is. Max must have taken a selfie after he stole my phone when we were filming for art class. It's blurry, obviously taken on the run as I was trying to yank it back off him. I haven't bothered going back through my photos to have seen it. Max is pulling a ridiculous face and his hair is a black riot falling over his eyes.

'He's just a jerk in my class. Don't worry about it.'

'So why do you have his photo?'

'I don't know! Just give me back my phone!'

I try to grab my phone again and he pushes me so I stumble. I start to scowl at him but his face is so much meaner than any expression I could wear, and I stumble back again, even though he hasn't touched me.

'What do you have to hide?'

I try to say something back, but it's hard, I have to force the words up from my throat like a stuck zipper.

'Nothing. I don't hide anything from you.'

I want to stop him when he starts to go through my messages, I want to be that person who yelled at him on our first date – the one who said, 'If you try to tell me what to do again, I'll break you.' But I realise I'm not that person anymore. The thing is, nobody ever tells you how brutal falling in love is. You think you have this living business worked out; your insides are firmly held up with bones and they're neatly walled in by skin, and you know what is you and what isn't you in this fundamental way. But then you meet someone, and it feels like you've met your missing other half. It's beautiful, but it's brutal, because now you're only half of who you used to believe you were. You're no longer whole.

Nobody ever tells you this.

So I'm not the girl I was when I said those other words. Now, it feels like I need Jared to make me complete. I hug myself to make sure that all of me is still here, digging my fingers into the flesh between my ribs, and my breathing's shallow as I scramble to make it better.

'Jared, stop being angry at me. You're, like, the most important thing in my life. How can you not realise that?'

Finally, he places my phone down on the car bonnet, but he doesn't step towards me. His fists are two balls by his side.

'How do I know that, Ily? You have a picture of another guy in your phone. I don't know what you're doing when you say you're at school. How do I know you're not screwing this guy? I mean, it's been two months and you won't sleep with me yet. Is it because you're getting it from somewhere else?'

I shake my head furiously. It's not that I don't want to

have sex with him. My body is wildly attracted to his body. Sometimes, when we're tangled up in the backseat of my car, our eyelids leaden and our breathing thick, Jared will run his hands down the valley of my back, his fingers nestled in between the ridges of my spine, and he'll begin to pull me to him and even though my body is screaming yes, screaming itself hoarse, I'll stop, and push him away. Not yet. I'll tell him. I'm not ready yet.

His gaze slides off me and he looks hard at something in the distance. Something that's not there. I feel him slipping away from me and it makes me move over to him and grab onto his shirt because I want to cling to him like a drowning girl.

'I want to sleep with you,' I tell him. 'I want my first time to be with you.'

His eyes return to me and they feel like life rafts.

'You're really ready?'

I nod, my fingers still clutching at the hem of his shirt and I pull him towards me so close that my nose is resting on his shoulder and when I breathe him in he smells like the sea.

'Tomorrow,' I tell him. 'I'm busy in the morning but I'll pick you up late afternoon, okay?'

'Okay, Ily,' he says and he holds me so I stay upright even though nothing inside me feels solid anymore.

After I've dropped him off and I'm driving home I watch the road spool red and long before me and I realise that Jared's made my insides feel so messed up I've completely forgotten to be afraid of my father.

fourteen

The next morning I wake and lie in bed for a while, thinking that this is the last day I'm going to be a virgin. My stomach is so fluttery, but I'm not sure if it's a good fluttery or a bad one. I think of the butterflies breeding like crazy somewhere inside my gut, and I think of how butterflies were just funny old caterpillars once, but then they broke free from their cocoons and they had wings. I steady my nerves by thinking that it will signal the end of my childhood once it's done. Once I've done it. I can properly tell my childhood to scram. But then I can't stop thinking of what I'll be like, once I've torn off the child Iliad and properly stepped into the adult Iliad's skin. Will I like her? I hope to God that the grown-up me will eventually emerge to be something like a butterfly and not a moth.

I silently make up a magic word. 'Butterflightflitting.'

Nope, I don't feel any magic.

Knowing me, I'll be a moth and I'll eat everyone's clothes out of spite.

I'm meant to spend the first half of the day learning how to film with Max, and I seriously consider cancelling. I don't want Jared to find out and hate me for hanging with another guy, but then I imagine showing up to his house in a few weeks time, laden with camera equipment, and I imagine his dimples winking at me when he realises he was overreacting about the photo. He'll realise that this was all for him. That I love him. I imagine his parents, too. I imagine filming something so good they'll realise that Jared was never meant to be an accountant and he'll be able to quit his degree and move to Sydney with me next year. I'm thinking all this as I lie in bed, and my closed eyelids are canvasses where I paint a future that is so much brighter and bolder and better than the life I'm living now. When I finally open them again, the room around me seems colourless and I realise that things only shift from your imagination into reality if you make them.

I drive around early to pick Max up from his house. He really needs to get a car and not just rely on his parents whenever they decide to lend theirs to him. I park at the end of his driveway and beep, and I watch him lope along the dirt track, a large duffle bag slung over one shoulder. He hops over his wire gate without bothering to even open it.

'You're not going to kick me out in the middle of nowhere again?' he asks as he buckles up. I roll my eyes.

'Depends on how annoying you are.'

He makes a tortured sound as he runs his fingers through his allergic-to-brushes hair and I ignore him and crunch the gears to get going. The landscape blurs past as we head towards Mary River. It's all red dirt and spiky green brush, and a hot, build-up-season humidity makes the road seem like it's breathing. The Mary River is off the Arnhem Highway and it has the notable reputation of having the highest crocodile-to-water ratio in the Northern Territory, if not the world.

'We couldn't do this closer to home? Really?' I ask, when we're only halfway there after more than an hour of driving.

'Nope.' And there's no more radio reception so Max keeps on tapping annoying tunes on his legs until I'm this close to leaving him to die of exposure on the side of the road. When we get to where Max directs me, I crunch to a halt and he walks over to an old, rusted caravan and bangs on the door. The man that comes out wears dirty khaki stubbies and has the sort of beard that would put Melbourne hipsters to shame, but the thing is, he isn't ironic. The outback hasn't got onto the irony bandwagon yet, it's too far away from civilisation to have gotten the memo – I mean, there isn't even phone reception. I watch from my car as he and Max have an easy conversation, then Max gestures for me to back my car towards the banged-up dinghy that sits on an old trailer nearby.

Oooh no.

'Do I look like crocodile food to you? I am not taking a boat into that water,' I tell Max when he comes over. He meets my gaze.

'Fine. Great. The world won't have to be inflicted with Jared Loves Himself's stupid script. Your decision.'

Max Selwyn is a jerk.

I scowl at him and after a few seconds' stand off, where I'm giving him my evilest eyes, I switch my car into reverse

125

and back up, and Max attaches the trailer to my bull bar, and hops in. I don't talk to him as we drive down towards the river edge at Shady Camp and I back the trailer down the boat ramp towards the water. Some people who obviously have no regard for personal safety are fishing on the nearby bank, their reels screaming whenever they hook a barra, while on the other side of the river there are at least half a dozen crocodiles sunning themselves on the water's edge. And they're just the ones we can see. The crocodiles stay hidden for the most part in the murky depths, hanging there invisible in the river's guts. You'd only really know they're there if they decided to pounce, and by then, it'd be too late.

Max, the suicidal idiot, unlatches the dinghy and pushes it into the water, wading in up to his knees, and the water chomps at the bottom of his board shorts. He dumps his camera equipment and other bits and pieces inside and then he hops in with all the ease of a kid that's used to jumping for footballs and dodging tackles. I park my car and stand watching him, my hands fidgeting about at my sides.

'C'mon!' he shouts.

'I am not croc bait!'

Max holds up a rifle.

'I'll shoot it if one attacks. Maybe. Depends on how annoying you are.'

I roll my eyes and I think about Jared. I think again about making a film that'd prove to his parents that he can be an actor, and he and I living in Sydney next year.

'If I do hop in, the prank war is on hold, just while I'm in the boat.'

'Fine, it's a ceasefire, the boat is Switzerland.'

I eye him warily, then, taking a deep breath, I roll my

jeans up and say a silent magic word – crapshiterous – and I run into the knee-high murky water with a scream. Max offers me his hand but I ignore it and pull myself in. The boat teeters unsteadily. He pulls the engine cord and the thing splutters to life. We speed through the water and the air licks our skin and I eye the rifle that's resting next to the camera equipment.

'Do you actually own a gun? Is that even legal?'

'It's my dad's old air rifle – a BB gun. Can't do much damage. Would maybe scare off a croc though. If we're lucky.'

It's funny out here, in the middle of nowhere. It's like the sky just swallows you whole. The sheet of water ripples, choked by lotus lilies and punctured by the splash of a jumping barramundi or the sly snout of a crocodile. Max kills the motor and shushes me, pointing to a saltie that's wriggling up the bank. He adjusts the camera and hands it over to me.

'Keep the camera steady and film him until he's out of the frame. Once you've done that we can cut away.'

I take the camera and do what he says. The insects drone and hover, and the jabirus wade about in the water, looking stately. The crocodile crawls up the bank until the end of his tail is out of shot, then I stop recording and hand the camera back. The boat lolls from side to side and I can feel Max so near. He avoids my gaze and takes the camera from me to zoom in on the next angle. I lie down on the hard tin seat, sweaty and bored.

'So you reckon you're the next David Attenborough? Ha!'

After a few moments he presses stop, then turns, angry.

'I'm documenting my country. What of it?'

I pick at my nails.

'This was your year-twelve art project, yeah? You did a painting of the river? So even after you've handed it in you

127

want to spend your weekend here? Why?'

Max plays with the setting of his lenses before looking at me.

'I dunno. I mean, because out here, where there's nothing else around, all that you're left with is yourself. I can understand why that's confronting for you, Ily, hey.'

I kick at the oars, offended. They make a din against the metal.

'I like myself,' I lie. 'It's just nature that I don't like. That's why cities are a thing, we build walls to keep it out. Stupid hippies go on and on about nature, but they forget that cyclones and snakebites and man-eating crocodiles are what nature's all about. They like to forget that.'

Max is silent for a bit and he's turned the camera back on and it whirs and clicks. The humidity is making little pools of sweat in the crook of my knees and my brow drips. Finally he looks over at me.

'You're wrong. Nature isn't cruel, hey, she's just . . . she's just wild. That's why I love her, you know?'

There's a raw honesty to what he's said that makes him look away, squinting out along the floodplains that are the same colour as his eyes, and I know he'd be blushing if his skin wasn't that shade of brown. This country is where his people come from, they've been here for tens of thousands of years, and there's a connection that comes with that. A connection to somewhere or something that I wish I had, instead of feeling so adrift all the time and needing to grasp onto something, like Jared's hand, to make me feel like I belong somewhere. I want to insult Max, but the insults lodge in my throat. It doesn't seem right to mock that rawness. It'd be like digging my fingers into an open wound.

I bundle my hair up on top of my head and change the

128

subject, asking about the camera's apertures and settings and lenses, and we look at the camera instead of each other. I tell him about milk thistle and chicory root and he takes the crystals from me and the hours pass without the clash that comes from fighting or the aching weight of shielding myself. The water just laps against the side of the boat and it reminds me of the sound of a white surrender flag snapping in the wind. For a little while, the war inside of me is quiet.

As we're driving back, Max goes on and on about a crocodile we saw.

'Did you see that saltie? It poked its head out about a metre from us and its head was half the size of the boat! Reckon it would have been at least four metres, hey.'

The memory makes me shiver.

'Don't worry, I remember. The motor scares them away though, yeah?'

He grins and wiggles his annoying black eyebrows.

'Nope. Sweetheart, the five metre crocodile that's stuffed in the Darwin Museum, it was famous for attacking motors and capsizing the boats. Never ate a person, but she hated motors.'

I press down on the accelerator and the landscape flies by.

'Thanks for telling me that now. Jesus.'

He's slapping stupid tunes on his thighs and I'm about to lose my shit at him when we finally get phone reception again. My phone beeps. And beeps and beeps.

Jared has tried to call me exactly twenty-two times.

'Shit,' I mutter when I see my call log, grabbing my phone from where it's buzzing to itself on the dashboard with received messages.

The radio reception's started to come back on through the static, and it sounds like it's coming from a ghost space. I don't even complain when Max switches it from Triple J to his lame hip-hop station. My ringtone starts blaring and Jared is calling me again.

I pull over and answer it. 'Hey you,' I finally say into my phone, trying to sound cool.

Max raises his eyebrows at me and I mouth, 'Jared.' He rolls his eyes, unimpressed. Whatever. Like I care about impressing Max Selwyn.

'Don't say "hey you", I've been trying to call you all day and it just went straight to voicemail. Where the hell have you been?'

I can't tell him I've been hanging out with Max. He wouldn't understand, and I want the Shortfest idea to be a surprise, so all my excuses catch in my throat before I can say them.

'Well?'

I scratch around for something to say back.

'I haven't had reception, I've been out bush doing errands. I'll be around really soon, I haven't forgotten. I can't wait.'

'Me too. See you soon.'

When I hang up, Max looks at me sideways.

'You know you should be allowed to do things without getting your boyfriend's permission, hey?'

'And you know you're allowed to shut the hell up if you don't want to be left by the side of the road, hey?' I snap, and I switch the radio back to Triple J and turn it up loud so I don't have to listen to him slapping those stupid tunes on his legs anymore.

fifteen

It feels like my heart is doing cartwheels while I'm driving to pick Jared up, and all I can think about is the condom in my wallet. I know that the whole concept of virginity is a relic from a bygone era where a whole woman's worth was based on her so-called purity, from when men wanted to own and control their bodies. I know that it's not something that I can lose, I hate that term, *losing your virginity*, because I know I won't be lesser for having had sex. I won't have *lost* anything. I won't suddenly become impure, as though I'm something that's soon to be soiled with a dark stain that can never scrub out. But it's a symbol, for me and me alone, that I'll have travelled away from the land where my childhood lives, and it's a place I can never return to. And the thing is, I don't even want to return to it. I want so badly to run from my childhood, as far away as I can. But there's a part of me that's scared about leaving it behind, now that I'm just about to, because despite everything, it's all I've ever known.

Jared's quiet in the car. His lips were as dry as paper brushing my cheek when he kissed me as he got in, and I wonder if it's because he's as nervous as I am. He's been with girls before, but I haven't pressed him for details. I don't want to know. Instead, we just listen to the radio, his hand heavy where it's resting on my knee, and I glance at the rear-view mirror occasionally to see the town dismantle the further we get down the highway, until there's nothing but scrub and red dirt and that towering sky.

When we finally reach my place I don't drive up the driveway. Instead, I pull over on the side of the road a few hundred metres past it, at the outer edge of the property. We get out and I turn to him and place a finger to his lips in a shushing gesture. I remember when my dad used to do this to me, when I was little and I was crying because he'd made my mother hurt. I wasn't allowed to go comfort her. Dad would hold me tight and put his finger to my lips, and he'd tell me that's why I had a dent there – he said it was from where the angels up in heaven were shushing us, when we were babies, before we were born.

'Shoosh, little Iliad,' he'd tell me. 'Shoosh now.' But I'd watch my mum over his shoulder and I never did learn to be quiet.

Our shoes crunch the undergrowth as I lead Jared through a path in the scrub to the edge of the clearing where the furthest bungalow squats. We don't have any clients this weekend and the place is deserted. Looking around to make sure neither Mum or Nan are nearby I creak open the bungalow door and gesture for Jared to follow me inside, then I quietly shut the door behind us. I'm rummaging through the teak drawer as Jared runs his fingers along the ridged bamboo wall, tinkles the wind chime and checks out the view from the window. I move past Jared and reach across with one hand to close the off-white cheesecloth curtains. In my other hand I have the fresh spare towels that we keep stacked in the bottom drawers.

'What are those for?' asks Jared.

I turn away from him so he can't see me blush. It blooms right down to my neck and flames as I spread the towels over the bare yellowed mattress.

'If things get, you know, messy . . .'

A grin creeps into his mouth and his dimples wink at me, then his face looks wolfish and hungry and I have to stop fiddling with the towels because he pulls me towards him and I know that this is it.

I wish it was darker instead of late afternoon. I wish the curtains were thicker. I wish it wasn't still daylight so he couldn't see all the things that are wrong with me. Jared doesn't seem to notice though. He doesn't notice that my breasts are too small or that I have too many moles or that my hips are too large. We're naked now, our clothes are puddles on the floor. He's grabbing at me and squeezing too hard and kissing me like he's starving. It's not soft. I try to push him back and guide his hands to be gentle, but he still isn't soft. He's hungry and it sort of flatters me, how I could inspire this hunger in someone. And then he rolls on the condom and we do it.

I brace myself for pain. I expect there to be pain, but it's not so bad. A little bit and then it's over. But then, after the pain is done with, I'm expecting waves of euphoria or some heightened sensations, or something to understand what all the poetry's about. It just feels . . .

Like there's something inside of me.

I close my eyes and try to focus on the *something* that is supposed to happen. The ecstasy. The throbbing. The crashing. The lifting up into a higher plane . . .

Nothing.

I think that I'm doing it all wrong.

Jared doesn't seem to notice that I'm doing it wrong. He has his eyes closed and he's making these mewling sort of sounds.

All I can think about is – I have something inside of me and this feels kind of weird.

I look up at Jared. He's thrusting and scrunching his face up. He still looks lovely. God, he looks lovely. Behind him, a gecko is scampering up the wall.

Focus, Iliad.

God, I'm thinking about the gecko, I must be doing this all wrong.

Focus.

Jared's brow is dripping and the sweat is splattering down onto my forehead. It'd be weird to wipe it away so I try to ignore it. Then he grabs me and he swings me around, so I'm on top. I don't know what to do, I feel exposed and awkward and he has full view of how buxom my breasts aren't. He gets frustrated.

'You have to move,' he tells me, and he grapples my hips. I don't think I do that right either, because then he flips me around so I'm on my knees and he's making these little grunting sounds and there isn't any poetry. It's not high-minded, it's as animal as you could imagine. Earthy and musky and base. It's like *rutting*. The gecko on the wall scurries and clicks.

I'm focusing on the gecko again. I'm really doing this all wrong.

Finally, Jared grabs my hair and pulls my head back and he makes this sort of exhausted moan and then collapses on top of me. It's over. That was it.

Goodbye childhood. Goodbye virginity. I had freaked out over . . . *that*.

If I had thought that this would change things, if I thought that he'd be nice to me again after our fight yesterday . . . then I was wrong.

He didn't even look me in the eyes.

We lie there in a sweaty silence. Sex has a smell, I've discovered. The room smells of it and it doesn't smell like poetry. It's sort of like mulch and tang and salt. Jared's on his back, his hands clasped together under his head. He's looking over at the breeze swelling the bellies of the cheesecloth curtains and the light's turned soft. I rest my head on his chest and I can feel his heartbeat below my ear, it hasn't yet slowed after all that exertion. The sweat pools around my cheek.

'What are you thinking?' I ask him, circling his belly-button with my fingertip. He reaches a hand down and pats my head, absentmindedly.

'My Shortfest script. I've only got another month before the entry's due. I'm thinking of who I should get to shoot it.'

That's it?

'I just lost my virginity to you and you treat me like that?'

I grab a pillow and throw it at his head and I'm about to get up and leave when he launches at me, his arms hugging me in a way that I would have killed for a moment ago. He looks me in the eyes, and he's so vulnerable.

'I'm sorry, I don't know why I said that,' he tells me, his eyes pleading. 'I wasn't thinking of my Shortfest film. I was wondering where you were all morning, when you didn't answer my calls, and I get jealous when I don't know where you are, and I get angry when I'm jealous, but it's only because I care. If I didn't care, you couldn't affect me like you do, Ily. You know that, right?'

And I look at him, the dreamy guy, wanting *me*. And he's right. If he didn't care he wouldn't get angry at me, right? And it's sort of flattering, how I can inspire this jealousy in someone, and maybe the bruises that'll bloom from where his fingers are gripping my shoulders so desperately right now are proof he needs me. I look into his eyes and he chews his lip, nervously.

'I care about you too much, Ily, that's all.'

He looks like a drowning man, and I know that drowning men are dangerous, they'll only pull you under with them when you reach out to save them, but I'm sick of the blazing war inside of me. I'd rather drown than burn.

'I care about you too,' I tell him, softening. Slipping. Cooling. 'Too much. Way too much.'

And he releases his grip on my shoulders to kiss me hungrily, then he pulls away and grabs a pen from the guest book on a side table and he begins to write something on his chest. It's wonky writing, but that doesn't matter a bit. Across his heart, he's written 'yours'. I reach out and trace the crooked lines with my fingers. I keep my palm pressed on the word even when Jared reaches the pen over to my small left breast, above where my own heart sits, and he writes 'mine'. I'm his. He's mine. We belong somewhere in this world, even if it's just with each other.

We lie there for ages, tangled up together, until the frogs

start croaking and the evening insects hum and the shadows slant so low it'll be dark soon.

'We should go,' I tell him, and sit up, looking about the room for my underwear. I'm wiggling them on when Jared looks down at the towel I was just lying on.

'There's no blood,' he says as I kick at his shorts to see whether my bra is hidden under them. Where is my bra?

'Huh?'

'There's no blood,' he repeats. I look over.

'There has to be.'

It was my first time, there's always blood, right? Jared sits up and examines the white towels. His eyes darken.

'You weren't even a virgin?'

And that was the first shot that started the war. I ball my hands at my side, I can feel my nails digging into the flesh of my palms.

'Maybe there isn't always blood the first time? I don't know.'

Jared looks angry, his hair mussed and his eyes vulpine against his high cheekbones. I pick up the towel and flip it over, confused.

'Why the hell would I lie about something like that?'

Jared's picked up the shorts from where I'd kicked them and he's stepped into them now, and he's tugging at his belt, clacking the buckle, not looking at me.

'I dunno, maybe to hide the fact that you've slutted around already? You tell me?'

And bang, bang, my baby shot me down.

'Fuck you.'

'No, fuck you, Ily. I bet everyone else has,' he shouts.

When he says that I wish that all the love I'd had for Jared just emptied from me. I wish he was forcefully evicted

137

from all four chambers of my heart. But wishes aren't real, I know that. The love doesn't budge, not even a little bit. I hate him, I fucking hate him, but hate can sit side by side with love just fine.

I love him in a way that hurts.

Instead, something funny happens. All the love I have for *myself* starts to pour out of me, even though there wasn't much there to begin with. I'm standing there, staring at him, and I can almost hear it dripping down through the gaps in the bamboo floorboards. *Splat.*

I feel emptied of all that was me.

I am empty.

Jared is tugging at his shirt, turning it back from inside-out, not looking at me, and suddenly I feel panicked. My heart is scrabbling about in my ribcage like a wild thing caught in a trap. He shakes my hand off when I touch him and he pulls the shirt over his head.

'Was it that guy whose picture's in your phone?' he asks me.

I shake my head because my throat's closed up and I don't want him to look at me like this. I'm there in just my underwear with my small breasts exposed and I feel so vulnerable. I don't know what else to do, I grab his face with both of my hands, forcing him to look into my eyes. To really look into them. I want him to see me here. Iliad, his girlfriend.

'I didn't lie to you, Jared,' I tell him, and the words are jagged at the edges and they hook at my throat on the way up. 'I love you,' I tell him.

I'm crying and I never cry. Never. This is the first time I've ever said I love you to any guy. My hands are like a vice against his face, and now he's looking into my eyes, but I wonder if he can see the real me. Because I'm looking into his eyes right now and I'm searching as much as I can to find him in there, but they remind me of the steely marbles I used to play with as a child. They may as well be metal.

'Okay,' he says and that makes me cry harder with relief. I let go of his face and clutch onto his collar and pull him towards me and I dig my head into his chest. His arms have been hanging dead by his side this whole time, but now he reaches up and strokes my wild, flyaway hair.

'Hey, hey Ily. Just don't lie to me again, okay?'

I didn't lie, he is my first, but I know that if I say that it'll set him off again, so I stay quiet. I don't know how long I'm standing there for in my black lacy underwear bought especially for this occasion. It's long enough for my tears to have stopped and for me to have wiped them dry on his shirt. I don't move from his chest, though. I breathe him in. I like the fact that his heart is so close to me right now, I can feel it through his skin. So we're standing there, like this, my face in his chest, my hands gripped around his collar, his fingers lost somewhere in my hair, when my mum walks in.

She's carrying a mop and a bucket as though she's here to clean, and she just barges in.

I'm practically naked.

'Oh! Excuse me,' she says but she doesn't move away or give us privacy. I jump for a towel and wrap it around me.

Jared hasn't met my mum or my nan. I haven't wanted to taint him with the weirdness of my home life, but Mum and Nan have Facebook-stalked him behind my back and they know full well who he is. I'm expecting Mum to tell me that she's deeply disappointed in me. I'm expecting her to tell me that she's speechless, even though whenever she says that she's speechless she's lying because she always has a hell of a lot to talk about right after she says that to me.

'Oh my God, leave!' I yell at her. She just stands there and she draws her face into a smile that looks real, but I know better.

'It's almost dinnertime. You should join us, Jared. You're welcome as well.'

I widen my eyes at her. *No*. Jared looks shifty.

'Ahh, we're about to go,' he says, and he glances over at me standing wrapped up in a towel, my face blotchy. Mum's mouth is still pinned up into a smile.

'Oh, that's a pity,' she tells us, 'but the thing is, Bob just popped around. Iliad, he saw your car by the side of the road and he thought you might need assistance. You left it unlocked, you know? He's looked around under the hood and there's nothing wrong with it, but I lent him the spare key and he's giving it a service. I'm afraid it might be a while before you'll be ready to drive anywhere. Dinner's in ten, I'll put out some plates for you.'

Her ankle bracelet jangles as she turns and walks back towards the house. I'm so nervous right now. Surely Jared can see she's faking being all right with the whole situation? I don't know how much she heard. He just watches her go.

'Wow, so, like, she was okay with that? You never told me how cool your mum is,' he says once she's left.

I find my bra behind the bedhead and I begin to get dressed.

'Cool as hypothermia,' I mutter, but Jared isn't listening.

I don't want to do dinner although I don't really have any other choice but to show Jared the path up to the main house and he seems impressed by the property. I crouch to splash my face with the dam water and I'm wary when we get to the clearing but the plover doesn't attack us.

'Your mum is a real hippie, huh?' Jared says as we're

140

stomping through the undergrowth in the fading dusky light. He's got his hands in his pockets and he's looking around the place. I can't believe his composure. All I can think about is what happened ten minutes ago. My heart still hasn't forgiven me, it's jumping at the slightest snap of a twig. Jared goes on talking about my mum. 'She even looks like she'd know about tarot and stuff. You're so lucky,' he says, stopping to pick up a stick and examine it.

I don't say anything back to Jared, I just trudge steadily forward as he uses his stick to whack at fern fronds and the occasional spider web.

sixteen

Dinner is the worst. We're sitting on the decking, around the heavy mahogany table, with the smoke of mosquito coils curling up from near our feet and staining all the food with a poisonous tang. Not that it would be very tasty anyway. Mum's cooked a vegetable ratatouille and a lentil and tabbouleh salad and I just wish for the millionth time she didn't inflict her vegan ways on the rest of us. It's not like she eats much of it anyway. My mother is not at peace with food, she just moves it around on her plate between talking. And God, tonight does she talk. She elongates her vowels and uses her hands a lot in that way she does when she wants to seem charming.

'So Iliad tells me you're a thespian?' she asks Jared, all smiles and pouring him a glass of water. 'How interesting.' When Mum says 'how interesting' it's always an insult, but Jared doesn't know this. He's like a rat in the trance of a snake. She can be like that sometimes, her gaze like a flood-light blinding whoever she turns it on for, and Jared, the actor, is just basking in this spotlight.

'Yeah, Mrs Piper, I played the lead in *Macbeth*.'

'Oh, don't be silly, call me Eve.'

'Okay, sure, Eve. So I'm hoping to move to Sydney next year where I'll get an agent. There's not really much scope to properly showcase your talent around here, you know? You need to be in the city if you're gonna be discovered.'

Mum smiles and nods her head slightly as she places a tiny morsel of food into her mouth. There are about three beans on the fork and it takes her forever to chew.

'So I'm writing a Shortfest film at the moment that I want to get filmed. I'm gonna star in it and when I win it'll be good exposure for really breaking into the Sydney acting scene, you know?'

Mum nods and makes a 'hmmmm' sort of sound. To other ears she'd sound like she was interested, but I know she's taking the piss.

'Yes, well, if wishes were money we'd all be millionaires, wouldn't we? Do you have a back-up plan?' That's Nan. She's hobbled around the table to grab the whisky bottle and now she's pouring a nip into her glass of ice water. Jared glares at her but Mum just places her fine, delicate hand on Jared's arm to settle him down.

'Don't pay her any attention, Jared. People who don't dream big can't understand how vast the horizon can be to people like us.' Oh God, there's another totally meaningless platitude she trots out for money. Jared, however, laps it up and nods at her, like she really understands him. It makes me feel small and outcast watching them and I can't believe this is happening. I look over to Nan for support but she's taking small sips of her whisky and laughing quietly to herself. I suddenly lose my appetite and I'm not the sort of girl who ever loses her appetite. I've never once come to the end of the day and realised I'd forgotten to eat any lunch. If anything, I'm the person who decides to eat two lunches. But tonight I'm so stressed out by how horrible this day has become that my food sits barely touched on my plate. I clank my cutlery down so loudly that Mum and Jared look over at me and I speak up.

'I'm moving to Sydney too, Mum,' I declare. 'I've decided to apply to the College of Fine Arts next year. My teacher thinks I'm good enough. I mean, my grades might not make it but he says my art portfolio could get me over the edge.' This is the first time I've said this out loud to my mum. I want the world to know that I'm not just a girl who struggles to even pass a subject.

Like Jared, I want bigger things than I'm living right now.

I *want*.

I hardly speak about it because I'm afraid that speaking it will jinx it, like the universe is waiting behind a rock, waiting to hear what my dreams are so that it can dash them before they leave my lips. I don't want all that *dreaming* and *hoping* to be spilling out of me for everyone to see, just oozing out, vulnerable, for someone to step in. But secretly, silently, I imagine Jared and me together next year, succeeding.

'That's wonderful, darling!' beams Mum. Her attention has flown from Jared, and I almost feel sunburnt from the shine of it. 'You are such a wonderful artist. I'm so glad.'

Jared pipes up. 'But you don't really take it seriously, do you, Ily? I mean, your major work was good, but to make it big, you have to really have genius. It's tough out there.'

Those dreams I was just talking about? He's treading on them. I focus on my glass. 'I don't know, it's just an idea,' I mutter.

Mum's mouth is hidden beneath her napkin, and she holds it still for a tiny moment before she returns to dabbing at her lips. When she places the napkin down her smile dazzles again.

'Jared, you simply must have read all about the Power of Attraction, am I right?'

This is one of Mum's favourite philosophies; it's all about how you can make the universe give you anything you want as long as you visualise it hard enough. The funny thing about that theory is – although it might work for rich people visualising a free car space in the parking lot, somehow those starving people in third world countries can't seem to visualise well enough to stop their children dying from malnutrition. Funny that. When Jared shakes his head, Mum explains the concept to him, all elongated vowels and dramatic hand gestures. I look at my own hands, knotted in my lap, and my fists are clenched so tightly my black polished nails almost pierce the skin of my palms.

'That's exactly what I meant!' exclaims Jared. 'You need that special something to be able to really attract success towards you!'

Mum does that 'hmmmmm' sound again, nodding slightly.

'Jared, it's refreshing to find a young person so interested in the metaphysical. You simply must come back to discuss it further – I'm looking at your aura right now and it's turquoise and gold, which is such a rare combination – turquoise means creativity and gold represents monetary success. You very rarely come across these colours together.'

I can't stand it anymore. I feel wounded and bloodied and forgotten and even Nan isn't making any snide remarks.

'As much as I'm sure you'd love to empty his pockets, Jared doesn't have any money, so you'll need to go fleece somebody else,' I snap at her. Mum keeps her composure, her posture perfectly upright, and she turns away from me and back to Jared.

'Iliad's being silly. Of course I wouldn't charge any fees from the boy that she's seeing. Do come along and chat with me about this, Jared, if you get time. It can be incredibly enlightening.'

I slam my chair back from the table.

'My car should be sorted by now. Jared, we're going.'

When I return from dropping Jared home I want to howl. Nan has gone to bed. Mum has collected all the dishes and I can see her in the kitchen, scraping them and dunking them into the suds. All her dazzle is gone. She picks at stubborn food scraps nervously and her hands fly about, they can't keep still, they're clattering pans, picking up and putting down the dishcloth, balling the material at the side of her dress. When she's like this her hands always remind me of a pair of long, scuttling crabs. She stiffens when she hears me come in, but I don't say anything. I stand at the doorway for a bit, leaning my head against the frame, then I walk up next to her and start drying the dishes wordlessly. After a while I notice the tension slip away from her neck and from her shoulders and all we can hear is the clinking of fork against fork in the water, the *chk chk* sounds the geckos make and a mosquito that whines somewhere close.

'I thought for certain you were going to yell at me just

now,' she finally says as she rinses a sudsy plate under the tap and passes it along to me.

I focus really intently on wiping it down. I pummel it with the dishcloth before jamming it in the drying rack just hard enough for it to clatter, but I keep my voice measured.

'I've got too much schoolwork to do so I can't scream and throw something like I'd love to. I literally don't have time to feel guilty later and have to make it up to you.'

She smiles wryly.

'So the fence isn't getting painted?'

I roll my eyes.

'Nope, but fix the lock on the front door. It's loose and it makes me nervous. You should use the deadlock in the meantime.'

We stand there in silence for a bit and work our way through the pile. The mosquito gets closer and I slap it between both hands. It's just a bloody black mess when I peel my palms open and I bump Mum aside so I can wash it off under the tap. Finally, I bring myself to speak.

'Why did you deliberately exclude me at dinner, Mum? He's the first boy I bring home and you act like that?'

She sighs and hands me the final pot before pulling the plug from the sink.

'I wasn't excluding you, Iliad, I was trying to get a measure of him. I don't like him. He didn't care if you felt ignored and he doesn't speak to you with the respect you deserve.'

I scrunch up the tea towel and throw it down.

'Like you can judge anyone's choices in men. You picked Dad and it was a terrible choice and now you can't help but project. He speaks to me fine, you're just angry at me because I'm having sex.'

Mum wipes her hands on her skirt and the wetness leaves

two dark marks, then she calmly picks the tea towel from where it lies rumpled on the bench and she smooths it out to hang off the oven handle.

'Don't be ridiculous, Iliad. It's your body and I would never be anything but pleased to know you're exploring your sexuality in a mutually respectful and emotionally healthy way.'

'Good. Because it is mutually respectful and emotionally healthy.'

Mum makes that *hmmm* sound like she doesn't believe it, fiddling with the tea towel so it hangs straight. Then she turns to me and her gaze is serious.

'I don't like the way you've stopped focusing on your studies since you started seeing him.'

I return her gaze, defiant.

'I've never really focused on my studies.'

'You've stopped hanging out with us, or your friends.'

'I've never had friends. I'm not a friendly person.'

I start taking the things from the drying rack and putting them away. I slam the cupboards louder than I need to and I only stop when I feel Mum's hand on my arm.

'Iliad, you've stopped doing art, you just spend all your spare time with that boy. You used to love art.'

I concentrate really hard on the earthenware mug I'm still holding. I'm gripping it so tight that my knuckles are turning white, because I don't have anything to say to that. It's true. Mum clocks the way my face has tightened and the way my hand is poised.

'Are you going to throw that mug?'

I take a breath and return it to the bench.

'No. Your fence isn't getting painted. Suck it.'

I stick my tongue out at her and she rolls her eyes.

'I'll finish up, daughter. You get some sleep.'

I nod, and go to leave, but when I get to the hallway I turn back. Mum raises her eyebrows.

'I love him, Mum,' I tell her. 'And he's not like he was at dinner. Not usually. When he's good, he's so so good, like, he's actually the nicest person in the world.'

She just rests her cheek in her hand and looks at me like she is staring hard into a mirror.

'Everybody's good when they're good, darling. You don't judge a person by that. It's how they act when things aren't good that tells you who they really are.'

seventeen

I wake up in the middle of the night from a bad dream I can't remember, but it still lingers in the way my stomach's churning, and then I remember the awfulness of yesterday and anxiety crashes down on me in waves, each crest peaking and collapsing before I can surface to catch a proper breath. I scoop myself out of bed and switch the bedside lamp on to examine my face in the mirror, watching my muddy brown eyes blink back at me.

This is the face of a girl who is no longer a virgin. I move my head side to side, watching all the different angles, trying to find the woman underneath the child's softness that still clings to me. I can't find her. I don't look any different. I don't feel any different. I especially don't feel like I've lost anything, except the thing is, I didn't gain anything either, like I'd hoped to. Not a sense of sophistication or any adult insight. Not Jared's trust. I realise dully that no matter what I do or where I am, I'm still going to be me. I can't do anything to climb out of my own skin, no matter how uncomfortably it sits on my bones.

I lie back down on my bed and kick at the sheets and try to calm my breathing as I watch the overhead fan whisk the air. I can't go back to sleep. I never have been a good sleeper. Instead, I pull out my English textbooks and scatter them across the bed to try to cram in some pre-dawn study. I'm lying there propped up on my elbows for so long that pins and needles are climbing up my arm, but nothing in the books is sticking, the words just slip away somewhere in that space between my eyes and my brain. I chew at my pen and start to sketch the characters from my English books instead of jotting notes, except the Macbeth I draw looks just like Jared, and all I can think about is how the frogs outside have never sounded lonelier than they do right now.

I'm a wreck when I arrive at school. Mia clocks my face as I dump my bag down, and she doesn't ask, she just offers to plait my hair. I tell her that I don't do plaits. Instead, we sit with our textbooks splayed out on our knees to cram in some study before class but my mind is a mess and all the words float around like they're letters in alphabet soup.

'Ily,' Mia nudges me.

All her bounce disappears when she sees Jared. I've never said a bad word about him, but somehow, as the weeks unfurled, the maniacal grin Mia wore at the night of the play has turned to a look of quiet concern whenever he's around.

I pivot my head to see him standing there, his proud posture slumped, hands hanging loosely. He looks as awful as I feel.

'I couldn't sleep,' he tells me, opening his palms upwards

like he's holding all the things he can't say. It suddenly feels like I can breathe again.

'Me neither.'

He's kicking his boots into the ground, upturning clods of grass.

'Can we go for a drive or something?'

I check my watch. It's only a couple of minutes until the bell.

'Don't you have uni today?' I ask him. He shrugs.

'You're more important.'

It's amazing how three words, five syllables, just sound and air, really, can turn the world from fuzzy to clear. I nod, and I shove my books back into my bag and I take his hand to pull myself up. Mia jumps up too.

'Ily, you have school today. It's almost exam time! You can't afford to miss class!'

I look from Jared back to the classrooms and I move towards him.

'I'll see you in a bit, Mia.'

She bites her lip and just watches us as we walk off.

We're sitting on my car bonnet near the cliff edge, and Jared unzips his bag and pulls out a bottle of wine and some plastic cups.

'It's just cheap sparkling. I can't afford champagne or anything, but I wanted something to celebrate. I'm sorry I was funny yesterday, when it should have been really special.'

My legs are pulled into me, my toes curled on the bonnet and my chin resting on my knees. I look across at him.

'You were awful.'

He nods, guilty.

'I was just in a mood. My parents told me that there was no way they'd financially support me if I quit my degree and moved to Sydney next year to be an actor, and then I panicked when I couldn't call you to talk about it.'

I soften and let him slip his arm around me.

'It doesn't matter if they won't support you,' I tell him. 'You love acting, right? So it's going to be harder and more complicated than you expected, but if something's worth it, you won't give up on it, even if it's difficult and complicated. That just proves to the world you love it more.'

Jared sort of smiles now, a serious smile.

'Could you think that way about me, and how I acted?'

I can't help myself, even though yesterday is still making my nerves jangle. I nod. I do love him. Complications and all.

We pop the cork and pour the sparkling into the cups and the bubbles hiss. I take a sip and it tickles my throat and it reminds me of the way I always feel when Jared's close. Like my insides are fizzy. Like he makes me unsteady. Jared threads his fingers though my hair.

'I was up all night on the internet trying to think of something to make it up to you. So I was gonna pick you flowers but I remembered you hate them. Why do you hate them again?'

I sigh.

'Because after you pick them, they can't pollinate anything and be useful, they serve no purpose anymore except to be decorative. They're pointless.'

'So's art though, decorative and pointless, really, and you like that.'

I shake my head.

'No. The purpose of art is to pollinate ideas and have them spread. It's the only way I can see the point in anything.'

Even as I say it, though, I realise that not even art can make things clear when Jared's mad at me. It reminds me of a science experiment we did once at school, where we put a compass near a wire coathanger that was attached to a battery so it got charged with an electrical current. The compass couldn't find north anymore when the current was switched on; the wire created its own magnetic field and made the needle swing towards it. Jared's like that for me. The electricity. The magnetic pull. The way I forget all directions except the one that leads me back to him. We finish our drinks and Jared refills the cups. The sparkling liquid feels cool in my throat.

'There's this thing that the Sydney Observatory does, where you can buy a star,' Jared tells me after a bit. 'I found it when I was on the internet last night and I wanted to get it so I could name a star after us, in commemoration, you know? To mark us being together. You get a certificate and it shows you the star's coordinates and everything, so you know where to find it when you look up in the sky, but it was three hundred dollars and I couldn't afford it. Not if we're gonna move to Sydney next year. And it's not official or anything. Like, our names won't be on any scientific documents even if I did buy it. But I liked the thought that there'd be a star that shone just for us.'

I reach out and muss his quiff, and he leans his head closer to my hand, like a pet when you scratch it.

'I don't need you to buy a star to remind me of us,' I tell him. 'And besides which, if it's not going to be on any official documents, why let the observatory pick the star? They'd probably choose some tiny one that's hard to find, and even if they chose a good one, we'd only be able to see it at night.'

I point at the sun.

'I choose that one to be our star. Screw the ones lost in a crowd. Let's have the best one. The one that shines the brightest.'

Jared smiles at me, a full, open smile where his dimples claim his cheeks, and we lean against each other and all I can think about is how good it feels to have the nice Jared back as we squint against the sun that shines just for us. In this mid-morning brightness where everywhere you look is stained golden, I can almost forget that the dark even exists.

eighteen

'Skipping class, Iliad?'

I'm sneaking back into school just before the end of third period and I look up to see Principal Lovett standing there, eyeing me off coolly with the kind of arched brows that are made for withering stares. Since the inauspicious start with the crates back in July, I've tried my best to avoid her, and it hasn't been too hard since Jared isn't exactly pro his family. Today, though, she's blocking my way and doesn't move to let me pass. I adjust the weight of my bag on my shoulders and shrug. School isn't compulsory for seniors.

'I'll get notes from Mia.'

I want to walk past her but the principal just taps her feet and stays where she is, and I get the feeling this is about more than missing biology. 'I saw you leave this morning with Jared. He was supposed to be at his lecture, but he hasn't been concentrating on his studies since he started seeing you.'

The sting of her accusation bites at me like a swarm of midges and I want to lash out, but I can't. Not with Jared's mum. I stare defiantly back.

'Maybe you should talk to him about what he wants? I know he's been concentrating on his acting career.'

She snorts and her eyes narrow as she looks me up and down, like she's not impressed with what she sees.

'Jared needs to focus on his degree and not be distracted by things that clearly aren't good for him in the long run.'

She says this pointedly and I know what I look like to her, with my black clothes, my half-shaved head and my reputation as the girl who everyone expects to fail. I lift my chin and square my shoulders.

'Or maybe you need to realise that you're wrong.'

The bell rings and kids start to spill from the wrappings of their classrooms, shouting and barging and elbowing each other. I have to ball my hands into fists to stop myself from giving Mrs Lovett the finger as I stomp away. My breath gusts out of me and I swear to myself that I'll make her eat her sharp words so they scratch her throat on the way down. I want to prove to her that Jared can make it as an actor, that he has so much more talent than spending his life in a neat little cubicle, tapping at spreadsheets. And most of all, I want to prove that I can be a good influence. That bad doesn't always have to be the adjective that describes me. I wasn't going to meet up with Max again, I was going to forget all about my Shortfest idea after the repercussions from last time, but I so badly want to make this work, and to prove Mrs Lovett and everyone who thinks like her wrong.

Everybody always underestimates the power of spite.

'*There is nothing alive more agonised than man / of all that breathe and crawl across the earth.* Or woman, as it may be in this case, Iliad.'

I've arrived at fourth period English and Mr Salmon says this to me after I roll my eyes when I hear the news that we'll be practising the creative writing component for our year twelve exams. It's a quote from Homer's *The Iliad*. I swear he's spent this year memorising whole passages of the book just to taunt me with them. I'm guessing he's trying to tell me I look agonised. Well, duh. It's English. He marches around the desks, trying to make eye contact with us, his bright shirt looking like a unicorn threw up on him and his ginger beard hanging puffed and springy down his chest.

'There is nothing more vital, more bursting with creative energy than youth,' he tells us, as we sit slumped, leached of energy, our underarms squelchy with sweat. 'Passion!' he goes on. 'Passion is what creativity is about. This is what I want from you.'

Our eyes glaze back at him, listlessly.

'Today, students, we're going to practise poetry!'

More groans. Max raises his hand.

'Can we write limericks? I have one, hey. There once was a teacher called Salmon, who's classes were really quite *gammon* . . .'

Mr Salmon cuts him off.

'Literary genius, young Max, the next poet laureate I'm sure, but I don't want you to write about what you dislike. That's not passion, it's apathy. Apathy is the death knell of the spirit. The project for today is to write about what you love. What makes your spirits soar?'

Max raises his hand again.

'But can it be a limerick? Because you're not gonna get

me writing a lame love poem. Shame job.'

'No limericks. We're not Irish.'

I am technically part Irish, from way back when, but I don't tell the teacher this. I just slump my chin on my desk and watch the time. The space in the click of the hand of the clock lasts an eternity.

'Acrostic poems then?' bargains Max. Mr Salmon looks exasperated.

'Acrostic poems are acceptable, but I'd rather sonnets. Sonnets are the poetry of love.'

We scratch mosquito bites and haltingly pull pens from pencil cases and open our notebooks. None of us will be writing sonnets.

I chew on my pen as I stare at the empty lines of my blank page.

What I love.

Jared?

As if I'm going to write a poem about Jared in my English book that Mr Salmon might see. As if I'm going to empty all of myself onto this page.

I try to think of what else I love.

Art? But I can't answer the assignment with a drawing.

I can write about what I hate.

I hate slow walkers. I hate infomercials. I hate people who want to taste all the ice-cream flavours when there's a line queued up behind them. I hate the colour pink. I hate hypocritical hippies. I hate that I can't whistle. I hate these stupid English assignments.

I am defined by what I hate.

What do I love?

Food with sugar and preservatives? But they account for my hips, which are way too large already for my liking. That's filed under the classification of a love–hate relationship.

My page stays blank and I'm surprised when I look back up at the clock and it's almost the end of the lesson. Shit.

'Pens down, all you passionate creatures. I know it's hard to temper that flow, but pens down.'

Our pencil cases are zipped up before he has the chance to finish the sentence.

'We have a few minutes before the class is up. Who wants to share with everyone the beating of their hearts?'

Silence.

'Max, our resident poet laureate?'

Max slams his hand across his notebook like Mr Salmon is a kid trying to steal the answers for an exam question and he shoves it deep into his bag.

'Na, can't sir. School's havin' an Indigenous dance performance and practice starts now. Gotta run.'

Mr Salmon watches him scoot out of the room and taps his fingers on the desk.

'Jasmine?'

Jasmine sits up straight like a ballerina and as she reads out loud some awful poem about sunsets I breathe a sigh of relief that he didn't ask me.

Mr Boaden has taken to sitting Max and I together in art because, despite his skater t-shirt and long black ponytail which both scream 'cool teacher', Mr Boaden is a jerk.

'We were all devastated that we didn't get to hear your poem about the joys of AFL,' I whisper over to Max as we're meant to be writing notes about how the cultural framework is evident in the art of Vivienne Dadour. He wiggles his shoulders like he's some R&B god.

160

'Not all of us can be deadly dancers like me.'

I roll my eyes.

'You got out of maths. Seriously. I wish I was part of some cool culture so I didn't have to spend last period learning about data and statistics.'

All of Max's dorky arrogance is gone. He looks at me like I am an idiot.

'Yeah, sure you wish you were Indigenous. Sure you'd love to have a life expectancy twenty years shorter than the rest of the population just so you could miss maths. 'Cause it's all about skipping class. Moron.'

'Jesus. I said it was a cool culture. Screw you, I was being nice to you, you moody shit.'

Max continues being a moody shit and runs his fingers through his crazy black mop.

'Yeah, I can see why you don't usually do nice,' he mutters. 'It doesn't suit you.'

We're sitting in the back corner and Max moves his chair so it's scraped right against the furthermost desk leg and he twists his body away from me and leans as far as he can towards the edge of the paint-splattered table.

I roll my eyes up at the overhead fan and stretch my arms out wide, pretending to yawn, pretending I like the extra space.

Like I care about Max's opinion.

nineteen

I send Jared a text while I'm waiting for Max to meet me at the front of his house on Saturday, when we're supposed to be filming again. I send him emojis because I think best in pictures: hearts and a yellow sun and the drama sign and a crocodile and a fish and a clapper and a cartoon couple, standing hand-in-hand. I string them together carefully like beads in a necklace. I'm secretly telling him my plan. I told him I'll be helping Mum out bush today. He shoved his hands deep into his pockets and looked pissed about it, because he doesn't like it when I'm not there next to him in my spare time, but I don't want twenty-two missed calls again. I don't want him to hate me again.

It's been fifteen minutes and Max still hasn't shown up, jerk, so I kill my engine and hop out. When I creak open his front gate the rust sticks to my fingers. It's so hot that I've forgone my trademark black jeans and I'm wearing denim cut-offs with my black Velvet Underground t-shirt. My legs glow a moon colour against the build-up season sun. It's strange walking up his long driveway. There are the same plants we have on our property – golden trumpets, dragon fruit, the grevilleas, all yellow-orange with flowers – but it's more unkempt. There's a wildness to it. I pick up a stick and as I walk I whack at the cobwebs that are strung between branches in giant shimmering nets. I'm whacking and whacking and then I drop my stick and almost scream when I spot two big emerald eyes staring at me through a thick knot of fronds.

It's a child of about ten, crouching, in a dirty buttercup-yellow cotton dress and bare feet. She must be more startled than I am because she springs up and runs, her waist-length black hair streaming behind her. In a moment she's disappeared into the bush.

Weird.

I reach the house, all plaster and corrugated iron, and when I knock on the front door a teenager opens. She'd be a couple of years older than me with the sort of long limbs you see on a runner, her black hair pulled back into a sporty ponytail. She looks like Max.

'Half a shaved head, black clothes, you gotta be the cudgerie who left Max by the side of the road that time.' Her voice is hard and mean as she stands with her face against the flyscreen, narrowing her eyes at me. I'm not equipped to deal with an overprotective big sister right now so I don't know what else to do but stare her down.

'Yeah, I'm Iliad. What of it?'

'Nobody screws with my little brother.'

She cracks her knuckles. They snap, one by one, like the clinks of ten toppling dominoes. I don't know whether to leave or what. I'm standing there, ready to snarl, when she drops the angry expression and the next thing I know she's showing me a full mouth of white teeth and her big smile scrunches up her eyes.

'Naaaw, just messing with ya. I'm Shana. Come in, come in, you're the famous Iliad. I've been *dying* to meet you.' She pulls my arm into the cool shadow of the house. A Marvin Gaye album is spinning on an old record player in the corner and Shana half dances along the terracotta tiles as she swings through the open-plan living room and takes two lemonades from the kitchen fridge. She cracks them open and passes one to me as she sips on hers, perched up on the kitchen stool, kicking her legs, and looking down at me like I'm a curious specimen in a museum. I take the can and feel it sweating cool beads of condensation onto my hand.

'Bet he deserved it, when you left him there on the highway! Took him down a peg or two. Too funny, watching him walk in from the storm like he'd been dragged out of a swamp. Ha! What'd he do to make you kick him out? Was he slapping some rap tune on his legs again? I bet it was that.'

I take a sip of the lemonade, the fizz tickling my throat. Shana is watching me, expectantly.

'He offered to show me his python . . .'

She grunts an 'ugh' sound as she makes a tortured expression and holds her can against her brow, pressing the coolness into her skin for a moment.

'Fluffy. I hate that thing. It has evil eyes. I'd let it out into the bush except I'm afraid it'd slither into my bedroom at night and get me. You're a deadly artist, yeah? Max was going on and on about your year-twelve major work, how

164

cool, all those army figurines and bullet shells, hey?'

Before I can answer, Max appears, laden with camera equipment. He looks over to the clock.

'It's after ten already? Shit.'

Shana slips down from her perch and bops him with her bony hip so he almost falls sideways.

'I've been making friends with *Iliad*.'

She says my name like it's significant.

'Shan!' He says it like a warning. He gestures to me with his head like we're going. She ignores him.

'Noooo . . . she can't leave yet. Mum would want to meet her.'

'We're late.' He says it warningly again.

She scrunches her nose at him like she doesn't care what he thinks and she takes my hand.

'Mum's been dying to meet you, too,' and then she checks herself, like she's said something wrong. 'Bad turn of phrase,' she corrects herself. Her voice flattens. Her bounce disappears.

'Shan,' Max barks.

Before she can respond a man dances through to the living room, singing along badly to Marvin Gaye's 'Got to Give it Up'. He looks like Max, those same swamp-green eyes, startling against dark skin, but he's stockier with thinning hair, and he's performing some classic dad dance moves. Shana perks up again and joins him in the impromptu boogie. Max bangs his head slowly on the kitchen bench, again and again, mortified. It just spurs the other two to dance harder.

'Talia!' the man calls out, looking over his shoulder. 'Where is my half-wild youngest? I thought she'd be in here with you lot.'

I step forward from where I'd been leaning against the wall.

'About yay high, big eyes, has a habit of hiding in the palm fronds and scaring the hell out of people walking down the driveway?' I ask.

The man notices me.

'That'd be the one. I guess she'll come in when she's hungry. You must be Iliad. I'm Ian, the respected patriarch of this household.'

How the hell does he even know my name?

His words have set Shana off, though, and she's hooting with laughter, thumbing her nose at her dad.

'Respect my authority, impertinent spawn,' he says with a grin. Max groans again.

'C'mon.' He grabs me by the elbow.

I wish everyone would stop grabbing me. I shake him off.

'Iliad.'

There's my name again. Why does everyone know my name? This time it's coming from the hallway entrance. It's a woman leaning against the doorway in a floral dress that falls, unfilled, along the bones of her body. Her skin is a smooth, rich brown, and her head – I can't stop staring at it. Her head is completely bald.

She shuffles over to the couch and, exhausted by her efforts, sits herself down on its padded arm, looking up at me, her dark eyes sparkling.

'I'm Rosie. All the cool people are shaving their heads, aren't they, love?' Her smile is full and mischievous, even if the rest of her is caving inwards. 'Pity Max won't let me come near him with the clippers. He could do with a haircut.'

'Guess I'm not cool enough, hey Mum?' he says as he cracks out a half smile for her.

I run my fingers through the shaved side of my head, and

I know this woman's hair hasn't been shaved off.

It's plain as day.

She's lost it through chemo.

Rosie can see the questions marks hurtling inside me. She's not the type of woman who misses much.

'Terminal. Yes. That's the fancy doctor word for deadly. I wish they'd just call it deadly. I didn't get no ordinary cancer, I got the deadly one, hey.' She says *deadly* the way that Max says the word. Like it's a synonym for cool. Like it's fun.

'Don't say that,' Max mutters.

She smiles softly and picks at something from near her knee. Imaginary lint. It's almost like she's trying to pluck a flower from her dress. 'I had a good laugh when I signed the two-year contract for my iPhone, didn't I?' Her eyes dance with mischief again. 'Not many people get the better of Telstra.'

I look up at Shana perched back on the stool, more legs than girl. Her mouth says she's smiling but her eyes say she's hurting. Ian is sawing at a hunk of bread, jaggedly, his back to us.

Max tugs at his hair so it pulls down over his ears. Like he doesn't want to hear her.

'I can still fix you,' he tells her, his eyes fierce. 'There's still hope, yeah? There is.'

Rosie pulls her lips into a kind smile.

'Of course there is, my Maxie boy, there's always hope.'

Max sets his jaw into a determined line and nods to her.

'See ya later, Mum.'

She presses her palms against both his cheeks after he kisses her goodbye, like she wants to hold him close to her for always. It takes her a few moments to let him go.

'Have fun, you two. Lovely to finally meet you, Iliad.'

'We will, Rosie. Thanks. You too,' I reply.

Ian walks with us out of the house. In one hand he's carrying a sandwich on a plate and in the other an orange tumbler of water. He sets them down on the bottom step of the patio, then scans the bush, eyes squinting, and sighs.

'Pastrami, pickled onions and mustard?' Max is crouching down, peeling open the top slice of bread from the sandwich Ian's just laid down. His lip curls in disgust. 'Talia is weird.'

His dad shrugs, like he knows it, and with a quick wave he turns around and heads back inside, the flyscreen chomping shut behind him. Max and I walk up the driveway towards my car, our thongs slapping our feet.

For once in my life I don't have anything to say.

twenty

We don't speak until we get into the boat. I even take Max's hand when he offers it to me as I'm climbing in. He pulls the motor cord and we slice through the river, parting the lily pads.

'It's liver cancer, isn't it?' I finally say.

He nods, eyes steadfast, gazing over at the white mangrove trunks that are piled on the riverbank like dinosaur bones. Near them a crocodile crawls up from the water, a living dinosaur itself. After a bit he kills the motor and pulls his camera from its case, blowing on the lens and wiping it down with his t-shirt, checking the settings. The sun slaps my pale skin.

'Talia's been hit the hardest,' he says, his words falling down from his lips as he presses at buttons. 'She's angry that she only gets ten years with Mum, while the rest of us got more.'

He looks up at me.

'It's not right that a little kid should lose her mum. I won't let it happen, hey. It's not right. She tramps around in the bush all day these days. She's furious at us for those extra years we've had.'

I know what it is to be a little girl, scared and angry at the world. I know how safe a cluster of ferns can feel.

I know.

'Mum and I used to come out here all the time. Go fishing. Dad and Shana weren't too interested, Talia was too little, but Mum loves it out here. We saw a croc once. A Godzilla of a thing. That's what we called it. Godzilla. It would've been seven metres, I reckon. We never saw it again, even though we were looking all the time after that.'

I look at him properly. I see the person there inside his eyes. I see him.

'That's why you keep coming back here, to film? You want to find Godzilla and show it to your mum?'

In his silence I hear my answer. I'm right. He just switches on his camera and starts filming.

I listen to the insects hovering. I listen to the tick of water against tin. I listen to the emptiness around us filled with everything.

'She can't help you,' I tell him, picking at my nails. 'I'm sorry, Max. Mum gallops around on her spiritual high horse. God, she should be in the Melbourne Cup the way she rides it. But magic crystals just aren't a thing. You know that, right? Kale can't cure cancer. Or chanting. I'm sorry for saying I could help you. Truly. I'm sorry, but I can't help.'

I don't think I've properly said sorry before in my life, but the word is spewing out of me. Again and again. I can't help it. I think of Talia hiding in the ferns and I'm sick with sorry.

Max swings the camera around to me. I can see his nostrils flaring underneath where his camera is perched at his right eye. He keeps it aimed at me, his left eye scrunched close, and I can't see inside him anymore, and I feel all exposed, being watched like this without being able to see back.

'Quit it,' I mutter, glaring at the camera. The camera light keeps glowing red.

'Quit it!'

Slowly, defiantly, he lowers it, then switches it off.

'Just because you're too snarky to believe in anything doesn't mean it's not true,' he says, finally, his voice low and harsh and determined. 'The doctors say there's no hope, that chemo's just buying us time, but fuck them. We made a deal, Ily. You said you'd teach me everything your mum knows. I'm not letting the doctors take my hope away from me, so I'm sure as hell not letting *you* do it. I can't look Mum in the eye knowing I didn't try everything I could. Jesus, I can't look Talia in the eye. So you can believe what you're telling me or not, I don't give a shit. But you're telling me!'

He looks away now, turning his back to me, and he reaches out of the dinghy and presses his palm flat against the surface of the water, not caring that there are deadly creatures waiting, hungry, in the murk. He just presses his hand there for a moment like he has the power to hold back the tide. I lean across and take his arm and I gently pull his hand back into the boat. His eyes are wild when they look at me. I shake my head at him.

Don't.

He begins to breathe again.

He breathes and he dries his hand on his board shorts, staining them with river muck.

He's settled down.

'Let's teach you how to win Shortfest, yeah?' he says, finally.

I shake my head at him again.

'Let's do an aura cleansing first.'

He nods, a small nod, and I can see so many things swimming in his green eyes. So many more than there are in the water that slaps against our boat. I try to remember what I've heard from Mum over the years as I hid underneath her massage table when I was small, or from when I was older and I'd roll my eyes during the holiday breaks from boarding school, bored, as she tried to teach me what she knew. As she tried to pretend we could be friends.

'Lie down,' I tell him.

He sprawls across the three benches, a plank that doesn't bend even in the gaps. I place my hands about ten centimetres from his skin and I slowly move them over his body. I adopt my mother's soothing voice.

'An energy field runs through us all, and if we accept negative thoughts or feelings about ourselves they create blockages. These blockages cause disruptions, which in turn affect the organs and cells in our physical body. Reiki heals by flowing through the affected parts of the energy field and charging them with positive energy.'

I sweep my hands along him, above all of his lanky limbs, then I return to the top of the boat and I kneel near his head, pressing my hands against his wild hair.

'This is your crown chakra.'

His sweat makes little eddies between my fingers as I work down along all of his chakras. The boat rocks a lullaby. The sun presses onto us. I keep going.

'This is your third chakra. This is where your mum's

blockage is. You need to dislodge it.'

I hold my hand against his navel. He flinches slightly at my touch, but after a moment he relaxes. His stomach is hard. The stomach of a kid who's always running and tackling. I'm leaning into him and it feels strange to be so close with neither of us poised to fight. I close my eyes, scrunching them, and try to tap into the oneness of the universe. I try to believe. But the thing is, belief isn't something you can switch on and off like a light. It's either there or it isn't. There's no in between, and I don't have it. I'm alone. So very, very alone. It's just my hands pressing against his belly and I think of the cancer eating at Rosie like termites and the thought of it eats at my insides, too.

After I've finished with the chakras I sweep my hands over him like I'm brushing the dust from a room. I'm standing, sweeping, and then I lose my footing and the boat teeters wildly below me and I lose my balance. Max jolts up and grabs my hand just as I'm toppling. His strong wrists pull me down against the seat with a crash. Safe.

My hands are shaking as I look at where I almost fell. Max sits up straight. He forces a grin at me.

'Don't worry, not even a croc would dare take *you* on, Ily.'

I roll my eyes at him, and my heart begins to slow again. I am safe.

The rim of the sky meets the horizon and everything is still.

'What causes the blockages?' he asks me as he bats away a dragonfly. 'What caused hers, and how can she fix it?'

I squint against the sun and bite my lip, not wanting to answer, but I do.

'Liver disorder is apparently caused by neglecting the solar chakra. That's the root of primitive emotions. The ability to love keeps the energy chakras flowing and open, and illness is the cause of accumulated negative energy in the body, through fear, negativity and selfishness.'

'My mum, fearful? Negative? Selfish? Not able to love? Fuck off.'

I shrug, knowing that Rosie is none of those things. A pool of water has splashed into the bottom of the boat and I dip my toe in it and draw pictures on the side of the tin bench facing me. I don't want to look him in the eyes. I know how the swamp creatures will be snapping inside of them. His breathing is getting raspier and raspier. I know his nostrils will be flaring. I don't need to look at him.

'Fine. Let's say she was negative and fearful and selfish. *Pffft.* But let's say that she was. How do I fix it, Ily?'

I keep drawing pictures with my toes. When I'm finished I look down at them. The first few are almost dried and disappearing already.

'Ily, how do I fix it?!'

I ignore him. I don't want to say anything.

Max grabs onto both edges of the boat and he begins to rock it dangerously. I'm sliding along the seat and the water's whacking the tin and splashing up onto me and he doesn't stop rocking until I speak.

'Fine! Reiki will help, like I showed you how to do, but the only way she can cure the blockage is for her to accept she's totally responsible for it. That's the only way she can learn the lesson the illness came to teach her and become free of it.'

'I have to make Mum admit to being she's all these things she isn't?'

'Yes.'

'Well, your mother is full of bullshit!'

174

I jump up.

'What have I been telling you all this time? I know!'

I turn around and grab the motor cord and I pull, angrily. It doesn't turn over and I pull again and again until Max grabs my hand and wrenches the cord from it.

'Damn it, you flooded the motor!'

He shoves me aside and pulls again.

Nothing.

I stand, my hands moving nervously at my sides like scuttling crabs, like how my mum's hands are, and I have to grab them to make them be still. I am not my mother.

'It's a prank. You're doing a prank. The boat was supposed to be Switzerland and I swear I will break you.'

Max just kicks at the oar and the boat metal shudders and clangs. I can tell this isn't a prank. I look down and realise there isn't another one. For some stupid reason we only have one oar. We can't row back. Panic tightens its grip on me and it pinches all my insides. I need to get off this boat. My hands are doing the full scuttling crab thing now and my breathing is jagged.

'I need to get off this boat.'

Max sits down with a thud. He starts to tap an annoying tune on his legs.

'We can't until the gas evaporates from the injectors. Half an hour, I reckon. Moron.'

The boat drifts aimlessly and my eyes are darting wildly across the rippling sheet of water and into the mangroves when I see it. Strangely I don't panic. Strangely I feel calm.

'Max, pass the video camera,' I whisper. He looks up, still angry. I point.

And there, half perched on a submerged log, is the biggest crocodile I have seen in my life. It's Jurassic. A good seven metres. And it humbles me.

Max drops the anchor and I feel the heat of him as he slowly leans next to me and switches on the camera. It's not a fiery, burning, blasting heat that I feel. It's not a heat acrid with gun smoke and cinders and all the things that come from war. We sit watching in a silence that seems holy and the heat that Max gives off just feels warm.

twenty-one

After dropping Max off, I drive down the dirt path of our driveway. I check Facebook once I've parked. There are more comments on Mum's Mystic Everbright page. *BITCH WHORE*, it reads. *I DON'T FORGET. I DON'T FORGIVE.*

Mum's out the front throwing feed at the chickens. They peck, bowing down at her painted toes, and they cluck and follow her like her kaftan-robed devotees do. Nan is sitting at the mahogany table on the decking, whisky in hand and a game of solitaire spread out. Neither of them look up at me as I slam my car door shut. Neither of them notice that the house is engulfed in flames, a fireball ravenous for wood. They're on fire, too. Their hair sizzles and their skin is blistering and then melting from their bones. They are turning to ash. They don't notice.

My hands are shaking as I hold out my phone to Mum.

'I'm going to ask you again, is Dad out?' The panic

attack is starting to hit me so bad it feels like even the light is biting me, and I rest my hands on my knees now, wheezing for breath. She rubs my back.

'He's not out, darling. You're okay. It's okay.'

I hate the way I react like this to internet trolls, and I take it out on her.

'Another one,' I say, holding up my phone again so she can see it. An accusation.

Her brow furrows as she reads it and a deep crease forms, like someone's just taken a sharp knife and sliced right down into her third eye.

'You don't need to worry about this, Iliad, you need to focus on year twelve.'

'What did you do to make someone hate you like this, Mum?' I hurl my words at her. 'How can I protect you when you keep making enemies?'

She tries to reach out to me, but I flinch.

'It's not your job to protect me, Iliad. It's never been your responsibility.'

That's a lie. It's always been my job. She pretends like it's always been her problem, not mine, but she chose my father. She chose to make it my job.

'You promised you could fix them, didn't you?' I say, my voice coming out brittle. 'You tell people that you've got magic hands and they give you money so you can enjoy your stupid organic quinoa that costs, like, a bajillion dollars, and you don't even care that you're selling them a lie. You don't care that it doesn't work because you can just tell them they weren't "open" enough or "evolved" enough to accept your positive energy. You tell them that it's their fault for not believing enough. If they die it doesn't matter to you, you've got your money.'

Nan keeps shuffling and snapping cards onto the table.

'There are so many things you don't know, you silly, ignorant girl,' she barks.

'Don't tell me you believe Mum can perform miracles. I know you don't. Be quiet, you're drunk.'

'Iliad!' snaps Mum.

'Don't *Iliad* me. Max's mum has cancer and he thought you could fix her, and when she dies he's going to think it's his fault he didn't believe hard enough, or that he didn't convince his mum to believe hard enough. And that's not fair. It isn't. It's not fair!'

I think of Talia, hiding, angry and afraid, and I know that I can't help her, just like I could never help Mum, and just like Mum never helped me when I was angry and afraid and alone in a different city. Tears push their way into my eyes but I won't let them escape. I won't let her see me cry.

Mum's hand flies to her mouth.

'Rosie has cancer? That's why Max came to me . . . Iliad, if I had known . . .'

I run my fingers through my hair, frustrated, and stomp at a chicken. It squawks and runs under the decking.

'If you had known, you'd have been as bloody useless as if you hadn't known.'

'I don't say I can cure cancer, I never say that. My powers don't extend that far. I just do what I can to help.'

'Well, why do you call yourself a healer then? A healer of what? Boredom?'

She pulls at her chunky necklace and she begins to open her mouth and I know she's about to defend herself. To make up some nonsense explanation that she'll actually believe. I won't let her explain. Before the words climb out of her mouth and into my ears I take a giant breath and I yell so that I can't hear anything she might say. A foghorn of a yell. An angry, animal sound. It blasts out of me and rumbles across the property. I clench my fists and squeeze my eyes shut, trapping in the tears, and I scream.

The sound feels like me. It's the sound of warriors galloping across battlefields, swords held high. It's the sound made when striking the final blow in a battle to the death. It's the sound of someone fighting for their life.

I scream until my lungs are empty, and I wish I didn't need to breathe and I could keep screaming forever.

When I finish I stand, breathing hard, defiant, and Mum is as silent as I was loud. She's staring hard into my eyes, like she's trying to connect with the real me inside of them, but I won't let her and I look away. I shift my gaze up onto the decking and Nan holds out her glass of whisky to me.

'Have a sip of this and calm yourself down, girl.'

I glare up at her.

'I'm underage. That is *not* good grandparenting!'

I can't stand being here anymore. I get into my car and I almost stall the thing in my rush to drive off. I feel like all that is broken inside of me have become gaping wounds. I need someone to stitch me together. I need Jared. I need love.

In the forty-minute drive to Jared's house my heart slows and it feels like it's beating just for him, because I don't understand my world anymore without him next to me. I pull up at his place and I notice Toby's finished working on the car out the front. It's not on cinder blocks anymore. I wish I could fix things that easily. That all things could be fixed with some grease and a spanner. Max's camera equipment sits in the back of my car and I can't wait to tell Jared my plan, that I know how to film now, and I can help make him a star.

His grey eyes are like storm clouds when he opens the front door.

'Hey, lover.' I smile at him, and lean in for a kiss. He lets me kiss him, but he doesn't kiss me back. It's like kissing a riverbed stone. I look up at him, confused, but his face doesn't give me any answers as he moves back against the door and lets me in.

'Shorts?' He's talking about my denim cut-offs.

'Umm, yeah, I caved. It's hard to be a hipster in the build-up heat so now I have to inflict my legs on everyone. Ugh.'

Jared doesn't even crack the smallest of smiles and I look down at my pale thighs and feel suddenly embarrassed.

'Inflict. Show-off. Tart around. Use whatever verb you want.' He doesn't say this like a compliment, he spits it out. I take a couple of steps back and lift myself up to sit on the kitchen bench and place my hands on my legs, spreading my fingers wide, as though I could cover them. Jared's eyes look sharp, cut against his high cheekbones and his beautiful face looks dangerous. There's something of a vampire feel about his beauty today, cold and mean, and it makes me wary. After a moment he flops down onto the couch in his living room, it's strewn with a notepad and pen and dozens of scrunched-up pieces of paper. Ignoring me, he picks up a scrunched-up ball and throws it at a wastepaper bin in the corner. It misses. Angry, he throws another one. It misses worse. He grabs a handful now and flings them all at the bin. Most end up on the ground, drifting lightly like impossible snowflakes in the heat. This enrages him and he strides over to the wastepaper bin and kicks it. It bangs into the kitchen bench, below where I'm sitting, and

I flinch. One of the scrunched-up balls flies up onto the bench and I take it and open it, smoothing it out across my lap. It reads – *Scene one. Day one. Coffee shop. Jarah, 18, handsome and misunderstood, sits drinking his latte while –*

Jared snatches it from my hand.

'Don't.'

'So you're working on your Shortfest script . . .'

I reach over to grab his hand in my own, and I open up his clenched fingers one by one and throw the paper onto the ground so I can draw little circles in his palm.

'I know whatever you write will be excellent. You don't need Silas's stupid film anyway. Screw Silas.' I smile up at him. 'I have a surprise for you. I've been learning how to direct and I've borrowed a camera and –'

He snatches his hand away from mine.

'I know. With that Max Selwyn guy. The one whose photo's in your phone.'

My smile drops.

It falls.

It splats.

'How do you know?'

Jared leans right in, his hands either side of me, holding onto the bench.

'Silas. I ran into him today. I heard you and Max have been hanging out a bit lately. Or were you *running errands with your mum*?'

It wasn't meant to be like this. He hates me. His eyes are cold marbles. My heart is scrabbling around in my chest and I try to make it better.

'It was supposed to be a surprise.'

'That's why you're showing off your legs. Because you were out with Max?'

'What? No. Don't be an arsehole.'

'How many times did you let him screw you?'

His words are bullets that are shooting holes in me. I feel all of me draining out, and I flounder, trying to plug up the holes. This is going all wrong.

'He was just helping me.'

'Helping you orgasm? Are you into jocks now, are you? Did you let him screw you just because he can kick a football? Did you?!'

He's leaning in so close I can feel his breath on my face. He's scaring me now, but despite the way his words are wounding me, I am not a person who cowers. I square my shoulders and lift my chin, defiant.

'Fuck you.'

'No, fuck you, Ily.'

He presses his finger into my left breast and it digs into me as he traces where he'd written 'mine' onto my chest in pen only last week.

'Mine. Not fucking Max Selwyn's!'

We stare each other down.

'I'm going home,' I tell him, my strong, lifted chin not betraying how weak I feel right now. I go to get off the bench but he pushes me back.

'No, you're not!'

He takes my keys from where they sit on the bench beside me and he sounds like my father and it feels so familiar and now I'm really scared.

I have to make it clear here. He doesn't hit me. Not once does his fist make contact with my face. I never feel his knuckles against my skin. He doesn't even slap.

Jared Lovett does not hit me.

Instead, he grabs my ankle and with a sharp, quick pull

he jolts me off the bench. I fall the metre onto the tiles and my head bangs back and hits the laminate.

My words get swallowed up as my teeth crash together from the impact.

For the second time today, I don't have anything to say.

I sit there, stunned, and he reaches for my arm, between my elbow and my shoulder, and he yanks me back up. I don't have time to regain my footing because he swings. He swings me around and I can feel the tight grip of his fingers digging into my skin and then he lets go and I'm flying, hurling backwards into the wall. My head hits again.

'Fuck you!' I scream at him. I will not cower. He pulls me up again and swings me so that this time I land hard on the tiles, my tailbone jolting.

'What were you doing with him?'

'Nothing! I told you! Stop it!'

He doesn't stop.

I am a rag doll.

The world is like some twisted fairground ride as it spins and the walls fly towards me, and I see stars, pinpricks of light twirling in front of my eyes as I swing and fall and am wrenched back up again, only to be thrown once more. My arms ache from where he yanks at them, my butt and thighs are swollen and sore from crashing onto the ground. I can feel eggs forming on my skull. I still don't cower. Adrenaline riots through my veins and when he comes for me again I lash. I'm not as strong as I think I am and I'm useless. He just pins me against the wall by my neck and we stay like that for a bit. His fingers latched around my throat, his nose almost touching mine.

We're both breathing harshly. I feel like a cyclone is gushing through me, my breath the whipping winds. His fist is raised to my face in a warning but I will not cower. We eye each other off like this, catching our breaths. I'm not sure what he'll do next. This isn't my boyfriend. It isn't. And then, slowly, as we're staring each other off, nose to nose, I see him. The storm clouds clear from behind his eyes and he crawls out of that dark abyss he was in and Jared comes back. I see him in there, and I think, strangely, that he looks like he's in more pain than I am. He doesn't move his hands. The storm clouds just push away and all that's left in front of me is a frightened child.

'Why did you have to make me do that?' he whispers, the words tripping at his throat.

I can feel the grip of his fingers loosen from my neck, and his fist is still raised, but its menace is gone. I can't reply. I don't know what to reply. I almost want to apologise to him, and that doesn't make any sense, but before I can unscramble my feelings I realise Toby's returned home and he's standing, watching us by the doorway.

'Get off her!' He reaches us in three quick strides and flings Jared off me with no effort at all. Gently he pulls me to my feet and I can see him noting my red, swollen limbs, the mess of the living room. I've never seen Toby look anything but good-natured, but today his easy grin is gone. Today he is all brawn and fury. I look up at him and he reminds me of the woodsman from *Little Red Riding Hood*, strong and brave and a hero here to save the day. But the thing is, I don't want him to kill the wolf. I love the wolf.

'Go home, Ily,' he tells me.

My eyes dart between the two of them, my hands shaking.

'I don't have my keys . . .'

Toby wrenches them from his brother's fist and places them firmly in my palm. I can see the fear in Jared's eyes.

'It was my fault,' I try to tell Toby. 'I upset him.'

He doesn't seem to register my words, he just cracks his knuckles and nudges me, not unkindly, between my shoulderblades towards the door.

'Ily, get out.' It's an order, not a request.

I'm walking backwards towards the door as Toby turns to Jared's cowering shape.

'I have never, in my life, *ever*, been ashamed to call you my brother until right now.'

I'm outside and heading to my car and I can still hear it. Toby's fist impacting with Jared, the blunt thud of it, and Jared's cries.

I can't look back.

twenty-two

I don't want to go inside to face Mum and Nan, so I park my car towards the edge of the property and creep up through the bush to the outermost bungalow. The sky outside is burning with sunset reds and oranges and I turn on the fan and slump down on the bare mattress, pulling a towel over me, and I feel my limbs, my tailbone, my back, my head, all throbbing from the pain. It's only now that I'm alone that I can let the tears out. They finally escape and spill down my cheeks. My chest heaves as I watch the geckos scuttle up the walls, unconcerned.

I wish I could stop loving Jared. I've stopped loving my father for what he did to Mum. I hate my father for what he did to Mum, and I hate Jared, too. I do hate him. But I hate myself more for still loving him, because love can sit side by side with hate just fine. I know this. I suddenly understand why Mum stayed so long. It's not always fear that keeps you with someone, it's love, and walking away from love hurts so bad, even more than bruises. You're not just losing a person, you're losing that whole, bright future that you've imagined for the two of you. The present right now feels so dark. I wish that hate was stronger, that it could engulf and conquer everything else, but maybe some of Mum's preaching is true. Maybe love is the most powerful.

Love is a jerk.

My phone beeps, and even though a part of me never wants to hear from Jared again, a deeper part of me desperately wants to hear from him and I desperately want an explanation that will make it all better, even though I'm not sure that anything he could say would make anything better again.

Love is an inconsistent jerk.

I scramble for my phone and I'm disappointed to see it's a text from Mia.

> Trial exams are soon, cue death star theme song, want to come around tomorrow for a study date, young Padawan?

I envy Mia, in a way, how she's a nerd who quotes *Star Wars* and how the only dates that ever concern her are study dates. There must be something so beautifully simple about that. I so don't want to concentrate on maths or biology right now. I reply with emojis — an unimpressed face and a girl with her arms crossed out in front of her. Within a couple of seconds she replies back.

> I take it that's a no. You do realise that you can't answer your exam questions with emojis, don't you?

I roll my eyes and chuck my phone back onto the bed and continue feeling sorry for myself.

Somehow I fall asleep, the whirr of the fan like a lullaby blocking out my thoughts. It's deep into the night when a hand nudges me awake.

My heart is in panic mode.

Dad.

'I will break you!' I yell at the intruder as I flail to turn the bedside lamp on.

It's Jared, his beautiful face looking knocked around by Toby, his right eye nearly swollen shut. He looks broken.

'I saw your car parked by the street and I figured you might be here.'

It takes everything I have to not reach out and touch where he's hurt, to not press my lips gently on the wounds to kiss him better like I'd automatically do if what happened today hadn't happened. He looks harrowed, and desperate, and pleading. He kneels, facing me, silent, though his face says so much. I have to ball my fists tightly to keep my fingers from going to him. I have to feel the sharpness of my nails digging into my palms, but even still, I'm about to cave when he reveals a giant bouquet of multi-coloured tulips from behind his back.

I hate flowers.

Does he not know me at all?

I roll my eyes and just before I tell him to piss off he plucks a bloom from its stem, deliberately, and while looking me right in the eye crushes it in his fist, his face begging me to forgive him. He crushes another one and another one.

'I know you hate picked flowers, so I'm destroying what you hate.'

I'm crying now and his eyes are leaking tears too,

through the bruising, and one by one he rips through the bouquet without once looking away from my gaze. It's the most romantic thing. Even bloodied and bruised, he's the one that I love.

The floor is strewn with torn petals now, they're scattered over the bamboo like wedding confetti, and the bouquet is a tangle of stems wrapped in brown paper. There's only one flower left. A red one. Jared doesn't tear this one apart in his fist. Instead, he plucks only one petal, and he looks up at me, desperately.

'She loves me . . .'

He tosses the petal on the ground. It falls like a drop of blood.

'She loves me not . . .'

He keeps my gaze.

'She loves me.'

He keeps my gaze.

'She loves me not.'

By the time most of the petals are gone we're both holding our breath.

'She loves me?'

I reach out to him, and nod, and pull him onto the bed.

'I'm so sorry. I'm so so sorry. I'm so so so so sorry.' His voice breaks as he curls up into me, and my shoulder feels wet from his tears. 'I don't know what happened. I just, I don't know, I just felt so hurt because I couldn't cope with the thought of losing you to someone else and then I sort of blacked out. I promise, Ily, I swear on my life that I'll never, ever, ever lay a hand on you again.' His voice is thick with emotion, and when I look into his tortured eyes and impossibly long lashes, I believe him. Nobody could look this distraught and not mean it. They just couldn't. He kisses me, hesitantly, like it's a question, like he's asking for permission. I kiss him back. The answer is yes. He's my whole world, and how can you walk away from your whole world? I smell his familiar smell and feel his familiar touch and his skin against my skin just seems like home. He's the only real home I have. The answer is yes.

This time he's gentle and soft, although no less hungry. In the lamplight flecked with darting moth shadows I watch how he wants me, and it still flatters me, how I could inspire this hunger in him. We both wince if the other one presses too hard, our fingertips flutter like the moths do. Every time a bruise is accidentally knocked I'm reminded that I hate him, but the rest of my body doesn't remember, or maybe if it does remember it's just choosing to forget.

He rolls on a condom and my body is arching forwards towards his body, and he draws me closer. This time I don't care about the geckos, because his eyes are reaching into mine, and I don't notice when his sweat drips onto my forehead, because it doesn't matter. Because all the poetry is making sense now. This time, when we do it, I understand what the bards were on about. I get it. And when Jared looks me right in the eyes, in the middle of it, the weight of him pressing down on me, he tells me he loves me. Nothing else in the world matters.

Love has won.

We wake early, when the sun's still young. I nuzzle into him.

'Do you think they have garrets in Sydney?' I ask him as he traces the moles on my arm. 'Actors and artists need garrets, you know.'

'If they don't I'll make them build us one.'

'And we can wear outrageously pretentious berets?'

He kisses my forehead.

'We can't not. Should I tip mine to the right side or the left?'

I analyse him, mock-seriously.

'To the left.'

He nods, then kisses the dip of my neck, and pulls away, unwillingly.

'I have to go, I stole Toby's car and I gotta return it before he finds out . . .'

'No!' I cry, even though the thin cheesecloth curtains are doing little to soften the harsh morning rays. I reach over and pull the towel over our heads, and the world is small and white and just big enough for the two of us, and nothing else in the world exists but Jared and me.

'It's not daytime yet,' I lie. 'It's an illusion, the moon's just bright.'

He knots his fingers with mine and they're so entwined that if it wasn't for my black nail polish I couldn't tell whose were whose. He raises our hands to his lips and kisses them, then rolls out from under the towel and the sun pours over us and he begins to get dressed. I don't want him to leave. I want this Jared to stay, and be like this for always. This sweet, kind Jared. My favourite kind. The one I fell in love with.

'I miss you already,' he tells me, stepping into his jeans.

'Me too, you,' I say as I watch him squash the fallen petals underfoot. The bungalow door swings shut and he leaves me alone with the discarded, torn-apart bouquet.

I sneak through the house and into my room without having to run into Mum or Nan, and I stand in front of my mirror, twisting myself around. The bruises are blooming, bright and purple, and they climb right down to my elbows and the back of my knees, as well as a small one circling my throat like I'm wearing a tight amethyst necklace, the type my mother might own. I chew my lip, analysing my reflection, then I try to figure out how I'm going to cover the bruises up. I can't explain them. Nobody will understand that it's not what it looks like.

It's not.

I ignore the jungle-hot heat and step into my trademark black skinny jeans, but my t-shirts don't reach down to my elbows. My long sleeved shirts from Melbourne are too much in this weather, and I scramble through my drawers, trying to find something suitable. Finally I pull out a top that Mum bought me once in an optimistic fit of charity. As if I'd wear it willingly. It's a flowing white cotton thing with loose, embroidered sleeves that drape halfway down my arms, and the material's light enough to let breeze blow through. My neck is still a problem so I dig around some more for a saffron silk scarf Mum had once bought in India. I stare at myself.

I look like a hippie.

Nan assesses my outfit sceptically when I stomp into the kitchen to make myself breakfast. She's standing by the kettle, bent over like a gnarled old tree branch, and I almost jump when she grabs me as I'm reaching up to the high cupboard for the oats packet. Her fingers claw my wrist as she straightens my arm and twists it around to show where the stupid hippie blouse has crept up, exposing the bruises. Her stare is hard and mean. I meet her mean stare and turn it up a notch.

193

I would totally win the glare Olympics.

With an aggressive jolt I pull my arm back from her grip and then pretend to act naturally.

'I fell out of a tree,' I lie, pouring the oats into the earthenware bowl and jiggling my shoulders so the sleeves of the blouse fall back down. The kettle's screaming now, but even though it switches itself off with a bubbling and hiss, Nan doesn't move.

'Oh you did, did you, girly? And why were you up in a tree?'

I slosh the soy milk into the bowl so forcefully that it splashes onto the bench. I don't wipe it up. I just dig my spoon into my breakfast and chew loudly, meeting Nan's gaze and answering with my mouth full.

'I was feeling whimsical.'

She narrows her lids.

'Bah!' she finally grunts, not believing for a second that I could be whimsical, and she hobbles from the kitchen without bothering to make her tea.

twenty-three

'You do one session of reiki and now you're some mung-bean-eating hippie?'

Max says this about my outfit when he opens the front door, confused to see me. I roll my eyes.

'Say one more word about it and I'll cast a spell and turn you into a cane toad,' I mutter, readjusting the weight of the camera equipment and tripod I'm carrying. Shana bounces up behind Max, all legs and ponytail and toothy smile.

'Hi *Iliad*!'

Again, she says my name like it's significant. Max shoots her a dirty look, widening his eyes in a warning, and before I can say hello back he's dragging me through the house, into his bedroom and away from his sister. He slams the door with a bang.

'Well that was rude,' I tell him, dumping his camera equipment onto the floor and scanning his bedroom.

'So this is the infamous Fluffy?' I gesture to the large glass tank that sits next to the bed. Inside it curls a giant carpet python, all twisted up around a fallen tree branch. The snake would be about two metres long if it was stretched out. It's olive and gold, and diamonds make delicate patterns down its back. It's frightening and beautiful all at once and I can't look away.

'I'd offer for you to pet it but I don't want you to go all psycho on me again.'

I scrunch my nose at him, unimpressed, and I walk over to the tank. Crouching down low I lean right in close, inspecting the creature's evil little face. It sticks its tongue out at me and I do it back.

'It won't bite?' I ask Max, tapping on the glass.

'Depends on how annoying you are.'

'Dork. Look, even Fluffy thinks you're a dork and he's sticking his tongue out at you.'

I stand and lift the glass lid, resting it against the wall, then tentatively reach my hand in and stroke the snake's back. I expect it to be slimy, but it's not. It's cool and smooth and it feels almost like I'm running my fingers along Mum's crystal collection.

He stands next to me and twists Fluffy's tail around his wrist. He wears it like it's some sort of bracelet.

'Not such a big deal, hey? And yet I had to walk a million miles home because of it.'

I groan and when we're both done patting the thing I return the lid to the tank.

'Exercise is important. Seriously, you should thank me. But, you know, as much as I'd love to stay and listen to you have a cry about it for the umpteenth time, I've got to go. I just came around to drop off your stuff.'

Max clocks the camera equipment and his bushy black eyebrows knit together.

'I thought you were gonna film that *gammon* Shortfest film for Jared Loves Himself?'

I shrug, making faces at the snake.

'Yeah, well, things change. Oh, and by the way, I really don't appreciate you telling everyone we were hanging out. It's not gonna happen again, so you can go and tell Silas to keep his mouth shut about it next time he runs into Jared, got it?'

I can almost feel the pierce of Max's gaze as he's trying to work me out.

'Did your boyfriend ban you from seeing me? He did, didn't he? That's what this is about. Ily, I'm tellin' ya, that bloke's a douche.'

I'm insulted.

'So's your face,' I sling back, childishly. 'Anyway, you've finally realised my mum's a fraud so our pact is done with, yeah?'

I walk around his room, annoyed, picking up and putting down his things, trailing my fingers along the AFL trophies on his shelf so I don't have to look at the stupid judgemental expression he's wearing. Like I care what Max Selwyn thinks.

'Sure, the deal's off, whatever,' he finally mutters, snatching his Best and Fairest trophy out of my hand and returning it to its place. 'But hey, look, I've been editing the footage we shot on the river. Before you leave and I totally massacre you again in our prank war you should check it out.'

I kind of want to see what he's done, and this is definitely the last time I'm going to visit him at his house, so I stand beside him at his desk and heave an exasperated sigh.

'Okay, David Attenborough. Show me what you've got.' I'm scrunching my hair into a messy knot on the top of my head but a few loose tendrils fall free and cling stickily to my neck like they're pasted on with glue.

I hate this weather.

'Soooo, are you planning on showing it to me sometime today?' I ask, tapping my feet impatiently.

Nothing.

I slide my gaze over at him but he doesn't move his mouse. He isn't concentrating on his computer. Instead he's staring at my arms.

The sleeves of the ugly hippie blouse are creeping back around my shoulders again now that I'm holding up my hair and he can see the bruises. Embarrassed, I release my hands and tug at the embroidery.

'I fell out of a tree, okay?' I mutter. 'Just show me the stupid video.'

Max doesn't move so I shove his hand away from the mousepad and I open the editing software myself.

'So, the sequence named *Ily*?' I ask, clicking on it.

'No, don't! That's the wrong one!' He tries to push my hand away but it's too late. The timeline starts playing.

And there I am.

I'm sitting on the boat, eyes squinting against the sun, and a small smile plays on my lips like I'm thinking about secret things you'd really want to hear about except I'm not going to tell you. It cuts to a close-up of my hair, ringlets dancing in the wind as the floodplains blur by in a thousand different shades of green. Another cut. I'm staring at the camera, angry, telling Max to quit it. There's a haughty stiffness to my posture and fires blazing in my eyes. Another cut. I'm lying across the benches, bored, hands reaching up at the sky, painting pictures in the clouds. Cut again. A close-up on my eyes rolling, so close that you can see the grains of gold there speckling the brown. The camera shifts in and out of focus. Cut. I'm cupping my chin in my hands and trying to keep a scowl pasted onto my face, but I can't and it cracks open as I laugh. It's a full belly laugh, head tipped backward and my throat all exposed. I watch myself and wonder why I don't laugh very often. I wonder why I stopped. It looks like fun. Cut. There's a close-up of my hands, tapping against the tin, all black nail polish and nerves, and finally, there's me getting out of the boat, swearing and screaming as I land in the knee-deep murk. I run towards the ramp, the river gripping my calves, but halfway there I stop and turn. I tilt my head to the side, wearing a face full of mischief, and I'm smiling as I stick my tongue out and kick water towards the boat.

Towards the camera.

Towards Max.

The splash doesn't quite reach him but he's slowed this footage down, and the droplets fall delicately in slow motion. They're sparkling clear and bright and beautiful. It's like I'm standing in a shower of diamonds.

The video stops.

Max's hands are shoved deep in his pockets and he won't look at me.

I don't understand what this video is. Why would he splice together all these shots of me?

'Is that something to do with the prank war?' I ask finally, confused. 'Are you going to make it into some humiliating video that you'll upload on YouTube? Because I swear, I will break you.'

Max slams down the lid of his laptop. He doesn't say anything. His nostrils are flaring and his swampy eyes are teeming with so many things that are swimming just below the surface, hidden so I can't see them. He stomps around his room, kicking at a pair of dirty boxer shorts, picking up a football and throwing it onto his bed. Finally he crouches down at his graffitied old school bag and pulls out his English notebook. He shoves it onto the desk in front of me and jaggedly flicks through the pages until he gets to the one he's looking for.

Most of the page is taken up by a sketch of a dragon. It's so lifelike, right down to the scales, and it's curled up around the writing on the page like it's a fairytale creature guarding a treasure. Its mouth is menacing and fanged. You can tell that most of the class was taken up with the drawing and not doing the task at hand.

But it's not the dragon I'm looking at.

It's the words.

It was written when Mr Salmon asked us to write a poem. When we had to write about what we loved.

There are only three words scrawled there in messy boy handwriting.

An acrostic poem.

ILY

I

Love

You

I stare at Max, and everything becomes clear now. The video. His family's reactions. He loves me?

'But you hate me . . .' I falter. 'You're my nemesis.'

Slowly, Max shakes his head.

I look down at the words again.

I. Love. You.

'Dude. You egged my car and threw water bombs at me.'

200

Max runs his fingers through his allergic-to-brushes hair, flopping down onto his bed.

'You started it! And you were way worse than I was. But, like, the prank war was the only reason you even looked at me. Jesus, Ily you walk around like you're too good for everyone and you never stop to give anyone the time of day.'

'Wow, so I'm up myself, am I?'

He makes a tortured sort of sound and begins picking at the laces of his football.

'Do you think I want to like you? Do you think I'm happy about it? You're snarky and you're angry, and you have really weird hair and you tried to make a green-ant nest fall onto my head, for Christ's sake. I don't *know* why I like you. I mean, some people are attracted to feet or inanimate objects. I must have some messed-up fetish for eye-rolls or something. I don't know. All I do know is that on your first day of school, the first time I met you, I just fell. Hard. And I've never stopped falling. It was love at first eye-roll.'

I'm just staring at him now.

'Thank you, Max. I was wondering how I was going to let you down gently, you know, given how *I have a boyfriend* and everything, but you just made it easy for me. All I heard was insult, insult, I love you for some totally weird and incomprehensible reason that makes no sense because you totally aren't loveable. Insult. So thank you. I can now tell you to get bent without feeling bad about it.'

I turn to leave but Max springs up and grabs my shoulder.

'Jared is a total douche, Ily. You're smarter than that. I mean, why are you even in love with him?'

I shove his hand off me and struggle with trying to put my feelings into words. How can you explain why you love someone?

'Because I have eyes, Max. And because whenever I think about him my heart starts racing. Because whenever I think about him my palms get sweaty. Because I can't imagine my world anymore without him in it.'

Max shakes his head and he yanks up my sleeve to expose my bruises staring angrily back at us.

'That's not love, Ily. It's fear. Beating hearts and sweaty palms are fear. He treats you like a possession and you let him control you because you're afraid how he's going to act if he doesn't get his way. Christ, look at what he did to you when he didn't get his way. You can't imagine your world without him anymore because he's controlled you the whole time you've been with him so that you've forgotten what it was like to be your own person. Love isn't supposed to be that, hey. It isn't. Love is calm. Love is security. Love is me standing here right now, looking you in the eyes and saying these things even though I know you're not gonna listen to me. Even though I know you're gonna hate me for saying these things. Even though it's true. 'Cause I'd rather have you hate me, I'd rather risk not ever talking to you again, than hold my tongue and let you think it's okay to go back to someone who does *this* to you.'

He gestures at my bruises and that makes me shove my sleeves back down over my arms.

'I fell out of a tree,' I lie again.

'A tree that leaves finger marks? Yeah right.'

I hug my arms around myself, tugging down at the embroidery.

'How are you suddenly an expert?' I ask him. 'I mean, Jesus, have you ever even been in a relationship?'

'Yes, Ily. For your information I have. Lots of times, but I swear none of my ex-girlfriends would've let me get away with half of the bullshit that Jared pulls on you, hey.'

I let go of my sleeves to scrape my fingers through my hair, so furious that I've stopped giving a shit about my bruises showing anymore.

'If they weren't able to put up with the bad parts, then you obviously never loved each other enough,' I hiss at him.

His gaze back is so intense.

'No, the girls just loved themselves enough to know their worth.'

I roll my eyes.

'I love myself,' I lie.

'Well then why don't you think you're worthy of it back?'

I glare at him. He out-glares my glare. It's kind of impressive, his glaring ability.

'Because he knows me better than you ever will!'

Max staggers backwards, because people who aren't damaged can't understand. My words hang in the air and they don't disappear like words should.

I don't say sorry.

I never say sorry.

I just turn with my raised middle finger lifted up at him and I storm out of the bedroom.

I am not sorry.

twenty-four

Mia is ecstatic to see me when I arrive at school on Monday morning. She's made herself a daisy crown again and she's wearing some ugly floral dress that would have been unfashionable even when it was new a million decades ago. It clashes wildly with her scuffed, no-brand pink sneakers and I realise to my horror that the kaftan robe I'm wearing over my black t-shirt, skinny jeans and Nikes complements her outfit perfectly.

'Look, we're exactly like twins!' she exclaims, cooing over the rosebud patterns on my silk scarf. We're hardly twins. I'm built of strong-boned Irish stock, she's bonsai-sized and her parents are from Vietnam. These minor details don't seem to register for Mia. She lives in a world of physics equations and abstract thinking, not in actual reality.

'Our exams are soon. You really should come around and study with me one of these days. It'll be fun,' she prattles on.

'Anyway, I made you a copy of the notes I did over the weekend.'

She holds out a giant stack of paper, each page crammed with carefully written dot points. Only Mia would believe that a weekend spent studying could be classified as fun. I think back to Saturday night in the bungalow, fingers fluttering like moths. The memory makes my heart catch mid beat, and I'm reminded again of all the unlucky people who don't know how pointless their lives are because they're not being kissed by Jared Lovett. Mia's still holding out the notes and she waves them in front of my nose. I grab them from her.

'Ummm, thanks,' I tell her, scanning what she's written. 'You really shouldn't have.'

I mean it when I say that. She really shouldn't have. Even simplified like they are, I don't understand the theories and equations and squiggles that she's painstakingly jotted down for me. Despite the fact she's doing extension maths, she's even gone to the trouble of writing notes for the standard maths curriculum. They're for the most basic maths level, but they still don't make sense. I look at the xs and ys and funny little symbols and they just remind me of the markings you see in the dirt sometimes, where a goanna has left its footprints. It's all the same to me. I force out a smile and shove the notes into my bag and while I'm there I pull out my phone and check it for the thousandth time to see if I've received any messages from Jared.

Nothing, even though I've sent him two already today — a selfie and a link I found to an article about cool small bars in Sydney.

Damn it.

I scroll through my Facebook, and Mum's Mystic

Everbright page comes up on the feed. She's always posting images of goddesses and dolphins and unicorns. Most of the pictures are in varying shades of purple and turquoise with clichéd inspirational quotes written in whimsical white fonts over the top of them. *Dream the magic in your heart. Believe in the impossible and the impossible will believe in you.* What surprises me today is that Jared has just liked her page.

Um, what?

I'm being antisocial and pretending to listen to The Zombies on my phone when really I'm obsessing over this newfound friendliness between Jared and my mum while Mia sits beside me watching some science TED Talk on her phone. Despite my earphones she keeps updating me about what the talk is all about, going on and on about hyperbolic geometry while I throw her a tight smile and go back to ignoring her.

I'm surprised when Hamish McDiarmid suddenly crashes his bum down beside us.

'Wow, is that the one about crochet and coral?' he asks, gesturing to the TED Talk.

Mia looks up from her screen excitedly.

'Yes! You've watched this one? I just love videos about applying maths to real-life scenarios!'

Hamish seems flummoxed by the force of her enthusiasm and he scratches at a mosquito bite smeared in calamine lotion.

'Ummm, yeah. I just really like corals. Corals are cool.'

'Corals are very, very cool,' Mia agrees.

My gaze is sliding between the two of them and I'm afraid that any minute now Max is going to come join us. He and Hamish are always together, throwing a stupid football and punching each other on the shoulder. I shoot Hamish my most unimpressed scowl to make him scram but he just picks at the grass like he's not going anywhere.

'So . . .' he goes on. 'You two are like the smallest group in the year. You should come sit with us sometimes. You know, if you wanna.'

He hangs with all the popular sporty people, and Mia and I aren't just the smallest group, we're also known as the weirdest. I mean, just look at how we're dressed. We do not belong in the group that sits near the janitor's shed. I wonder why he's asked us, and I might not be the smartest girl in the year, I might not even be able to understand standard maths, but even I can see that it's obvious Max has put him up to this. I think about Max telling me he loves me and I want to scrape all that love from my skin and have a shower to wash it off. I put away my phone and decide to deal with this.

'Look. Hamish. I know what you're trying to do and it isn't going to work, so you can go back to your stupid best friend and tell him I'm going to smash eggs onto his face.'

Mia and Hamish look at me like I'm a crazy girl, and Mia shrugs her shoulders as though she has no idea what I'm going on about. I roll my eyes.

'All right, I'll translate it into Mia-speak, shall I? Tell Max that I'm onto your *modus operandi*, so will you kindly get lost?'

They're both still just staring at me.

'So, umm, what has Max got to do with anything?' Hamish asks me, still acting all innocent. I'm not buying it.

'Well why else are you here, asking us to come sit with you? Everyone else in the school is scared of me and nobody chooses to talk to Mia willingly, so it's obviously got to do with Max. Seriously, just get up and go back to the rest of the footy heads and leave us alone. Go.'

The silence that follows my outburst isn't nice.

'Okay . . .' Hamish finally says. 'I guess I'll see you later, Mia. And Ily.' He hauls himself up and lumbers off back to where he came from. Mia watches him leave, then her face crumples as she turns to me.

'Nobody chooses to talk to Mia willingly? Is that how you feel?'

Shit.

I want to say sorry but it's like trying to roll my r's that time I had to study French. I just physically can't do it. My tongue doesn't know how.

'I didn't mean it like that,' I try to tell her. I just meant that she's an acquired taste, like a rambutan fruit or something. She's weird and most people don't get her. I can't explain it properly though. My words just get tangled in my brain before I can order them.

She doesn't stay to hear what I might have to say for myself. She just stands up, brushing the grass from her knees, and she walks away from me, over to where the school garden grows wild, and she plucks flowers from the vines until the bell rings.

I never feel guilty. Ever. But right now guilt is moving in and making itself home in my chest, and as I watch Mia in the distance, gathering blossoms, I can't help but feel like I've just thrown dirt at something pure.

My sense of unease worsens when I go to art first period and I see Hamish sitting by himself. Max isn't even at school today. Mia spends recess and lunch by herself in the library and I'm hating on the day until I finally receive a text from Jared. A dippy little smile latches onto my face.

Hey Ily. Let's meet up at East Point after
school. I need to see you.

Jared Lovett needs to see me. Because I am necessary
to his life. Even with no other friends in the world, that is
enough to make everything okay.

I reply with an emoji of a face blowing a kiss.

He is enough.

twenty-five

I see him sitting on the embankment. The sun that shines just for Jared and me glints over the Arafura Sea behind him, a backdrop of turquoise and gold, and he's facing away from me, watching where the ripples flash and dip. I sit down beside him and the first thing I notice is the silence. He doesn't say anything to me, he just keeps on squinting out at the horizon and even though I look out to where he's gazing, I know that he's really looking at something I can't see.

'You clearly don't belong,' I tell him, nudging my shoulder playfully against his, and I wait to hear him say my lines, our in-joke, from when we first met. I wait for him to tell me that he doesn't want to belong.

Nothing.

I just sit there staring stupidly at his bruised profile, feeling the sweat pooling at the back of my knees and the sogginess under my arms while the sun barrels down on us.

He doesn't even turn his head to face me when he finally speaks.

'Ily, I'm breaking up with you,' he says, and the words are directed out towards the sea, but like cruiser missiles they swerve sharply off course and I almost lurch back from the force of them when they hit.

They're the most brutal six words in the world.

My heart begins to drum so loudly.

Kerthump.

Kerthump.

Kerthump.

It crashes around my ribcage.

I just don't understand.

'No, you're not,' I try to tell him, desperately. 'Only yesterday morning we were talking about moving to Sydney . . . Living in garrets and wearing berets. Remember?'

I reach to take his fingers but he's too quick and he tucks them away into a fist.

'I'm still going to Sydney, Ily, just not with you. I'm leaving next week.'

A knot begins to tie up in my throat.

'Next week? Why can't you just wait 'til my exams are over?'

Finally he looks over at me. His grey eyes are bursting with moisture like too-full clouds, but his face is determined.

'Because I can't have a girlfriend in Sydney if I want to be a successful actor. I need to focus my energies a hundred per cent.'

Bull ants are swarming around the dirt and he grinds one under the toe of his sneaker then wipes a tear that's running down his cheek.

'I've just learnt that Jupiter's about to ascend into my

career sector and it's apparently a really auspicious set of circumstances and I need to already be auditioning in Sydney by then. So that my destiny can manifest itself, you know? It's all I've ever wanted. More than anything.'

'Even me?'

'More than *anything*.'

I blink up at him and it all becomes clear. Just like skin lesions were believed to be the marks of the devil during the Salem witch trials, Jared's words right now are proof enough for me. Mum's left her mark.

'Jupiter ascending? Manifesting your destiny? Oh God, my mother put you up to this. I hate her for this! Please don't listen, Jared, she's a liar. She just wants to break us up!'

Jared's voice cracks, but he's determined.

'She said that you probably wouldn't understand. That's another reason why we'd never work out, Ily. Not in the long run anyhow. You're not an intuitive person like I am. You think with your head too much and your heart chakra is blocked so you're not open to anything.'

'Of course my mother would be against people thinking with their heads!' I try to sound sensible but my voice is edging on hysteria. 'Jared, look, she encourages people to switch off any kind of logic so that they don't see through her bullshit. Jesus, you can't possibly be falling for her crap? You can't!'

The Arafura Sea becomes really interesting to him again as he avoids eye contact. I'm not getting through to him. You know how you have those dreams sometimes? When you're trying to run but you can only move in slow motion? It feels like that now. It feels like Jared is racing out into the distance and I'm stuck running in resin, watching him get further and further away from me.

'Remember how I told you, the first day we met, that an old lady reading my tarot predicted I would be a star? This is my one chance to make it happen. Ily, I love you, but this is all I've ever wanted. Eve and I had this really intense discussion about my aura and what the universe had lined up for me.' Even though tears are rolling down his face and doing little dives off his chin, his eyes are still looking glazed like he's had some sort of religious epiphany. 'I mean, I ran into her on the way back to my car after I left you yesterday, and, like, we talked for hours and it just opened me up to a lot of things about my acting potential that I'd always sensed were there but, I don't know, I wasn't properly open to. She's really attuned.'

'Just shut up about my mother!' I want to take a pair of scissors to his tongue and make him stop. Tears are springing hot and itchy under my lids but I won't let them fall. I despise him for his tears, and the fact that despite them, he can still say what he's saying. 'And anyway, how could you have been talking to her for hours? Didn't you need to return Toby's car before he saw it was gone?'

He goes back to killing ants. He won't look at me and the tears are plopping off his chin.

'Yeah, I returned it late. What was he going to do? Hit me again? I don't give a shit about what he thinks of me. I wish I wasn't related to any of them.'

I reach out and grab onto the collar of his shirt but he leans the other way and he doesn't let me pull him into me. He just keeps talking as I tug at the material and he keeps crushing bull ants with his toe.

'I wish I wasn't born in this backwater town. People just want to pull you down, you know? I can't wait to prove to my family that I'm going to be someone.'

213

He pries my fingers away from where I'm clinging to him. He's properly crying now and he kisses my fingers before he lets them free.

'Ily, stop it. I can't be around you. You're holding me back.'

And then he leaves, beautiful, the sharp angles of his face cutting their way through the humidity and his shadow dragging behind him. He leaves me sitting on the wooden perimeter fence, and I want to run after him but I can't convince my body it's capable of movement. It feels like I can't breathe and I just stay sitting there and the sky gets so heavy I can't bear it anymore. I lean forward onto my knees so I'm almost completely folded, and the sobs burst out of me, and they crash and crash and crash.

She must have expected what was coming when I got home. They both must have. Nan is sitting at the table taking a pair of nail clippers to her craggy old claws and they fall like yellowed crescent moons onto the hardwood. Mum is chopping up basil at the bench. She doesn't believe in mainstream things like pesto bought in jars. Her hands fly about and her posture is particularly rigid. She jumps and the knife goes clattering when she hears me open the door.

'Iliad,' she says in her fake, breezy voice, and when she clocks my expression her smile just kind of hangs from her face for a few moments before she stops pretending everything's okay.

My eyes are swollen and red from crying and my cheeks are sticky with half-dried tears. There's a small framed print of an om symbol sitting on the dresser next to the front door and without saying a word I grab it and fling it at my mother. A terrible throw. It smashes into the wall and the glass shatters.

'Enough!' That's Nan. Her shrivelled sultana eyes are glaring at me something fierce as she bangs her chair back from the table. 'Your mother did you a favour, you stupid girl!' She hobbles over to where we keep the dustpan and brush.

'So it was your fault, you admit it?' I scream at Mum. She pulls at her chunky crystal necklace but she doesn't look sorry.

'I may have spoken to him about the forecast for Scorpio, yes, and how one might go about harnessing vibrational frequencies to manifest one's potential. Yes. If he chose to use that information to continue on a journey that doesn't involve you, well that was his decision.'

The tears are running freely down my face now. They're angry tears, and I ball my fists at my side and my blood is thick with rage.

'You're a fraud!' I scream at her. 'You didn't summon some glittering future for him, you can't see his aura, stop lying!'

Mum takes a few steps towards me, the fan blows at her hair and it hangs thick like a mane and right now she looks anything but sorry.

'A person doesn't need to read auras to be able to see that boy's true colours,' she spits. 'He was toxic. I know the signs, more than anyone. I lived with a toxic man for fifteen years. And I was not having that Jared boy anywhere near my daughter.'

'You're the toxic one! You're so toxic I feel sick just looking at you. What sort of mother tells her daughter's boyfriend that she's spiritually stunting him? You're evil, you are, and I

215

wish they still burnt witches at the stake!'

I do feel sick. The emotions are piling and piling up inside me and they're poisonous. I want to throw up. The tears keep spilling out and I wipe them angrily with the stupid silk scarf Mum gave me and fling it to the ground. She picks it up, calmly, and begins to fold it.

'Do you think any of us believe that you *fell out of a tree*?'

'I fell!' I scream. 'He's not Dad, and I'm not you, it's *different*. Stop punishing me for once for your own terrible life decisions!'

Mum looks hard at me.

'I fell out of lots of trees too, darling. There were so many trees. Don't think this will be a one-off. Those branches have a way of getting more and more fragile over time, and after a while they just snap so easily under your weight. They're always just, *snapping*.'

Nan's crouched down, sweeping up the final shards of broken glass. 'That vain, idiot boy . . . We had him believing he was going to be the next Liam Hemsworth by the time Eve had finished with him.' I throw her my most hateful glare and then turn back to face Mum.

'So you went to him behind my back like a snake and made him leave me? I'm your *daughter*. You didn't even think about coming to me first?'

Nan snorts loudly. Mum places the folded scarf on the bench and wipes her hands on her skirt and she must have had olive oil on her fingers from the pesto because it leaves a shimmery mark.

'Iliad, the surest way to make you do something is to tell you that you're not allowed to do it. Asking you to keep away from that boy was never an option.'

That might be true but it doesn't make it right. My

words are all stuck inside my skull, clashing together angrily, the loops of the y's and the g's knotted and tangled. No words could be enough to express how betrayed I feel. I just scrape my fingers through my hair as my shoulders quake with sobs and Mum's face looks evil and distorted through my tears as I glare at her.

'I hate you!'

Mum just holds my gaze.

'Yes, I suppose you do, but it's my job to be your mother, not your friend.'

'Argh!'

I storm into my bedroom and slam the door and blast The Ramones at full bore and muffle my screams with my pillow. Slowly, the world stops flashing red with rage. The fury begins to darken, then it dirties to black, and then despair just swallows me whole.

The days pass and run into each other like a string of ugly black beads on a necklace. I watch my bruises fade from purple to green to yellow. I don't want them to go away because they're reminders of how long it's been since I last saw Jared. Now they're just pale smudges, they're almost not there at all, and it scares me how quickly things disappear. He doesn't answer my phone calls and he's blocked me from Facebook, so I text, and I text, and my message history looks like the ramblings of some crazy girl.

I wish I hadn't loved him.

I remember how carefully I'd guarded my heart before meeting Jared, but I was stupid. I was careless. I'd unlocked my ribcage for him because he'd asked me to, and then he'd just taken what was left of my heart and he'd looked at it and thrown it into the bin like it was an apple core.

And now he's gone.

And I'm left here.

And I'm hollow.

twenty-six

I'd forgotten how immense a day can be when you don't have anyone next to you helping to fill it. I wear the days like they're oversized garments that desperately need to be taken in. It's awful. But still, I keep on trudging to school and back every day because, first of all, I want to get into the College of Fine Arts next year.

I imagine running into Jared in Sydney, and I'll be this sophisticated art student, one who even understands theory, and Jared will see me manifesting my own dreams. When I run into Jared he'll be surprised, but he'll make some joke about clearly not belonging. A joke we'll both laugh at and it'll feel intimate, because it's just ours. Then he'll ask me if I have time to go for a quick drink at one of the small bars in Surry Hills, for old time's sake, even though it'll still be early afternoon. I'll arch my eyebrow, and after pretending to consider it for a moment, I'll agree, and then while I'm sipping my wine, being charming, he'll wonder why he ever thought to leave me. He'll crush a whole florist's worth of flowers to beg me to be with him again. I cling to this fantasy while I'm zoning out in English and maths and I cling to it while I'm wearing the oversized days.

The second reason I go to school is because, despite everything, I still have a steady reserve of spite to fall back on. If nothing else, I still want to prove wrong all the people who've ever thought I'll fail and quit. That's the whole world, remember, if we're keeping score here. Everyone always underestimates the power of spite.

The day after the break-up I stopped for a while outside the front gates before walking in. I scoured the bushes for hibiscuses and bottlebrush flowers, because I knew that I'd treated Mia wrongly. I'd been a bad friend. Let's chalk that up as another way the word bad is used as an adjective to describe me.

I'd hated myself for being the type of girl who picks flowers, but I did it anyway, for Mia, and I saw her sitting by herself where we usually sit, and I was holding the flimsy bouquet and I was going to give it to her as an apology. She was looking around, and I knew she was looking for me, but before I could walk over and try to make things better, Hamish approached her, and he was holding a blossom that looked so small and delicate in his big footy player hands. He gave it to her, and I watched her smile grow so large, it didn't seem like such a small human could own a smile that huge. So I stayed hidden around the corner and I threw away the flowers I'd picked and I mushed them with my sneakers into the concrete. I didn't sit with her in biology and she didn't force herself back into my orbit like she usually does. So that was that.

She and Hamish are a couple now. I watch them walking through the school grounds and despite him being a guy who can cause real damage with just one tackle, when he's with Mia he looks like the gentlest person in the world. She sits with him by the janitor's shed and I've been avoiding her. We caught each other's eyes once as I was walking past and she was mid-bite, her sandwich in her mouth. I thought I saw her go to say something but I quickly turned away and hid myself in a remote corner of the back oval. She probably wants nothing to do with me. And besides, it's not like I could sit with her anymore. She's part of Max's crew now. Max and I aren't having anything to do with each other either, and I've even stopped bracing myself for pranks.

I didn't know how much I'd actually miss Mia when I was sitting with her. I'd always thought that I didn't need friends, but now, when I'm sitting by myself and watching YouTube videos on my phone, it sort of feels like I've lost a front tooth. You don't really notice your teeth when they're there, you just chew without giving them much thought, but when one's missing, you notice, I've discovered. You can't really smile anymore.

After school I'm trying to make the facts stick to my brain but they slip away. There's no glue inside my skull for things like facts. I was born without that kind of glue. The build-up season is horrendous and the fan slicing the air above me isn't making much of a difference. My window is flung open and I watch the curtains, praying for a breeze, but nothing happens. All there is are the dead blowflies that scatter the windowsill, everything is still, and I think that it's no wonder I can't remember anything. Nobody could think in this heat.

I stomp out into the living room where Nan is doing a terrible job at dusting. She just bats at the surfaces like they've done something to offend her. I'm still hating on both Mum and Nan, and I avoid them as much as I can. But right now I want some ice or some frozen thing to cool me down, so Nan will have to be endured. Before I open the freezer I wrap my limbs around the outside of the fridge, pressing my cheek against it, trying to steep some of its coolness into my skin.

'Why can't we be like normal people and invest in air-conditioning!' I say, but mostly to myself.

Nan's stopped attacking everything violently with the feather duster because she's come to an old clay ashtray that my mother made as a child. It's so weird that in the olden days ashtrays were a thing they'd get children to make during craft. Like, the school authorities were actively encouraging smoking. It sits on the coffee table and Mum's filled it with ancient coins from far-flung places. Nan handles it gently, almost reverently, as she cleans it.

'We can't afford air-conditioning, you ninny,' she snaps back at me.

I let go of the fridge and scoop out an ice cube from the freezer and make my way over to the living room to plonk myself down on the ground beside her, running the ice over the back of my neck.

'Of course we can,' I argue, enjoying the melted water trickling down between my shoulderblades. 'Boarding school cost, what, thirty grand a year? Minimum. Think of how much you guys are saving by having me home this year. There must be heaps of money for air-conditioning in my boarding school slush fund – whatever's leftover from selling your place in Wollongong. You're just not getting it because you like to see me suffer.'

Nan keeps wiping down the ugly old ashtray.

'Ha! Boarding school slush fund? There was never any slush fund, girly. After taxes, selling my house didn't nearly cover the cost of this one, and your mother had to scrimp and save and remortgage the damn property to send you to those places, not that you ever appreciated it. Money got so tight we had the electricity turned off once because we couldn't afford the bills, and you, Miss Muck, didn't even bother turning up to class half the time.'

I'm staring at her now. Sweat is forming little rivers down the crevices of her wrinkled old face but I can't look away.

'There's no slush fund?' I say, my emotions making the words come out all trembly. And then it dawns on me. 'That's how much you both hate me? You'd rather have gone without electricity than have to deal with actually having me in the house?'

The truth of her words stabs at me and there's violence attacking my insides and I don't know how to calm it. I drop my ice and snatch the ashtray from Nan's hand and I fling it. It's the only way I know to express how I feel, and there's satisfaction in seeing something become as broken as I am. But I still regret it almost immediately. The ashtray lies smashed on the exposed wooden floorboards and the coins scatter in haphazard piles. I almost can't look at them.

Nan heaves herself up and moves over to the shattered clay pieces, and her hands shake as she tries to place them back together. I pretend like I don't care that she's hurting.

'We don't hate you, Iliad Piper,' she tells me, finally, as she holds the utterly broken pieces, her face looking like it's completely fallen inwards as she stares at them. 'But, girly, don't you try your best to make it hard for us to *like* you?'

I've always tried my best to make it hard for people to like me. It started off when I was a little kid, and I didn't want friends to know why I couldn't invite them back to my home, because of my dad, so I made damned sure nobody would want to come visit me.

I sit by myself in class, pretending I'm fine with being alone. We're in biology and Mia's sitting up the front with Hamish. They're looking disgustingly adorable. I pretend I don't miss her. Mrs Patel taps at her desk and she raises her eyebrows at us.

'Trial exams are almost upon us.'

I sigh and open my notebook. I know. She taps her painted nails on the desk and doesn't start the lesson like she should. Instead, she just looks intently around the class.

'I had a copy of the exam paper in my desk drawer.'

I look up from where I'm drawing evil amoebas on my notebook, and wonder where she's going with this. She just keeps tapping.

Rat-a-tat-tat.

'And strangely, somehow, the paper's gone missing.'

I scan the classroom, and Mia catches my eyes. Instead of sitting up straight and focused like she usually is, she's shifting in her seat, playing with her crooked fringe, head low, feet jiggling. She isn't acting like Mia.

Mrs Patel keeps tapping.

'It's curious, because the paper was in my drawer before recess, and the only class it'll benefit is you, the year twelves. But don't think I'm accusing you. Surely nobody here is a cheat.'

She says it like she doesn't believe it. I keep staring at Mia. Mrs Patel goes on.

'So nobody will mind if I look through your school bags?'

Jasmine pipes up, 'You can check mine, but we all know who's responsible.' She turns around to smirk at me and I have to grip the edge of my desk to stop myself from throwing a chair at her ugly, over-plucked eyebrows.

'Let's not accuse anyone just yet,' sighs Mrs Patel, but she says it like she doesn't really mean it, like she's just reading from the script of things a teacher has to say to be politically correct, and she begins the search at the far end of the classroom. I see her making her way in a perfunctory manner through satchels and backpacks, taking out pencil cases, lunch boxes, flicking through textbooks. I keep looking at Mia and I know that something's not right. I know Mia. She never squirms, she always has a straight back and raised hand. The teacher works her way through the school bags, and Mia sinks deeper and deeper into her chair. Her parents have been on her case to get the marks she needs, but they could never be harsher on her than Mia is to herself. The truth slams me. She stole the exam, I know it, and I know that I have to save her. Even if she still hates me. It kills me to see her hurt, because she is the purest soul I've ever met, and if you can make it seventeen years without letting the world dirty you, that's special. That's something. It dawns on me what I have to do, and I don't want to, and my face is flooded with red from the thought of it, but it's the only way. The teacher is just one desk away from checking Mia's bag.

'I need to go to the bathroom, miss!' I blurt out, standing up so suddenly the chair crashes back behind me.

'You can wait until after the class, Iliad.' The way she says it makes it obvious she agrees with Jasmine. This whole checking bags charade is just her acting out the checklist of things teachers have to do until they catch the obvious culprit. Me. My face keeps flaming, but I know what I have to say.

'I can't wait, miss. It's my period, it's arrived early. I *need* to go now.'

The class cracks up, their laughter directed at me. Nobody talks about their period out loud. Girls make up excuses, like headaches or vague nausea, but that won't work right now, not for the prime suspect number one. Mrs Patel zips up the bag she's been checking and dumps it on the ground and I know Mia's next, but thankfully the teacher's distracted by me.

'Well that's convenient, isn't it?' It's an accusation. Female teachers aren't as easy as male teachers when it comes to period stuff. There'd be no questions with a male teacher, but Mrs Patel isn't buying it.

'Don't shame me for my normal bodily functions,' I snap. The class is hurling laughter now, and the sharpness of it digs at me. I try to keep my armour up so the scratches don't cut, but it's hard. 'And I need Mia to come to the bathroom with me. I don't have a tampon and I need to borrow one.' I shoulder my bag, staring at the teacher defiantly. She's certain she has her culprit. She would never in a million years suspect Mia, the dux of the year, every year.

'All right, Iliad, but you won't mind if I go through your bag before you leave?' She smirks as she says it, triumphant.

I glare at her.

'Fine.' I stalk to where she is at the front of the class and dump my bag at her feet, grabbing Mia. 'You can check it while I'm gone. We're off to the bathroom.'

Mrs Patel picks up my bag like she's been given a prize, and I sort of wish I could be there to see her face when she discovers nothing, but all I can focus on is saving Mia. She lets me pull her out the door.

When we reach the toilet I drag her into a cubicle, locking it behind us.

'What the hell?' I snap at her, snatching her schoolbag from her arms, unzipping it, and I rummage around until I find what I'm looking for. I pull out the offending exam paper and wave it in her face.

'I'm meant to be the stupid one here! Not you. You're the smart one and smart people don't do dumb shit like this. What the hell were you thinking?'

Mia's face crumples as she buries her face in her hands and her black side-ponytail bobs up and down as she sobs. She looks so tiny.

'You need a mark of more than 92 to get into the Mechatronic Engineering course to study robotics.' The words drop down at our feet. 'It's all I've ever wanted, and I saw Mrs Patel leave the exam there, and . . . and . . .'

Tears spill down her face, plopping from her chin, and I stop being angry. I pull her towards me in a hug, even though I don't do hugs, and my pats on her back are awkward.

'You've got this, Mia,' I tell her. 'If anyone has this, it's you. You don't need to cheat. Leave the stupid stuff to me.' While she's gathering herself and wiping away snot with the sleeve of her ugly polka-dot onesie I tear the exam paper into little pieces and stuff them into the sanitary bin, where no one will ever find them.

When we return to class, Mrs Patel's face is unimpressed as she hands me back my bag.

'Did you sort out your women's business?'

I meet eyes with Mia.

'Sorted.'

I can hear Jasmine snipe from the other side of the room. 'Makes sense the angry girl is always on her rags.' The class titters. I am never going to live this down, but I can deal with their laughter. My armour holds. Knowing that Mia's okay is enough.

When I get home I open my biology textbook to prepare for the trial exams, and I attempt to let the words sink in but they won't. I'm never going to get into uni next year. My whole life I'd always been so preoccupied with family stress or trying to figure out ways to be kicked out of boarding school that I could never concentrate on class. Then, for the final few months of year twelve, when I really needed to be knuckling down, when it really mattered, Jared had made sure I spent all my free time with him instead of studying. I realise that I'm going to prove everyone right. Everyone who always thought I'd fail. I want to scream and rip everything up, I want to rage at the world, but then as I'm flinging everything out of my school bag and watching each item crash, I find the notes Mia made for me crumpled up at the bottom. I smooth one out and try to decipher it. It just looks like a jumble of words for a while, but then, after staring at the dot points for a good amount of time, they start to string together into something. It reminds me of those 3D picture books you'd look at in primary school. They'd just look like an ordinary picture, but after a bit, like magic, an image would suddenly jump out at you. The information that Mia's written down starts to become clear to me. I start to get it. I scramble for the rest of the notes and slowly little scraps of facts begin to take up residence in my brain.

I think of her spending her weekend jotting everything down and it kills me, how I shoved them into my bag and told her that nobody would choose to speak to her willingly. I'm not surprised that people usually don't like me. Often, I don't like myself either. I take out my phone and stare at it, wanting to send her a text. I want to say sorry but I can't say it in words. I send her a stack of books, a question mark and a confused yellow face, then a picture of a happy black-haired girl who looks like Mia, and a notepad and a pencil and a lightbulb, then a face blowing kisses and an exclamation mark. It's the only way I know to properly express how I feel. It's the only way I have to say sorry. When she replies, two seconds later, with a smiley face and two girls holding hands, I want to cry. I don't know why Mia never thinks to grow thorns after being crushed underfoot, I don't understand how anyone could be like that, but I've never been more thankful that she hasn't.

About an hour later, Mia arrives at my house and I'm confused to see her standing there. She's still wearing a polka-dot onesie that probably once belonged to a child, coupled with that side ponytail and a pair of Crocs with rainbow socks, but ugly fashion has never looked so adorable. Her arms are filled with a stack of books so high that she has to rest her chin on the top of them.

'Hamish told me you lived next to Max and gave me directions,' she explains as I move back from the doorway to let her in.

We're lying on my bed, textbooks splayed out in front of us, our feet kicking at the sky as we're studying. She's chewing on the end of her pen and occasionally leaning over to correct one of my maths equations, explaining it in a way that makes sense. I nibble at my nails and stare at her.

'Mia, don't feel like you owe me anything,' I tell her, finally. 'You have a boyfriend now. You don't have to hang with me anymore. I'm awful.'

She rests her chin on her hands and looks up at me, her face doing that innocent, open sunflower thing, and she shakes her head at me like I'm wrong.

'You try to make yourself out to be awful, but you're not. Everyone used to pick on me before you arrived, and you never had to stick up for me, but you did. Every single time. Even when it meant dealing with Jasmine's backlash.'

'Jasmine is a jerk.'

'Agreed. She's not an optimal human being.' Then Mia looks down and bites her lip and starts to pick at the plastic laminate on the history textbook. 'And you told everyone you had your period just to save me from being caught cheating. That's big. Really big. And I'm not stupid, you know. I knew that you didn't want to sit with me that first day. You made some excuse to leave after you realised how unpopular I was, but then you saw me sitting all by myself and you came back. Because you knew I didn't want to be alone. Even if you *did* want to be alone. And that means something, Ily. You pretend to not care if anyone likes you, but I like you. So that's why I'm here.'

I think of all the times I've rolled my eyes at her, and all the times I've snapped, and shame stretches out inside my chest because being mean to Mia is like kicking a kitten.

'I'm not good at having friends,' I admit, quietly.

She just shrugs.

'Everything takes practice. Speaking of which. Let's go over the biology notes again.'

230

She heaves open the biology book and smiles, and it wriggles through my wall of cynicism. My lips can't help but tug upwards in return. We continue studying in a comfortable sort of silence and I realise that the afternoon doesn't feel like it's so oversized anymore.

twenty-seven

It's late and Mia's left and I've grabbed a bunch of food from the kitchen while Mum and Nan weren't around. Manuka honey on spelt sourdough, an apple, some buckwheat crackers and a handful of macadamias. It's hard to mindlessly snack in this house, everything is so disgustingly wholesome. I've been avoiding family dinners and Mum doesn't press it. She just leaves my serving in an earthenware pot in the fridge for me to reheat and eat when I want to. I can hear her and Nan clattering plates about in the living room, and Mum's playing a CD with the sounds of waterfalls and dolphin calls.

I suck the honey off my thumb and flick through the pages of my textbook, then bite into the apple. I wonder how long they're going to be out there for, Nan sipping on her whisky, Mum moving the food about on her plate. The waterfall soundtrack is making me thirsty but I don't want to have to walk past either of them to get to the kitchen.

I'm surprised when I hear the front door rattle, then open, and the deep rumblings of a man's voice. This house is steeped in oestrogen; we never have male visitors unless they're Mum's clients.

I hear Nan pass through the hallway on her way to the toilet and I tiptoe over to my bedroom door with my plate of food, holding a buckwheat cracker between my teeth. With my free hand I creak open the door a tiny bit. I didn't think my snooping was so obvious, but as Nan hobbles back past again she presses an eye against the door crack so it's only centimetres away from mine and she hisses in a low whisper.

'I've just called the police. Hide yourself, girly.'

I'm about to ask why, because my hands have started shaking and my heart has begun to drum, but she shuffles away quickly, and then the man in the living room talks louder. I would recognise that snarly voice anywhere.

It's my father.

My heart jumps into my mouth and I can almost taste blood. It tastes metallic.

'Don't you tell me to leave, you slut. You are *my* wife.'

Mum's tone stays impressively calm and measured.

'Troy, we have been divorced for years. Now would you kindly step off this premises?'

'Well, where is my daughter? She's mine. You stole her!'

I can almost hear the strain as Mum tries to remain Zen.

'Iliad's at boarding school. Like she has been since you broke my ribs. Now I'm going to ask you again, Troy. Leave.'

I can tell Dad's drunk. I hear him stumble a bit and his voice is mean and slurring.

'Bitch. Whore. You can't take what's mine and think you'll get away with it.'

I've seen those words before. Now I know who's been

233

posting those threats on my mum's website and I know that Mum and Nan lied to me. He must have been out of jail for years. My chest is shuddering loudly and my fingers won't work anymore. The plate just slips from my hands and the crash when it hits the floor feels like it echoes forever.

'So Iliad is home? I knew you were a liar. Come out here, Iliad! Come say hello to your dad.'

The way he says that last sentence sends shivers down my spine. It's like we're still allies. It's like he misses me. I crouch to pick up a shard of smashed plate from the ground, slipping it in my back pocket, and I say a magic word under my breath, *Pierceacutaswipe*, a silent prayer that it's sharp enough to slit a throat, then I square my shoulders and hold my chin high so he doesn't see how scared I feel right now, and I walk out into the living room to stand next to my mum and Nan.

There is my father, the same lean, knotted muscles and prickly stubble that I remember. The same hawk face. Now, though, his clothes look slept in and his eyes are wild, and my heart lurches a bit when I see he's wielding a metal post, one of the ones that Mum's used to steady a sapling. I can't stop staring at it, there're still clods of dirt caked on from where it must have been ripped out of the ground just a little while ago. My hands are moving like scuttling crabs by my side, and Mum's are the same, but then she clasps her fingers into mine to still them and I let her grip me. I've never been so glad to have her holding my hand. Dad analyses me, his gaze scraping my skin as he looks me up and down.

'Iliad . . . My baby . . .' He reaches out to me but I stay by Mum's side. He looks puzzled that I'm not choosing him like I used to, but I know that even if I fight with my mum, even if we do nothing but fight, I won't be used as his weapon against her anymore.

'She's grown up to be just like you, hasn't she, Eve?' He reaches out again but I stay put. His face darkens. 'Iliad, have you turned into a bitch like your mum while I was away?'

I stare back at him, ignoring my thumping chest.

'Depends on whether they deserve it.'

I feel my mum's fingers claw mine in a warning. I still don't cower. All of Dad's softness leaves his face now and he replaces it with a mean smirk.

'Is that so? And are you a whore like she is?' His face is mottled red from the alcohol as he drunkenly glares at my mother. 'She's been whoring around with that Bob Millerd bloke. I've been in this town and heard the talk. You think you can be with another man and get away with it, Eve? Do you?! You're *mine*.'

I look over at Mum with widened eyes. Bob? The client Bob? What?

Mum pulls me slightly behind her, but her posture still stays as rigid as the metal rod that Dad keeps tapping on the hardwood.

Tap.

Tap.

Tap.

He reminds me of a wild dog whose bone has been taken away from him.

'It's been enough years, Troy. I am allowed to start dating other people. You don't own me anymore. You can't hurt me anymore. Now leave.'

Dad keeps tapping, and he cocks his head to the side, that ugly smirk still latched onto his mouth.

'Wanna bet?' he snarls, and then before I know it he's barrelling forward and Mum throws me behind her and she raises her spindly arms up as the metal comes crashing down. I scream when I see her on the floor, just a jumble of silk and saffron, and she's nursing her arm, which is bent in the wrong angle. I can see her bone, white and awful, nosing its way out through the skin. Nan races to her daughter and kneels down, her gnarled hands burying themselves in Mum's hair. The look she shoots Dad is venomous.

'Enough, you bastard! Enough now!'

Mum's face is pale. She tries to stand up, but she can't, she's hurt her ankle in the fall, but her mouth is still a determined straight line.

'All right, Troy. You've hurt me. You've punished me. Now you can go.'

He keeps tapping the metal rod.

Tap.

Tap.

Tap.

'Sweetheart, that was just a taster.' He spits onto the ground and I'm not sure if he's on drugs as well, or just out of his mind, because he's skittish and he's got crazy-person eyes. I look from Mum to Nan, and I know with a sudden certainty that I'm the only one who can protect them. Slowly, I step towards him, with one hand out, fingers splayed, like you'd approach a snarling animal. The other hand I keep behind my back, resting against my back pocket, poised to grab the shard of plate.

'Dad, it's okay, calm down, it's okay.'

Mum tries to grab at my ankle to keep me back, but her fingers just clutch at air.

'Iliad, no!'

I'm close enough to touch him now, and I gently place my hand on the sleeve of his flannel shirt. He flinches and looks down at me, but when he stares at my face, it seems to settle him, to take him back to a time when we were friends.

'It's me,' I tell him, and I reach out like I used to, when I was only little, my fingers curled so the back of my hand is grazing his face, and the stubble feels rough against my knuckles. He lets me, and his face softens, and I think I've calmed him, but then I scream when he swings around and latches onto my wrist. I try to struggle free, but I can't, it's like a manacle. He pivots to glare at my mother.

'Sweetheart,' he spits at her as his fingers tighten. 'I'm gonna make sure that your decisions will haunt you for the rest of your life.'

Mum braces herself for an attack again, but he doesn't hit her. Instead he looks at me, and it dawns on all of us. We all know how he can hurt her best. The air is clogging our lungs with the truth of it.

The best way he's always used to hurt her is through me.

He raises the iron bar, but before he can strike I use my free hand to pull the ceramic shard from my pocket and with a battle cry I swing around to slit his throat.

It doesn't work.

I barely pierce the skin, but it's enough of a shock for him to let go of my wrist and hurl me away so I go skidding across the hardwood. My breath is gusting out of me as I watch him touch the scratch, then look at his fingers and the small smear of blood that bubbled up from the wound. His face when he looks down at me is all fury and menace, and my limbs just stop working. I'm completely frozen when he raises that hard, metal post and I'm too numb to even say a magic word as I wait for it to crash down and crack open my skull like an egg.

'Girly, run!'

Nan barks the words out, and it jolts me out of my para-
lysed state as Dad lunges towards me. She springs like some
rabid marsupial and jumps up at him, all gristly old skin and
scraggly white hair, biting with her false teeth and clawing at
his face. I scramble to my feet and I don't want to leave them
but there's nothing I can do. I'm powerless.

'Run!' screams Mum.

I run.

I'm sprinting out the front door when I hear it. The sick-
ening thud of Nan being thrown and her head hitting the
ground. I look back. I can't help but look back, and there's
blood. So much blood, and there's my father with the rod
raised over his own head, sprinting towards me.

I sprint faster.

'Safeickity,' I hiss under my breath, trying to find a magic
word that'll keep my father from catching up with me. My
legs burn as I try to make them work harder and the bush
races thick and shadowy towards me.

'Invisibrackendart.'

But there are no magic words. I know that.

Thankfully my father is drunk and he keeps stumbling
as the undergrowth twists around his boots. He swears as he
pulls himself back up again and staggers after me. I've never
been a good runner. Tick. Another thing I'm not good at.
But I know the property, even in the dark. After being adrift
for so long, it hits me. This is my home.

'Iliad, it's your dad. We're friends, remember?' he calls
out into the blackness, his voice rumbling across the landscape, and it's almost kind, the way he says it, like back when
he used to pretend we were allies. I keep running. The moon

glows, haloed and bright tonight, and the stars crowd the sky like a dot painting, but there are trees and there is grass and there are ferns. My bare feet hate me as I navigate the thorns and the twigs, they snap like cracked knuckles underfoot, but I keep running.

I'm past the back bungalow and my lungs are wheezing and I know the police won't get here for a while. We live too far out. I just hope I can avoid him for long enough. All I need is long enough. I hear him swearing, pulling a vine from where it's wrapped around his leg and he's thrashing at the fronds with that hard iron bar. I circle my way over to where the grass grows long, higher than I am as I crouch low. The moon throws down the shadow of the turkey-bush branches and I hope there's enough foliage to hide the light from my phone. I write Max a text.

> Help send Ian Dad come to kill me am hiding out back help

I press send and switch the phone onto silent and as I hide it back in my pocket I feel something small and smooth against my fingers. It's the tigereye crystal Mum gave to me weeks ago. I remember her ridiculously earnest stare as she asked me to hold onto it, for her sake, for protection. As I hear my dad nearing closer and closer I clutch the stone so tight that my knuckles must be turning white, and I try to stop the grip of panic strangling me and I try to believe as best I can. I try to have faith that a crystal is any protection against a drunk, angry man who wants to see my brains splattered against a metal rod because I'm not his anymore. I think of Mum, and her exposed bone pointing white and sharp towards me. I think of all the times I'd wanted her to be as hurt as I felt, but right now, in this moment, I'd give anything to keep her safe. I think of Nan, and all the times I've flippantly asked her when she was going to die already, and I think of the blood. So much blood. And I want her to be alive so badly. I clutch the crystal to my chest.

I want.

I want.

I want.

'You don't need to be scared of your dad. *Come over here!*' he yells.

I squeeze my eyes shut and I pray silently to the universe that I don't think gives a damn about me. I try to not feel so small and alone as I hear Dad's footsteps getting closer and closer. As I hear the metal bar thwack violently against the flapping leaves.

'Pleasepleasepleasebelieverous,' I whisper, under my breath. The only real prayer I know.

Dad's footsteps get closer.

'Zapplewhackawayshay.'

Dad's footsteps get closer.

He's only metres away from me, but the grass grows long and thick, and I try to stifle the harsh whoosh of my breathing. I still keep the crystal close.

I try one last word as he's almost on top of me.

'Savelavenberrybophope.'

And it works.

It works.

A flashlight shines onto my father's ruddy face and there's the sound of a gun firing, the crack of it so loud that it makes the birds wake and jump out from the branches, their wings scudding noisily against the sky. Dad jolts, startled, and I hear the thud of the metal rod being flung onto the ground, and the quick, retreating stomp of his boots as he disappears into the distance.

The flashlight dances around the grass until it's beaming into my eyes. I stand up, squinting, and I try to make out who's standing there in front of me.

It's Max.

All the fear crashes out of me now. I stand there vulnerable and shaking and tears are spilling out of my eyes, and when he moves forward to hug me I bury my face into his chest and he feels like safety. He feels like calm.

'My dad wasn't home,' he tells me, his arms hesitant like he doesn't know how to hold me. 'He's at the hospital with Mum.'

I look up at him, at his murky green eyes, his worried, furrowed thick eyebrows.

'You do seriously own a gun?'

He shines the torch on the BB rifle he's holding.

'Probably wouldn't pierce the skin, but I figured it might scare something off, if we were lucky.'

I stare at him, dumbfounded, then I bang my fists into his chest from the stupidity of it.

'You're a suicidal idiot!'

He just pulls me in properly now, so I don't have leverage to swing at him anymore, and my forehead is pressed tight to his t-shirt and his chin is resting on top of my head and his thumb lightly grazes my cheek as he tucks a wild spiral behind my ear.

'You're welcome, Ily.'

We head over to the house, huddled close to one another. Max swings the torchlight around and he holds the gun poised and we both jump every time a nocturnal creature scrabbles through the leaf litter. He slams the flyscreen open with his foot, like how you see in the movies, but Dad isn't there. Mum is still nursing her broken arm to her chest, and her ankle is useless, but she's dragged herself across the room and she's using a tea towel to stem the bleeding from Nan's head. Nan's conscious now and her gnarled fingers are clawing at her knees.

They both jump as we bang our way in, but when they see us Mum starts crying, and Nan blinks furiously as she purses her lips into a thin, trembling line. I race over to them and take the bloodied tea towel from Mum's hand, pressing it down against the cut on Nan's skull.

'You're not dead . . .' I say, but mostly to myself.

'Worse luck, hey?' she replies, and her eyes are sort of smiling when she says it. She sticks her tongue out at me and I stick mine out back, before this half-sobbing, half-laughing sound escapes me from the relief of it. I should never have doubted she'd be okay. She's the strongest woman I know.

'Your father?' Mum asks as Max deadlocks the front wooden door and then makes his way around the house, securing everything. I unfurl my fist and show her the tigereye, small and round and catching the light in my shaking palm.

'Weird. Apparently magic crystals are a thing after all?' She sobs again.

'Do not mock me, Iliad.'

Max is on the phone to the ambulance, and moths flick against the overhead light, and outside there are frogs calling to one another, sounding lonely. But the night air is still, it's disturbingly still, and it seems to be holding its breath, like we all are, as we wait.

The police arrive. Apparently they picked Dad up on the highway. He was driving erratically, swerving in and out of the oncoming lanes. The ambulance people bundle Mum and Nan up, and I'm going to drive my car over to meet them at the hospital in town.

'You want a lift home?' I ask Max as I stand on the driveway with my keys jangling in my hand. He shakes his head. His eyes look like they're swimming with a thousand unsaid things.

'Na, I feel like walking.' He kicks at the pebbled ground. 'Hey, Ily, about last time you were over . . .'

I cut him off. The memory of how I acted burns at my insides, and I've discovered that shame is a nastier sort of fire than rage is. I'm not surprised it's an emotion I've always tried my best to avoid. It feels awful. I pick at imaginary lint from my shorts.

'I'm sorry, Max. Can we please never mention it ever again? I was out of line. I'm sorry.'

'No, I need to tell you something –'

I want to make him stop. The shame licks at me, white and hot.

'Look, it's been the worst night of my life, can we not make it any more awful by bringing that up? Tonight you saw me cry, and I never cry. And I said sorry, and I never say sorry. Here . . .'

I open my car door and grab a pen from the glove compartment. I take his forearm, and he lets me take it, and I press the pen against his skin. He stands still and he watches me as I chew my lip and concentrate. I write a big, cursive *SORRY*. It's artistic, like a python snaking its way down from his elbow to his wrist. When I'm done, I look up at him.

'See. Proof that the angry Iliad does apologise.

243

Sometimes. Depends on how annoying they are.'

He smiles, but it's a serious smile.

'I may have to get that tattooed, hey. No one'll believe me otherwise.'

I roll my eyes at him.

'Dork.'

And he stands there, gun slung over his shoulder, and he's silent as I get into my car and drive away.

twenty-eight

I watch my hair spiral thick and brown above me as I hold my breath under the water. I try to see how long I can stay, but my lungs start to scream and I push off from the clay bottom and into the air. The dam water is low, it's been months since the last rain and I'm floating on my back when I hear snapping twigs. I open one eye and squint against the sun to see my mother picking her way over to me. Her arm's in a sling but her sprained ankle is better, and her skirt is catching on the undergrowth.

'You look like a yawkyawk,' she tells me as she smoothes down the grass and sits down under the rosewood, her chin resting on her knees. A yawkyawk is an Indigenous mermaid spirit, and I spit water out of my mouth in reply, then start to slowly breaststroke towards her. I'm in just my bra and undies and when I get to her I kick the clay from my feet and bits splatter onto her.

'Iliad!' She flicks a clump from where it's landed on her ankle. I roll my eyes.

'It's organic, Mum. You'd pay, like, a bajillion dollars to have that smeared over you for some skin treatment.'

I plonk myself beside her and squeeze the water from my hair.

'Your exams are soon,' she tells me as she picks at a beetle climbing the grass. It stays on her finger for a moment before taking flight.

'Study break,' I shrug. I lean over to her cast and water drips from my forehead as I analyse it.

'When we get back I'll decorate it.'

She nods and smiles a small, tight smile.

'I'll miss you when you leave next year,' she tells me. I roll my eyes, but it's strange. I think I'll miss her, too. I pull at the grass and curl my toes into the earth and try to find the strength to say the word that's been sitting inside of me my whole life, stuck in there and heavy as a stone in my chest.

'I'm sorry,' I whisper, dredging the word up and out of me. 'I'm sorry I hit you, at the shelter. I'm sorry I always took Dad's side instead of yours. I'm sorry I made you want to send me away.'

Mum just shakes her head slowly, and gently releases the grass I'm gripping tightly in my hand so she can lace her fingers in mine.

'Darling, you've got nothing to apologise for. Nothing. You did what you could to survive. You were the bravest little girl I knew. He'd be yelling and screaming and you'd take his hand and calm him down to protect me. I was always so proud of the courage that took.' She's looking at me, distraught. 'Don't you ever think I sent you away because of that.'

I stare at the sky to keep in the tears that are pricking at my eyelids, and I feel the years of guilt and shame rise out of me like a balloon disappearing into the clouds.

'It was all Dad then?'

She nods, releasing my hand to fiddle with her skirt hem.

'Troy only got a few months in jail, with parole, and I was so scared. Mother and I discussed it and we thought that dragging you around on the run would do you damage, you needed stability, and we decided the risk to stay settled somewhere and make an income was small enough for her and for me, but not for you, Iliad. We weren't going to risk you. Boarding school was the safest place.'

I think of my heart when I was sent away. How guilty and shredded it felt. How unwanted I'd felt.

'I knew those Facebook posts were from him. Why did you lie to me?'

Her hands are balling her skirt material, pulling at her chunky necklace.

'Iliad, an obedient daughter you are not. It was near impossible to make you to stay put at those places as it was, you've always wanted to protect me, and then your anxiety was so bad, we wanted to shelter you from that.'

My face starts to crumple now and looking at her I think of how a mother crocodile carries her babies around in her mouth. It looks like she's eating them, all those teeth and scales, but sometimes seeing isn't really seeing. Sometimes you have to look past the teeth to know that she's actually caring for her young.

'I hated myself. I thought it was my fault.'

Mum shakes her head furiously and I dig at the grass again, thinking of all the rage I flung at her, not to mention the various household items over the years.

'And I hated you.'

The tears are creeping down my cheeks now and I wipe them off with my forearm. Mum's quiet for a bit, but then her bony shoulders start to shake in small, soundless sobs, and her neck's bent so her words tumble out into her lap.

'I know you hated me. I know. Don't you think I wanted to explain it to you and comfort you? Don't you know I could see you hurting? It wrecked me to see you like that, but I understood your hostility. I understood.'

She stares at me, her dark eyes drowning. She chokes her words out.

'I could deal with you hating me for sending you away, because, at the risk of repeating myself, it's my job to be your mother and to make sure you were safe, not to be your friend.'

Her skirt is scrunched-up tightly in her fists and her knuckles are white. I lean over to her, our shoulders supporting each other. I watch our hair fall together in matching dark curls so you can't tell whose is whose, and I wonder how we could have been, if things had been different.

'Why did you fall in love with Dad? Was he always so bad?' I ask. Mum sighs and her eyes become faraway, focused on the flame tree on the other side of the dam, as though the memories are tangled up somewhere in those red-orange branches.

'Oh Iliad, he was the most charming man in the world, your father. He promised me the moon and the stars, and I thought I was so lucky. It's ridiculous looking back, isn't it?'

I shake my head.

No.

I get it.

'Then when the cracks started to show, when he started

telling me who he really was, I ignored it, because I was in love with the memory of who he could be, instead of the person standing before me, smashing a wall. I focused on the good parts of our relationship and ignored the very wrong parts. The bad behaviour just built up and built up over time and I thought I had my line in the sand, the line of what was unacceptable to me, and what I'd always thought I'd walk away from. But every time he crossed it, and I forgave him, that line moved further and further back, until I found myself in a hospital ward and that line didn't exist anymore. And I thought it was my fault when he snapped. That if I could just change myself or my behaviour, our relationship would be like it was in the beginning. But there was always something to find fault with, always something I'd do wrong, and changing myself never helped, because he never changed. All that happened was that I eventually changed so much of myself to try to please him that one day I found there was none of the original me left anymore, and no part of me left with the strength to walk away.'

I remember Mum, with her eyes that were like they'd been turned the other way around so they were always gazing inwards, and I shudder.

'Nan knew there was still strength in you somewhere.'
She looks hard at me.
'Yes. Mothers often do.'
I chuck a pebble in the water, hearing it plop.
'He'll be out again one day, won't he?'
She nods, and she's back to fiddling with her skirt hem.
'One day he'll be out, Iliad, but not for a long while now, not after what he did.'

Her words are a comfort, but not completely. I watch the ripples from where I threw the pebble, and I know that ripples spread out for ages, and it takes a while for the water to be calm like how it was before.

'When he's out, you have to tell me,' I say to her, and I mean it, even though the nerves are making my hands scuttle like hers, like they're mud crabs. 'This time, can we deal with it together?'

She nods, and I believe her, because she's looking at me like she knows the strength's in me somewhere.

'Speaking of all these secrets. When the hell were you going to tell me about Bob?'

Mum laughs but it sounds more like a hiccup.

'Bob is a good man.'

I think about him. How I'm glad that Mum will have someone worthy of her.

'I like him too.'

She looks across at me.

'You like him? Well, wonders will never cease, Iliad Piper.'

I roll my eyes and stick out my tongue. She reaches out, tentatively, and we're not quite at the hugging stage yet, but when she runs her fingers though the shaved part of my head I let her.

'Hey, Mum,' I begin.

She meets my gaze and I scrunch my nose up and pick at my nails.

'Do you think we could maybe work on the friend bit?'

She just nods, and her smile is still tight and her face is still strained. She nods and she nods and she nods.

'I'd like that very much.'

We're silent for a while.

'But I'm still allowed to think you're ridiculous, right?'

She does the hiccup laugh again, then sighs her

exaggerated sigh and dabs her eyes with her pashmina.

'Daughter, I'll take what I can get from you,'

'It's just that I'm an Aries. We're too practical to believe in nonsense like astrology.'

It's her turn to roll her eyes now. I look at her cast again and I think of how her bone pointed out of her skin, sharp and white.

'Do you think your arm's going to go back to how it was before, once it's healed?'

She leans her forehead on mine and stares me right in the eyes so I see my own reflection in her dark irises.

'Not like how it was before. When bones break, and they heal, they always become stronger in the spot where they've once been broken. Don't you ever forget that.'

She picks herself up from the grass and straightens out my t-shirt, which I've tossed haphazardly over a branch.

'I'm going to blend some Gerson's therapy juices for Rosie now. Do take it over to the Selwyns next time you visit, please. For me.'

I nod, and when she leaves I stand, examining the indents on my legs from where the twigs have dug into me, then I run and bellyflop back into the water.

The sun is a fat blot in the middle of the sky as I crunch through the bush back to the main house. My clothes are slung over my shoulder, and the light is tinged green here, in the thickest bit. It makes me think of a word I learnt once at one of the schools while I stretched itchy jumpers over my fingers and glared at the walls penning me in. *Komorebi*. It's Japanese and it stuck in my brain because it reminded me of the property, and Mum and Nan being here without me. It means *the sunlight that filters through the leaves of trees*. There's no English equivalent, and I wonder if maybe that's one reason why I'm no good at expressing myself. Sometimes I feel like there just aren't any words in the whole dictionary that will fit properly. Some things are too messy to be boxed into sounds, wrapped up in syllables, and delivered like parcels from person to person. I rip a leaf from a tree, crunching it between my fingers, and I know that the most important things can't be lassoed with language. The most important things can only be felt.

My phone beeps when I get to the clearing and I slide it from where it sits in my zipped-up shorts pocket, expecting it to be another exam-related text from Mia. She's getting overly preoccupied with 'optimal study strategies', and when she arrived at school the other day with mismatched shoes, I don't think she was even aware of it. I glance down at the screen, thumbs poised to emoji.

It's from Jared.

Hey you. Sydney's like Darwin, except with a bigger pool of philistines. I really miss you.

I just stare at it, and I brace myself.

I wait for my heart to start lurching.

I wait for it to swell twice the size, then constrict until it hurts. Rinse. Repeat.

But there's nothing.

Curious.

All I can feel is the slow, regular thump, and I start to realise that somehow, he doesn't live in my heart anymore. He'd been evicted from all four chambers while I wasn't looking, and now, when I see his name flashing up on my screen, he just feels like some horrible person that I used to know.

I go to my contacts, and when I come to his name I don't even pause. I swipe *delete*.

When I was dating him, I used to think that the most romantic thing in the world was unconditional love, but as I purge Jared from my phone I realise that love, real love, comes with three conditions – respect, kindness and trust. It isn't, and should never be, unconditional.

I scrape my fingers through my hair and stomp at a skink, and I begin to run because the big and messy truth is overwhelming me.

It's not Jared who I want.

twenty-nine

I hold out the flask of smoothie when Max opens the door.

'Mum made it for Rosie. It's meant to help with cancer treatment, but seriously, it's gross. Basically I think that the way it works is, when you drink it, the cancer will run away because it won't want to share the same body with something as disgusting as this smoothie.'

That small, serious smile tugs at his lips as he takes it and lets me in. When he walks over to put the flask in the fridge, I watch him like a creeper. The strong knots of his muscles, the hair that falls wild, like nobody could ever tell it what to do. That skin which is the kind of brown that catches and throws out the light. My palms don't get sweaty, my heart doesn't start racing, but it does pump stronger. It does feel fatter. It's swollen to make room for Max, because he lives there now. I have feelings for Max Selwyn, and that's so weird, and I don't know what to do about it.

I pull myself onto the kitchen bench and swing my legs, trying not to act awkward.

'Will she be coming home soon?' I ask.

He just shakes his head slowly and the swamp looks like it's going to spill out of his eyes, but he blinks the tears away and tosses his hair out of his face.

'No,' he says quietly and from the way he says it, I realise she's not going to be coming home at all. He looks over at me. 'The others have gone to see her, I've been there the last couple of days but Dad reckoned I should take a break and do some studying today, he'll take me 'round tonight. But I can't concentrate, you know? 'Cause all I can think about is that another minute is passing, and that's another minute closer to when she's not gonna be here anymore, and I can't do anything to stop it.'

He grips the benchtop and his face is desperate. I think of all the sci-fi movies where people invent machines to travel through time, and it always seemed so fantastical, but I realise that we're all time travellers, really, when you think about it. We're always hurtling into the future, sixty seconds per minute, and we can't do anything to hit the brakes, even if we wanted to.

'Time is a jerk,' I tell him, and he nods.

'Time is a massive jerk.'

He looks so hurt and angry and all of those emotions that are too big to hang words on them. I don't know what else to say, so I just start to unbuckle the watch from around my wrist, the one Mum bought me for boarding school once because we weren't allowed to carry our phones with us. I jump off from the bench and rummage around his kitchen until I find a chopping board and a rolling pin and a pestle. I place the watch on the chopping board and hold out the utensils towards Max.

'Choose your weapon.'

He looks at me like I've cracked it, but I just shrug and with a battle cry I smash the pestle down onto my watch.

'Take that, you jerk!'

Max cocks his head to the side and a smile creeps out as he takes the rolling pin from me. He readjusts my broken watch on the board, then slams the rolling pin down onto it again and again and again until it's nothing more than a mess of black leather and glass and little metal cogs and screws. His breathing is harsh as he wipes his brow then scans the house and looks up at the clock in the living room. He bounds over, unhooks it from the wall, then places it onto the block.

'Fuck you!' he screams at it, and he starts pulverising it.

'Fuck you!' I join in, and we take turns. Me with the pestle, Max with the rolling pin, until the clock is in the same state as the watch, and we stand there heaving, sweat dripping from our brows and onto the twisted clock hands.

We both slide down onto the kitchen tiles, breathing hard, our heads rested back on the cupboards and the terracotta smooth against our legs. Max looks over at me.

'Have you ever thought about how weird it is? That, like, an infinite amount of time happened before we existed, and an infinite amount of time will happen after we're dead, and we're sitting here, living our lives, just a tiny blink of existence sandwiched between infinity?'

I shake my head.

'I can truthfully say I have never once thought about that at all.'

He brushes his hair off his forehead and watches the fan

cut the air to pieces above us, and I think of people, and how they're like words, too. You see them walking and talking and wrapped up in skin, but there is so much more to them than what's standing in front of you. Max is so much vaster than the space he takes up right now, legs all askew on the kitchen tiles.

'Hey, Max . . .'

He turns to me. I pick at my nails.

'Since we happen to be sharing this blink between infinity, I need to ask you. What was it that you wanted to say the other night when I wouldn't let you?'

He's looking at me properly now, his serious eyes darting around all the features of my face.

'I was gonna tell you that I didn't mean what I said, that day you came around to drop off the camera equipment.'

And there, that there, starts the painful constriction of my chest.

He doesn't love me.

Of course he doesn't.

I am not a loveable person.

'Oh,' is all I can force out. I can't look at him, I just start blinking too much, and I quickly pull myself up from the ground, all stiff and awkward.

'I should go,' I tell him, and I just want to leave as quickly as I can. He jumps up too, and I turn away from him, my hands scuttling nervously at my sides and I want to get out of this kitchen but he blocks the way.

'Hey, Ily,' he says.

I can't look at him.

'Hey,' he repeats.

He reaches out and knots his fingers in my hair, gently pushing my head up and tipping my face to look at him.

'Ily, I lied when I said I didn't know why I was in love with you. I do know why, and it's not because of the eye rolls. Well, it sort of is the eye rolls, but it's heaps more than that. You're funny, and you reckon you don't give a damn about anyone but you stick up for Mia like no one's ever done. And like, you're the deadliest artist I've ever seen.'

All the emotions are coursing through me. The big, important, nameless ones. My face is flushing against my freckles and I don't know how to do compliments, so I roll my eyes, embarrassed.

'Another eye roll. *Jesus*, stop flirting with me.'

I try to scowl to hide the smile, but it doesn't work, the smile wins.

'Dork.'

'And you're always complimenting me, hey.'

I laugh and go to roll my eyes, but then I catch myself and stop before he accuses me of flirting again. Although I desperately want to flirt. Max is looking at me really intently now. He's really looking at me.

'I dunno, Ily, you're just, like, the kind of girl who makes you understand why cyclones are named after people. And you're beautiful.'

I look away again and scrunch my nose up.

'All right, I know you're a liar now. The first couple are debatable, but I'm definitely not beautiful. I mean, I have eyes. I sure as hell don't look like a Victoria's Secret model or anything.'

I'm focusing on the tiles and he takes a curl that's hanging down in front my face and he tucks it behind my ear. His thumb grazes my cheek again as he does it, and his touch blazes through my body. The best sort of fire.

'Na. You don't, hey.'

I'm about to shoot him an annoyed glare, but he keeps going.

'You look like you, and I like that better.'

I glance up now, and I look into his eyes and I just want to dive into them, because I know that whatever creatures swim around inside his irises, they're not vicious. He leans closer and I can feel his body heat, and the space between us is crackly, like how the air gets charged with positive ions right before it storms. He dips his head low so he's resting his forehead against my forehead, and we stand there for a moment, tingling with the electricity that's zinging between us, and then he leans closer, and closer, and then his lips touch mine. It feels gentle, and safe, and calm, and right. His fingers move up my neck and into my curls, and his thumb sweeps across the shaved part of my head, and I slide my hands up under his shirt and cup his shoulderblades to pull him in to me. We kiss, harder now, and it feels so much closer than just our mouths discovering each other for the first time. Time passes, it has to tick forward, but neither of us are aware of it. Right now, we're just glad that we exist.

thirty

I'm sitting on the front steps, studying. Nan hobbles over and sits beside me, whisky in hand.

'How's your head?' I ask her.

'It'd feel better if I didn't have to listen to that damn Enya album Eve's playing.'

We look up at the sky, the clouds like dirty rags against the sunset pinks and purples.

'I don't know if I'm going to get the marks I need,' I admit, looking up from my textbook. Nan spits past the railing and it splatters onto the ground below.

I respect Nan for not assuring me that I will.

'If you don't, you don't, girly. But I'll let you in on a little secret. Sometimes you fail, but that doesn't define you as long as you pick yourself up again and keep on going. Life is much longer than seventeen years.'

I scrunch my nose up.

'You'd know. You're what, a hundred?'

'Bah!'

I swipe her whisky and take a sip before she cuffs me on the back of my head and snatches it back. I flick my fingers against the edges of the book, feeling the pages skim across my thumb. There's so much there to cram into my skull, and I'm not sure that there's enough space left for so many words. I lean my head against the railing and look at Nan.

'If I don't get into art school, do you think that it's because it wasn't meant to be? Do you think that Mum's right? That there's a meaning for everything that happens?'

Nan squints against the setting sun, and takes another sip.

'I reckon that things happen to people, and people like to hang meanings onto things that happen to them. Which comes first or second is debatable. I wouldn't know, girly, but I do know it gives your mother a sort of solace to believe in what she believes, and if the science hasn't figured out yet if it's true or not, what does it matter? Because the people she helps feel helped, and who are we to say what they feel isn't real?'

I mull her words over. I know that people pay Mum money because they're searching for the answers, and they might believe it and Mum might believe it and that may work for them, but I kind of like Nan's interpretation best. Maybe we can't know. Maybe we're not meant to know. And maybe that's okay.

Mum steps out to join us.

'Dinner's ready. Zucchini pasta with cashew cheese and pesto.'

She calls it pasta, but really it's grated-up vegetable. What I would give for carbs and gluten. I stand and follow my nan and Mum inside. I watch them, and I think of how I'm made up of them. I am my mother's hair. I am her scuttling hands. I am my nan's tongue. I am the way she narrows her eyes. And when I hate them, I'm not really hating them. I'm hating myself, and the parts of myself I see in them. And today, I choose to love them.

It's night and Max knocks on my window to wake me. I jump and panic like I always do, my heart does the automatic *kerthump, kerthump, kerthump*. But then I look up to see him there, forehead pressed against the pane, and I realise that I don't have to be afraid anymore. For the first time in my life, I know that home can be a place where I feel comfortable and safe, and my own skin can be a place where I feel at home. I join him on the decking and he doesn't say anything, he doesn't need to, the things in his eyes are swimming on the surface tonight. I take his hand and he grips it as we walk. The air is fat to bursting with humidity, and in the distance lightning is cracking. If I close my eyes I can still see the flash of it through my lids.

'Mum knew I couldn't fix her, hey,' he says, finally, the clouds rumbling in the darkness above us. His voice is colourless. 'She knew. But she let me try, because she knew that I had to.'

I keep hold of his hand.

The ions charge and bounce around us, making everything active. The air tastes coppery and it wants to split open. The wind whips, pulling at our clothes, jerking our hair, and the trees are going wild. We stand there, facing the elements together.

And then it happens. The clouds just give up. Water

crashes down and everything becomes looser. It's the first rain to herald the coming wet season and it's not cold, but it soaks us, and it hides Max's tears.

I keep hold of his hand.

If you or someone you know is experiencing domestic
or family violence, you're not alone. Call 1800RESPECT
any time to access free counselling, information and support
services by qualified, experienced counsellors.
www.1800respect.org.au

ACKNOWLEDGEMENTS

Heartfelt thanks to Laura Harris and all the brilliant team at Penguin Random House. Thanks to my editors, Lisa Riley and the word-wizard Amy Thomas, who kept tugging at the story strands to help weave a tighter and tighter novel with each draft. I'm forever grateful for your insights. Thank you to Marina Messiha, my talented cover designer. I'm so in love with the covers you've created and I'm so lucky to have them adorning my words.

Thanks to my agent extraordinaire, Tara Wynne, for taking a punt on me, and for all your support and advice.

To my parents, Patricia and Garry, for being first readers, and for all your encouragement, always. To my sister Nicole, my Darwin expert, who patiently answered my million questions, and who could tell me the names of every plant and bird. This book owes so much to you. To my other sister and brother-in-law, Kelly and Crosby Rechtin, for all your medical knowledge. A shout out to my brother, Rick, as well.

Shari Sebbens, thanks cuzzy for being my sensitivity reader, and for all your advice when it came to writing Max and his family. Thanks to Will Stubbs at Buku-Larrnggay Mulka Centre for your help with Indigenous art styles of the Northern Territory. Special thanks to the writing community I've been so lucky to get to know, and who have been so generous with advice, support and friendship, especially Nick Earls, Melina Marchetta, Tony Cavanaugh, Samantha Strauss, Kirsty Eagar, Justine Larbalestier and everyone at YAWSS.

To Joh-Joh, Sungi, Elva and all the rest of my beautiful, darling, funny friends. Your unwavering support makes my heart go boom.

Mostly though, this is a big thank you to my readers, for letting me share with you the musings of my imagination. It's a giant honour.

If fourteen-year-old Kirra is having a mid-life crisis now, then it doesn't bode well for her life expectancy. Her so-called friends bully her, whatever semblance of a mother she had has been drowned at the bottom of a gin bottle ever since her dad left them for another woman, and a teenage ghost is speaking to her through a broken phone booth.

Kirra and the ghost make a pact. She'll prove who murdered him almost twenty years ago if he makes her popular, gets her parents back together, and promises not to haunt her. But things aren't so simple, and Kirra realises that people can be haunted in more ways than one.

'I raced through this book, reading it in great big, wonderful chunks. A ripping story with fabulous characters and an imaginative plot . . . (that) rings with a strong teenage truth . . . with just the right amount of grit, adventure and emotion.' *Herald Sun*

Shortlisted for the Children's Book Council of Australia Book of the Year Award for Older Readers, 2017.

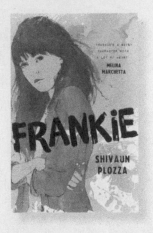

Frankie Vega is angry. Just ask the guy whose nose she broke. Or the cop investigating the burglary she witnessed, or her cheating ex-boyfriend or her aunt who's tired of giving second chances . . .

When a kid shows up claiming to be Frankie's half brother, it opens the door to a past she doesn't want to remember. And when that kid goes missing, the only person willing to help is a boy with stupidly blue eyes . . . and secrets of his own.

Frankie's search for the truth could change her life, or cost her everything.

Shortlisted for the Children's Book Council of Australia Book of the Year Award for Older Readers, 2017.